PENDRAGON

Page Cloverly leant towards Pendragon.
'Rambolt had the answer, dear fellow; enemies of
the state simply disappeared. To where? I have
no knowledge, nor want of such. And therefore,
John, this is what is expected of you; by myself,
by Sidney Herbert, by Her Majesty's Government,
and no doubt certainly by Her Majesty Queen
Victoria, if she were to learn of the matter. You,
John Pendragon, must remove the Queen's
enemies. If he is guilty then commence with
Count Selo Mikhailovich. In which case I suggest
you do it secretly, with discretion, and in a
manner which in no way involves Her Majesty's
Government, nor which causes international
embarrassment to the Crown.' He paused briefly,
then almost hissed the words: 'But kill him.'

Pendragon
Late of Prince Albert's Own

Robert Trevelyan

CORONET BOOKS
Hodder and Stoughton

Copyright © 1975 by Robert Trevelyan

First published in Great Britain 1975 by
Hodder and Stoughton

Coronet Edition 1976

Printed and bound in Great Britain for
Coronet Books, Hodder and Stoughton, London
by Richard Clay (The Chaucer Press), Ltd,
Bungay, Suffolk

ISBN 0 340 20812 0

For my good friend
Desmond Elliot, with thanks

1

THERE WAS THE metallic scent of blood in the air; Pendragon could taste it on his lips as surely as if it existed. And yet the blood was still unspilled, and the long wide valley silent and empty, as the men waited for their orders. Pendragon's clothing was still damp from the early morning mist and Dasher Charlie's grey bulk beneath the saddle was comfortingly warm. Pendragon made a soft slicking noise with his tongue, and Dasher Charlie swung his ears back and fidgeted his forelegs, working his shoulder muscles in anticipation.

Time ceased to exist. Pendragon had the feeling he was part of a painted tableau; even the wings of a distant hawk, hovering above the ploughed ground ahead, seemed to slow down and finally stop. Then the hawk fell in a twisting spiral, sweeping away out of sight close to the brown earth.

There were movements. The oil painting disintegrated. Cardigan swung his horse ahead of John Pendragon and rode forward until he was five yards in the lead of his officers. Pendragon heard him say, in a rather bored voice, 'Well, here goes the last of the Brudenells.'

Pendragon, looking younger than his twenty-four years, turned his head slightly and winked at Ashley, who grinned back. Old Cardigan might be an obtuse and pompous fool, but he was certainly no coward.

The valley, almost a mile wide, was an open-ended coffin. To the left of the Brigade, which was now aligned with parade ground precision, were eight battalions of infantry, fourteen guns, and four squadrons of cavalry—all Russian. To the right were thirty Russian heavy guns, a few field batteries, and eleven more infantry battalions, some of the men being sharp-shooters armed with a new and highly effective Belgian rifle. Ahead was a mass of Russian cavalry three lines deep, protecting a further twelve cannon. And on the Russian flanks were six of their lancer squadrons.

Ashley's saddlery creaked. Pendragon looked at him again. Ashley was leaning sideways, polishing a smear of mud from his boot with a silk wipe. He straightened himself, pushed the kerchief back into his sleeve and adjusted it so that a couple of inches trailed elegantly below his blue cuff. He looked satisfied with the result. Pendragon wondered which of Ashley's conquests had given him the favour, then felt immediately guilty as he remembered the silk square given him by his Aunt Georgina and still in his trunk back in camp. He'd promised he'd wear it for her.

Lord Cardigan drew his sword a couple of inches and pushed it back into the scabbard with a metallic click. In the silence the sound carried as a signal to prepare. There was a slight sigh, like the passing of a gentle breeze, as the Brigade took a breath of anticipation. Saddles groaned as men gripped harder with their knees.

Cardigan pulled out his sword with a broad flourish and moved his horse forward at a slow walk. There was no shouted command. The brigade followed; 636 men and horses of the finest light cavalry in Europe, disciplined and proud.

Captain Pendragon wanted to look back at his men, to admire them, view them behind him in their wide straight lines. He could hear their harness jingle and the pad of hooves on the soft ground. With laughter and chatter, it would be the sound of Rotten Row in London's Hyde Park on a spring Sunday. He resisted the temptation to turn his head, remembering countless times in training when he'd been ordered to 'Keep your head forward, Sir. Never look back, Sir. Looking back only makes the men think you're uncertain, Sir. Just keep looking ahead, Sir, and keep steady-like.'

He noticed movement on the hillsides: Russian infantry forming themselves into hollow squares, expecting the British brigade to wheel suddenly in attack.

Lord Cardigan ignored them, gently spurring his horse to a trot.

Pendragon was surprised. Cardigan was taking a straight line down the centre of the valley, towards the Russian guns at the far end. Dasher Charlie snorted and changed his pace without encouragement from his rider, lifting his knees high as though he were trotting the circuit of a show ring. With the trot, the sound of metal harness ringing increased. Pendragon half expected the brass band of the Guards Regiment to strike up a musical ride, and some hidden audience to applaud and cheer.

Pendragon's sabre, which had seemed heavy and clumsy in training, now felt light and positive. He was conscious of a feeling of mental keenness sharpening his senses to bring the Russian positions into a clarity as though viewed through a telescope. Colours, the grass, the ploughed earth, the sky and the uniforms of the distant troops were brighter.

There were flashes of yellow flame from the muzzles of the guns on the hillsides, and then the thunderous roaring of shot passing overhead like steam escaping from a boiler, terminating in sharp explosions above the trotting cavalry. Ball shrapnel scattered viciously downwards amongst the men. Pendragon kept looking forward, knowing there would have been casualties amongst the troopers, knowing gaps in the lines would have already been filled, and that men were still riding in their correct positions. It was the way of a Hussar regiment; it was expected of them.

An officer galloped across the front of the men, in complete breach of all battle etiquette, aiming himself at Lord Cardigan.

Nolan, thought Pendragon. Damned show-off. He might be a fine rider, but he was too self-opinionated. A difficult man at the best of times, he'd gone too far now. Cardigan certainly wouldn't let him get away with it.

Nolan was shouting something, wildly waving his sword as though he intended to attack Cardigan himself. Whatever he was shouting was lost in the roar of the Russian guns.

Just as the man neared Lord Cardigan a shell exploded close to him. Captain Pendragon heard his scream, high pitched and weird. Nolan swung his horse round and charged back past Pendragon into the advancing ranks of cavalrymen. As he passed, Pendragon saw the whole front of the man's tunic had been blown away; white rib bones gaped outwards from a bloody hollow.

The brigade was still trotting, though the urge to turn the trot into a charge at full gallop was almost irresistible. The

17th Lancers were pressing close behind Cardigan. He waved the Lancer Captain back impatiently and called, 'Steady, steady the 17th Lancers.'

Pendragon was pleased the 11th were holding their lines correctly.

The strength of the bombardment increased and Cardigan, as though he realised it would be impossible to keep the men at the slow trot, increased the tempo to a canter.

The noise was now incredible; shells whistled, screamed and exploded across the open ground. Shrapnel hissed and sang through the smoke, to rattle and bounce like black hail. A part-spent bullet rang against the guard of Pendragon's sword, stinging his gauntleted hand and bending the metal guard tight against his fist. A heavy fragment of metal thudded into the pommel of his saddle, knocking Dasher Charlie a foot sideways in mid-stride and almost unseating his rider. The metal was red hot, threatening to set the saddle stuffing alight. Pendragon banged it away with his rein hand.

There was no time for fear; little enough time for thought.

Suddenly the Light Brigade was in full gallop. A riderless horse, gushing blood from neck and shoulder wounds, swerved past Pendragon whinnying shrilly, and was blown to pieces as a shell burst under its stomach.

For a brief while it seemed for Pendragon as if he and Cardigan were the only two men in the charge. Cardigan was the only fellow rider Pendragon could see, and he forced Dasher Charlie hard to keep close behind the man, who was pressing his own charger furiously.

The Russian guns were now a hundred and fifty yards ahead. Pendragon found himself watching one man, a tall Russian gunner standing at the side of one of the guns. He could see the gunner's bearded face. He aimed himself at the man as though he were the one personal adversary behind the enemy front.

There were shouts. 'Close in! Close in to the centre! Close in!' Pack the charging cavalry tight; force a wedge right through the Russian infantrymen!

Pendragon was now only fifty yards from the guns. They opened up in a terrifying salvo of grape-shot. Pendragon was lucky to be close enough to find a safe channel between the expanding cones of fire. Behind him, only fifty troopers of the front line of cavalry lived to reach the enemy.

Pendragon dug his spurs into Dasher Charlie. The horse leapt the first gun and Pendragon struck downwards at the tall Russian, who tried to ward off the sabre blow with one of the cannon's ramrods. The sabre caught him dead on the top of his toughened bearskin, and Pendragon was angry to feel the jar in his wrist as the sword blade failed to penetrate and glanced off sideways. There was no time for a second blow, the next line of cavalry had now reached the guns and were forcing themselves into the mêlée, making a better job of sabreing the gunners than the decimated first line.

Someone was yelling orders. A non-commissioned man, with a broad Lancashire accent. 'Strike at their faces, lads! Strike sideways at their damned faces!'

A Russian officer, armed with an eight-foot spontoon, thrust the wedge-shaped blade up at Pendragon's face. He parried the blow with his sabre but found it torn from his grasp. He snatched out the double-barrelled pistol from his saddle holster and squeezed a trigger. The huge ten-bore ball lifted the Russian officer clean from his feet and threw him backwards against the struggling crowd. The shock of the pistol wrenched at Pendragon's arm. He used the second barrel on a Russian lancer driving in from his left; the heavy lead slug weighing over an ounce doubled the man forward so his lance point skewered one of his own infantrymen through the spine.

A thick-set man in a long greatcoat dived at Pendragon, grabbing at his leg, trying to pull him down from Dasher Charlie's back. Pendragon swung the pistol barrels at the man's head and spun Dasher Charlie sideways. The man disappeared screaming beneath his hooves.

Pendragon looked for a weapon. There was a stack of lances, propped vertically, point to point, a few yards ahead. He urged Dasher Charlie forward and suddenly found himself in an open space behind the fighting. He snatched at a lance, breaking the leather thong strapping the pile together, turned Dasher and charged back into the fighting from the rear of the guns. There was a hussar on the ground, standing between the legs of his dead charger, trying to fight off a bunch of Russian infantrymen who stabbed at him with long-bladed bayonets on their empty muskets. Pendragon dropped the lance and leant his weight on to the point as he hit the nearest man. The point entered between the man's shoulder blades and drove clean through, to spear a second man in the thigh before Pendragon was unable to support the weight. He shouted encouragement to the trooper.

A trumpeter sounded a call; the retreat! Pendragon swung his horse and saw Lord Paget waving on the other side of the guns. He knee'd Dasher Charlie alongside the officer.

'Fall back,' Paget shouted. The man's tunic and face were splattered with blood and his sword blade was crimson and dripping.

The guns began again. Dasher Charlie was tired, his mouth foaming green, his flanks running with sweat and blood. Pendragon kept him at a gallop. There were other troopers alongside; few of them, scattered. The bombardment was even more severe now than on the approach. The flat plain of the valley was littered with debris, dead horses and troopers.

Dasher Charlie swerved at a shell hole. As he did so, something seemed to hit Pendragon with the force of a sledge hammer on the hip. He was thrown sideways from the saddle. It seemed to happen slowly, as though it were a dream. He felt himself going, but was unable to regain his balance; the ground lifted and he turned his head slightly to try to get his shoulder down first. When he thudded into the ploughed earth, it seemed to close in on him as darkness.

* * *

A trooper of the 17th Lancers, already wounded himself by a Russian gunner's spear, hauled his charger to a stop, jumped down and gathered Pendragon from the red soil, tossing him across his saddle. The trooper ran the last half mile of hell, leading his horse by the bit ring. He collapsed exhausted only when he was beyond range of the Russian guns.

It had been a life-long twenty minutes, from start to finish.

Only seventy of the original cavalry rode back. The 11th Hussars, Prince Albert's own, now consisted of two officers and eight mounted men.

Pendragon was one of 125 wounded survivors.

It was a brave battle, a heroic battle, a glorious battle, a damned foolish battle. It did not win the Crimean War.

* * *

Sergeant Major John Grieve, of the Royal Scots Greys, Second Dragoons—the Heavy Brigade—won a Victoria Cross, the highest British award for gallantry.

Sergeant Henry Ramage, also of the Royal Scots Greys, won a Victoria Cross.

Surgeon James Mouat, of the Inniskilling (6th Dragoons), won a Victoria Cross that day.

Lieutenant Alexander Robert Dunn, of the 11th Hussars, Prince Albert's Own, Pendragon's troops, won a Victoria Cross.

Sergeant Joseph Malone, of the 13th Hussars, won a Victoria Cross.

Troop Sergeant Major John Berryman, of the 17th Lancers, the Duke of Cambridge's Own, won the Victoria Cross.

Quartermaster Sergeant John Farrell, of the 17th Lancers, won the Victoria Cross.

Sergeant Major Charles Wooden, of the 17th Lancers, won the Victoria Cross.

It was a brave twenty minutes, a damned foolish twenty minutes.

* * *

The trooper of the 17th Lancers who had saved Captain John Pendragon's life won no award. He lay for a while recovering his breath before he carried John Pendragon over to the surgeon's tents. He passed the unconscious officer across to a medical orderly, who was stained chest to knees in blood, and then he walked away with his horse. A few moments later he was seen to be riding back up the valley, no doubt with the thought of bringing in more of the wounded. He disappeared into a cloud of battle smoke as thick as the London pea soup fogs. He was never seen again. No one made a note of his name; he would be remembered simply as a trooper of the 17th, who had been willing to give his life for others. There were many like him.

* * *

Lord Cardigan, having led his men right through to the Russian guns, considered his duty done and rode back almost at a walk, alone through the gunfire. He ignored the barrage aimed at him, a solitary rider in the valley. He was pre-occupied and furious; too furious to notice the shrapnel that scattered and shrieked around him. He was thinking of Captain Nolan and the man's outrageous behaviour. When he was out of range of the guns he saw James Scarlett of the Heavy Brigade. His first words were, 'Imagine the fellow; screaming like a woman when he was hit.'

Brigadier Scarlett shrugged and made a more dignified reply. 'You should say no more, my Lord. You have just ridden over Captain Nolan's body.'

Cardigan turned his own animal and stared up the long valley, waiting until the few survivors returned through the smoke of the bombardment. When the first of the troopers reached him, exhausted, sweaty and blood-soaked, Lord Cardigan nodded them a greeting as casually as though they had returned from a Windsor Park exercise. Almost apologetically he said, 'Men, it is a mad-brained trick, but it is no fault of mine.'

One of the troopers grinned. It was the first time in the six years he had served with Lord Cardigan that the officer had ever spoken a word to him personally. He saluted him. 'Never mind, my Lord, we are ready to go again.'

* * *

Lancer Wightman had been taken prisoner behind the Russian guns. He had been wounded four times, but had accounted for several of the Russian gunners. He was hauled before the Russian General Liprandi.

General Liprandi eyed the lancer. The man was a foot shorter than the General, thin as the haunch of a starved chicken, but despite his wounds he stared back at him contemptuously.

'What did they give you to drink?' asked General Liprandi, having heard of the troopers' fighting ferocity. 'Did they not prime you with spirits, to come down and attack us in such a mad manner?'

Trooper Wightman saw no reason to give the enemy Russian General the respect he would have automatically shown his own officers. 'You think we were drunk?' Trooper Wightman's voice was contemptuous. 'My God! I tell you, if we had so much as smelled the barrel, we should have taken half Russia by this time.'

* * *

Captain John Hawkdale Pendragon recovered consciousness to find himself lying on a heap of wet straw, covered by a lice-ridden piece of bloodstained blanket that smelt of uncleaned stables. His head was aching as though he were suffering from a brandy hangover. He tried to move and found himself stiff and sore.

As mist cleared from his eyes he recognised the hospital section with its brown tents. The area was crowded with wounded, some groaning, some simply sitting or lying silently against the low earth wall that ringed the area. Out of sight, inside one of the tents, a man shouted in pain. Orderlies moved from wounded man to wounded man, offering water laced with rum, cutting away bloody and torn uniforms in preparation for the doubtful hands of the overworked surgeons.

Captain Pendragon tried to twist himself into a sitting position. A spear of agony drove itself up his left leg and seemed to bury itself in his groin. He bit hard on his lips to suppress any sound. There was an orderly an arm's length away.

Captain Pendragon called him. The man looked round. 'Sir?'

'What time of the day?' asked Pendragon.

'Late afternoon, Sir,' answered the orderly. 'Would you be wanting anything, Sir?'

'A cigar and a glass of wine,' said Pendragon.

The orderly laughed. 'Good for you, Sir, but there's none of either here.'

'What of the battle?' asked Pendragon.

'A damned waste of time,' said a languid voice behind him. 'Who are you, Sir?'

'Captain John Pendragon, 11th Hussars,' said Pendragon over his shoulder. He couldn't quite see the man who was speaking, but guessed from his voice he was a fellow officer.

'Napier of the Scots Greys,' drawled the voice. 'Jove, your men went in hard. We stood off and watched you a while. You rode in fast over that bad ground. We came in a couple of minutes later. Damn me, there aren't many of you left now.'

'Did we hold the guns?'

The man behind him laughed. 'Hold 'em? Five minutes after we left 'em they were firing again down the valley. God knows what happened to the infantry. How in God's name can you hold ground with cavalry? We needed infantry right behind us.'

'The valley was too long,' agreed Pendragon. 'Did you ride back?'

'All the way,' said the voice, sounding more tired. 'It was easier than walking without feet.'

The orderly interrupted them. 'Major Napier had his feet blown away, Sir,' he explained. 'He's had his operation. He should be sleeping, Sir.'

'Rot,' said Napier. 'My family always claimed I was foot-loose, I just didn't realise what they meant; damned things all but fell off. Lost a good horse at the same time. One of my troopers fetched me another and gave me a leg—half a leg—up. Where are you hit?'

'I'm not certain,' said Pendragon. 'Leg and side, I think. I don't know, I'm still pretty numb.'

'You won't be by the time the butcher finishes with you,' warned Napier. 'If he wants to chop something off, refuse him permission. Dashed chap is about as hygienic as a sewer scavenger's backside. His hands are covered in blood and guts, and there isn't a clean towel in the hospital.'

There was a shout from the nearest of the tents. An operating assistant lumbered into the daylight and paused for a second looking around the group of wounded men. 'Next one,' he called, as though he was an assistant to a working man's barber.

'It's you, Sir,' said the orderly beside Pendragon. He waved a hand towards the operating assistant.

'Good luck,' offered Major Napier.

* * *

They carried Pendragon around the brown canvas tent. The walls of the farthest side were rolled up, exposing the operating table and giving the surgeon working light. A man was being lifted from the table, naked down to the waist. There were large wounds, still open, on one side of his chest. The wounds were gurgling horribly as he was moved; he was limp and obviously dead. The surgeon was standing back from the table wiping his gory hands on his thighs. One of the assistants was washing instruments in a bucket that had once contained water, but which was now mostly blood. Another was tidying a pile of amputated limbs threatening to roll underfoot.

'Name please, Sir?' One of the assistants, less bloody than the others, waved a large leather-covered ledger at Pendragon.

'John Hawkdale Pendragon,' said Pendragon, waiting while the man scowled down at the book and laboriously wrote the information with an indelible pencil which had stained his lips purple. 'Captain of the 11th Hussars. Prince Albert's Own.'

'Age please, Sir?'

'Twenty-four,' said Pendragon. He couldn't see the use of that piece of information.

'Date of birth please, Sir?'

'Fifth of April, 1830,' said Pendragon. Clerks! If the man had any brains, he could have just asked the date of birth and worked the age out from that. It was typical. No wonder there was a shortage of fodder and materials if it was left to men like this to do the book-keeping and indenting.

The surgeon leant towards Pendragon. 'Good afternoon, Sir,' he said. His voice was sepulchral and reminded Pendragon of an undertaker's, although the man looked more like a slaughter-house artificer. His hands were huge and his face unshaven and ruddy-complexioned. 'What have we here?' The monstrous fingers felt at Pendragon's leg, stabbing him with pain. He winced but remained silent. The surgeon held a hand out behind him and brought it back with a huge pair of tailor's scissors. The scissors cut away at Pendragon's breeches, slitting them from the tear over the wounds, up to his waistband. 'Ah,' said the surgeon.

17

Pendragon lifted his head. There was a long deep puncture in his left thigh, with a fragment of yellow bone sticking sideways from the torn flesh.

'Here's one for a start,' said the surgeon, with rather too much satisfaction for Pendragon's comfort. The scissors slit downwards.

'Not the boots,' ordered Pendragon. 'They're a good pair. They'll be impossible to replace. Get a man to pull them off.'

'As you will, Sir,' said the surgeon. He signalled to an assistant. The man moved down to the end of the table and jerked at Pendragon's foot. Pendragon was unable to suppress a yelp of agony. There was darkness again.

* * *

Above was a brown ceiling, cracked and discoloured, with a piece of plaster hanging downwards, supported only by the pigs' hair of its mix. It moved, swaying like a pendulum, in a strong cold breeze blowing through the glassless windows. Outside it was raining. Inside, dirty rainwater trickled down the walls and formed pools on the muddy floorboards. Pendragon lay motionless for a long time, hardly daring to move, not knowing what sort of agonies he would find when he did so. Very carefully, very gently, he flexed parts of his body. First only the toes of his right foot, the one he was sure was undamaged. The toes worked well, and without pain. He tried the foot, then the knee; no pain. His hands and arms worked and so did his shoulders, although they were sore and stiff. His head and neck still seemed to be joined together. He tried his left toes and ankle. Now there was agonising pain. He let his left leg relax, and eased his shoulders up off the mattress.

It was a long ward, crowded, the beds so close together there was barely enough room for a man to move between them. The beds were all full. The air stank of rotting flesh, of gangrene and vomit. There was a soft rumble of conversation. Somewhere else, in another ward, or below, there was more noise. Loud talking, shouting, children crying, laughing.

The man to Pendragon's right was asleep, his face the pale green colour of approaching death. There was a fresh scar, probably from a sabre slash, running down his head from shaved scalp to throat, stitched but unbandaged.

The man on Pendragon's left was sitting up in bed, his back propped against the wet brick wall. He was reading a book so soggy with damp that the glue of the binding had softened, allowing the pages to come away. The cover of the book was mouldy and looked as though it had been fresh dug from a grave.

The man turned his head slowly and looked at Pendragon. 'Scutari. Barrack Hospital, if you're wondering where you are. You were brought in three days ago. You're Captain Pendragon, I believe. Your orderly's quartered below. I'll get him sent up for you.' The man didn't wait for Pendragon to reply, but simply shouted loudly in the direction of the ward doorway. A private soldier stuck his head around the doorpost. 'Captain Pendragon's orderly, and sharp too, my lad.' He looked back at Pendragon. 'These fellers don't know they're born. You'll find them all scavengers; layabouts, slackers. Oh, and they are all thieves, so keep a sharp eye on your belongings.' He reached a hand across the narrow gaps between the beds. 'FitzPatrick, Grenadier Guards. I'm due out on the first ship available. Been here since the attack on the Great Redoubt. Be glad to go. This place is a hell-hole, not fit for a damned pig, let alone a gentleman. Here's your orderly.'

Pendragon could hear the clank of Corporal Willie McQuire's spurs as he marched his way down between the line of beds. It was a comforting and familiar sound. He watched the man, proud to see his uniform with the cherry red breeches was as smart as ever. He was suddenly surprised; Corporal McQuire had been in the charge, in the leading line of troopers, and he'd survived! Pendragon was pleased. McQuire reached the end of Pendragon's bed, stamped himself to attention and saluted, smartly. He grinned down at Pendragon.

'Glad to see you alive, Sir,' he said.

'And I you,' said Pendragon.

'I thought you was a dead 'un,' smiled the corporal. 'Along with Dasher, Sir, but he's all right, too, Sir. Down in the stable, right as rain, 'cept for a few scars and a bit of deafness.'

'Water please, Corporal,' said Pendragon. His mouth tasted dry and foul.

'Oh, blimey, Sir,' apologised Corporal McQuire. He unslung a waterbottle from his shoulders and pushed himself between the beds until he was beside Pendragon. He poured water into the top of the flask and passed it across. 'Sorry, Sir. Right careless of me; unthoughtful. Here, have a drink, Sir.' When Pendragon had emptied the small cup from the top of the flask, McQuire refilled it and passed it back. 'Here, I'll leave the bottle beside you, Sir. And I'll bring you up a little of what does you good, Sir. And would you be feeling like a little solid refreshment yet, Sir?'

'Later,' said Pendragon. He felt his cracked lips with his tongue.

'You seen your sabretache, Sir?' asked Corporal McQuire, cheerfully. He reached beneath Pendragon's bed and pulled out the ornate pouch that all Hussars wore hanging on their left side. A huge piece of shrapnel which must have weighed three pounds still stuck through it, spearing the crown and the identity scroll with its words 'Prince Albert's Own Hussars'. The jagged piece of steel protruded six inches from the layers of crimson leather. 'Good souvenir, Sir, ain't it,' chuckled McQuire, holding it up in admiration. 'Saved your leg, Sir. If it weren't for the sabretache, the blooming bit of shell would have taken it right off at your knee.'

'How did the day go for you, Corporal?' asked Pendragon.

'Easy, Sir,' said McQuire. His moustache, with its drooping ends, seemed to bristle as he remembered. 'Just followed you, didn't I, Sir? Said a little prayer before we went. I was somewhat lucky, Sir. There was only me and seven other troopers on our mounts at the end. Oh, and a couple of the h'officers. Bit warm, wasn't it, Sir?'

'Lord Cardigan?'

'What, old ... er, His Lordship? Oh, he's all right. They say he rode back, went straight to his bally yacht and 'ad a bath before dinner, cool as a cucumber.'

'Have the surgeons told you anything about my wounds?' asked Pendragon. He made his voice deliberately indifferent, as though the wounds were about as important to him as the price of lamb in Smithfield Market.

Corporal McQuire looked uncomfortable. He fidgeted for a moment before he replied in a quiet voice. 'I asked them, Sir, and they told me as how you wouldn't actually need to lose your leg, Sir. And as how it would heal all right so long as it didn't go rotten.'

'And?' persisted Pendragon, realising there was more that Corporal McQuire was unwilling, or nervous to tell him.

'Well, Sir.' McQuire paused, his face deepening in colour with embarrassment. He looked down at the floor. 'Well, Sir, they said as how you was finished with the cavalry, Sir. I'm sorry, Sir. Dreadfully sorry, Sir. They said as how you wouldn't be able to sit a horse for long. Me, and me missus, she's down below, Sir, with the other men's wives and kids, well, us and the other troopers, Sir, we're all very sorry about it.'

Pendragon let himself relax back on to the mattress. The cracked ceiling seemed close, bearing down on him, pressing him into the ground.

He heard Corporal McQuire's voice distantly. 'Well, Sir, I'll be off, Sir. If you want me, just shout. I'll be back later with food, Sir.' There was the click of boot heels and the sharp jingle of spurs as the Corporal saluted and clumped away down the ward.

'Hard luck. Dashed hard luck,' commiserated the Guards officer in the next bed.

* * *

The hours passed slowly. At first, for Pendragon, much of the time was spent asleep, as though the experience of the battle had drained months of energy from his body. He had no appetite for food, and as he had been tall and lean to start with, now he was thin. But he was glad of the sleep; it shortened the periods of pain.

It was three days before he saw a surgeon. The man made a hurried and cursory round of a few of the beds at the far end of the crowded ward. Pendragon, awake, waved the man across to him. The surgeon looked down at him, his eyes angry at the summons.

'This is an officers' ward,' Pendragon told the man, coldly. 'I would have expected at least some small amount of your time.'

'You're getting more than many,' answered the man, curtly.

'There are four miles of beds in this vermin-ridden hospital, every one of them occupied. We've so little time we don't even bury amputated limbs, we toss them into the harbour. If I divided my time equally between patients, you'd be entitled to exactly ten seconds a day—if I worked twenty-four hours. I work twenty; your time's up.' The surgeon, in a brown-stained apron, turned his back and strode away.

FitzPatrick, sitting on the edge of the next bed, laughed. 'Now you know why I dress my own wounds,' he said. 'Why don't you let me do yours for you?'

The wounds on Pendragon's thigh itched furiously and he could feel the flesh bulging above the bandages, as though about to burst apart. He nodded to FitzPatrick. 'I'd be grateful.'

FitzPatrick moved across until he was sitting on Pendragon's bed. He rolled back the bedclothes and looked down at the injured leg.

'Do you happen to have a clean shirt I can use for fresh bandages?'

'I'd better have, or I'll find a new orderly,' said Pendragon. He shouted McQuire's name, and the corporal appeared almost immediately. He must have been sitting waiting outside the ward in the narrow hallway. 'Get me a shirt, please,' called Pendragon. Corporal McQuire saluted from the doorway and disappeared. 'It'll be clean all right,' said Pendragon. 'His wife looks after my linen, for five shillings a week.'

FitzPatrick had pulled out a pocket knife and was cutting away the bloodstained bandages. He peeled them back. 'God!' he said. 'They used moss on you, sphagnum moss! I wouldn't use it on my horse. Damned peasants! What the hell is this army coming to? No food for the men, no clothing, no boots, no fodder for the horses. Sphagnum moss for wound dressings. You'd think we were fighting at Agincourt, not in the year eighteen fifty-four. The French have got everything—good at administration, the frogs.' He gently tugged the strands of moss padding away from the wound. 'Not bad stitching,' he said. 'There's some pus, but not too much. Can you stand a bit of brutality?'

'Of course,' said Pendragon. He winced as FitzPatrick squeezed the edges of the jagged scar and mopped at it with a corner of the bedclothes.

'Good boy,' congratulated FitzPatrick. 'That's a damned lot better. Were you conscious when the field surgeon saw you?'

'Yes.'

'Do you remember what the wound looked like open?'

Pendragon nodded. 'Just a bloody hole, with splinters of bone sticking out.'

FitzPatrick groaned. 'That's what I suspected,' he said. 'It's not just a wound, it's a break as well. The damned fools haven't splinted you. No wonder it's been giving you troubles. Ah, Corporal, just the lad I want.'

Corporal McQuire saluted again and passed FitzPatrick a neatly folded white shirt.

FitzPatrick looked quizzically at Pendragon. 'Do you have any money?'

'A little,' answered Pendragon. 'I haven't drawn pay for a long while, but neither has anyone else. I think I've about ten guineas in my trunk.'

'Ask your orderly to get it,' FitzPatrick told him.

'Would you mind, Corporal?' asked Pendragon. He wondered what FitzPatrick had in mind.

'Of course, Sir.' Corporal McQuire began to leave.

'Hold your horse,' said FitzPatrick. 'Just take out five guineas. Go down to the Turkish sector and find the best bone-setter there is. He probably won't want to help, so bargain with him with the gold. Get the best man, and fetch him back here as fast as you can; even if you have to help him on his way with your sabre.'

'It's done, Sir,' promised Corporal McQuire. He saluted, turned smartly, and left.

'A Turkish bone-setter!' Pendragon was horrified.

'You won't get any help from the British surgeon,' said Fitz-Patrick. 'You've already met him. I don't think he cares for officers. Better a Turk than a life as a cripple. I hear they're quite good. We've been using them to cure horses. Excellent with croup.'

*   *   *

Two months later Pendragon was out of the hospital, although on crutches, and in a small room of his own in the near-by barracks. Winter was drawing in fast and the weather was bitter. There was a shortage of firewood; there was a shortage of everything.

Pendragon hadn't seen Lord Cardigan; in fact he never saw him again in the Crimea. But he'd had an interview with Lord Lucan on the day he'd left the hospital. Lucan, visiting the barracks, looked surprisingly well-fed, well-groomed, and too clean for an officer who liked to claim he shared the same hardships as his men and was crawling with as many lice as any of them. Lucan read the hospital surgeon's letter, raised his eyebrows, and stared across his desk at Pendragon.

'We'll send you home, my boy,' he said as though it were a reward for good behaviour. 'First available berth on a British ship—unless you care to arrange your own passage. Would help if you choose to do so.'

'If I can draw pay here, I can arrange one,' said Pendragon.

'Of course,' promised Lucan. 'See the paymaster. Tell him it is on my orders. When you get back, report to your barracks in London. See what we can do for you then. They'll be happy to welcome you at home, they like heroes. You lads of the Light Brigade are heroes already. *Times* newspaper saw to that, I'm told. Did you get a gallantry award, my boy?'

'I did nothing to win one,' said Pendragon. 'Simply rode my horse.'

Lord Luccan laughed. 'I watched you all,' he said, his eyes bright with enthusiasm. 'By God, what a show, what a sight to set hearts on fire! What a glorious memory.'

Pendragon, balanced on his crutches, looked down at the man. 'It will be remembered by many,' he said quietly, 'as the most perfect example of wartime crass stupidity; the obliteration of two regiments for no useful purpose.'

Lord Lucan's face hardened. 'Young man,' he said coldly. 'You make the mistake of inexperience by judging the whole with knowledge only of a part. Such acts of valour may not in themselves serve an obvious purpose, but consider the effects in future battles, when such known bravery will strike fear into enemy troops of all nationalities.'

'Forgive me, my Lord.' Pendragon stiffened himself until he was standing as straight and erect as his crutches would allow. 'I was under the impression that the purpose of our charge was to attack and capture the guns of our enemy. Had I known it was for example, I would have ordered my own troop to form a circling star in the valley centre, and had them ride singly, one at a time, to their deaths before the Russian guns. That way, the lesson would not have been driven home once, but many, many times.' He gave the purple-faced Lord Lucan no time to reply. 'And now if you will excuse me, my Lord, I will make arrangements for my return to England, and to sanity.'

* * *

Almost three weeks later, on the 10th of January, 1885, Captain John Hawkdale Pendragon and his charger, Dasher Charlie, embarked on the Dutch schooner Julianna, bound for Vlissingen in Holland. From there he planned to cross to Breskens, and then travel by couch to Oostende, and again by ship across the channel to Britain.

It was a long journey, made worse by storms that hit the Julianna shortly after she left port. Pendragon, still suffering badly from his wounds, could not have survived but for the kindness of the ship's crew and the medical help of her able captain. Had he ever felt misgivings about the former and traditional enemies of British sovereignty on the oceans, they were gone for ever. After seven weeks at sea with them, he could happily trust his life in the hands of a Dutch seaman.

The ship's course took her slightly southwards until she was off the North African coast, making use of the light winds blowing westwards. The weather was mild; English spring. Pendragon was able to rest in the warm sun on a long seat specially made for him by the ship's carpenter. The sea voyage gave him time to relax; and the first real comfort in many hard months of campaigning.

2

THE TEMPERATURE IN the narrow strip of shade beneath the compound walls was ninety-eight degrees, and the sun glared off the whitewashed mud with terrifying ferocity. It was April, 1830. The place was the military fort of Rhotuck, India; headquarters of the 5th Bengal European Cavalry. The time was noon, and twenty-one Bengali pipers stood in two rows in front of Major Nathan Pendragon's living quarters, playing the Lament of the ClanRanald Widows. The piping was customary on these occasions; to drown the cries of European officers' wives during the labours of childbirth. It was unseemly that such sounds should be heard by native troops or tradesmen.

The pipers played continuously until three forty-seven in the afternoon, when they were silenced by a music-tortured aiya, who scurried out on to the veranda and screamed furiously in their direction.

In the sudden quiet, Major Nathan Pendragon appeared on the steps of the officers' mess, on the far side of the parade ground. He was swaying slightly, having been plied with wine by fellow officers since ten that morning. One of the Indian troops, a Lance Dafadar who had been standing guard with a New Land Service musket beside the pipers, ran across to Major Pendragon, shouldered the weapon and saluted.

'Beg to report, Major Sah'b.'

'Do so,' said Major Pendragon.

'Sah'b is father of a male child.' The Lance Dafadar let only the briefest hint of a smile show on his lips; an indication he approved of the masculine issue.

'Very satisfactory,' acknowledged Major Pendragon. 'Please convey my best wishes to Memsah'b Pendragon. Tell her the boy's names will be John Hawkdale. I hope I shall see her at dinner. Dismiss.'

* * *

John Hawkdale Pendragon was the sole infant to reach puberty from his mother's eight successive children. Indeed he was the only one to reach the age of twelve months. The remainder lay in a neat and pathetic row beneath white stone slabs in the regimental burial ground outside the small township huddled around the fort. The children did not lie alone; the death of such a proportion of European military children was normal in India, and in the graveyards they frequently outnumbered those who had fallen in the many military campaigns.

John Hawkdale Pendragon's growing up was therefore watched with interest and pleasure by almost every member of the Regiment. English and native troops, they were his friends, his playmates, his guardians. His clothes, from the moment he was big enough to walk, were miniature regimental uniforms, carefully made for him by Aloke De, the officers' Bengali tailor.

At three, he was taught to ride by Sergeant Major Freddy Bowers; a man of a terrible reputation for severity and discipline. The Sergeant Major was a gentle nursemaid to John Pendragon, and would, when they had both ridden out of sight of the fort and other troopers, spend hours in kindly play with the boy.

By the age of four, John Hawkdale Pendragon could carry and use a small lance at full gallop, from the back of a rather reluctant but sturdy hill pony of some ten hands, and with legs as thick as the stockade posts. His score at hunting with the weapon was proudly recorded by Sergeant Major Bowers. It consisted of three rabbits, a civet, and a cobra; the latter having earned young Pendragon one of his few cuffs around his ears. He had stuffed the dead reptile into one of the commanding officer's dress knee-boots.

His fifth birthday present, from the armourers, was a small sabre, which he wore with assurance when allowed to ride out on patrol with the cavalrymen. The sabre proved useful; three months later he defended himself with it admirably, when attacked by a rabid dog whilst visiting a neighbouring village with his father.

Young Pendragon's father Nathan was a stern but just officer; just, that is, by the standards of the day. At seven years, John Pendragon had seen men flogged with wetted leather harness, for drunkenness; packdrilled in the sun, until they collapsed delirious, for insubordination; and one Indian sepoy of an infantry regiment blown to pieces, tied spread-eagled across the mouth of a regimental cannon, for murdering a European non-commissioned officer's harlot wife.

Major Nathan Pendragon, a slim and ramrod stiff military figure, believed men became men by being treated as such, from the moment of their birth. Affection and outward signs of love were feelings to be kept for the secrecy of one's mistress's or wife's bedchambers. Any smiles he gave his son were rewards for jobs well done. The only time John Pendragon heard his father laugh aloud was when he first tried to fire his father's double-barrelled game rifle. He managed to snag both triggers at the same time with his small fingers. The hammers snapped down on the two copper percussion caps simultaneously; the Joe Manton seven-bore lifted the boy clean from the ground and hurled him four yards backwards into a dry stream bed. Major Nathan Pendragon picked up his hunting rifle and examined it for damage before he attended to his dazed and bruised son.

Although much of John Pendragon's learning was military, his scholarly interests were by no means neglected. There had been an influx of fresh officers, transferred from another regiment. There were children amongst the families, and with them John Pendragon shared the ravings, rantings and scoldings of a sour-faced tutor, whose loathing of India was equalled only by the man's hatred of the creditors in England who had forced him overseas to work.

The man was Seton Yoxall; haggard, malaria-ridden, brilliant scholastically. An eccentric, who wore the clothing of a lower-class London clerk in the heats of India; his only head protection a black umbrella with warped whalebone ribs and a covering that had provided countless termites with sustenance. He had two weaknesses; cards and native women. He lost in the first, and gained in the second; the gains were far more unpleasant and unhealthy than the losses. He lasted until John Pendragon was nine years old, then one day he rode several miles up into the hills, alone, and blew his head off with a stolen ten-pound barrel of gunpowder. There was no official funeral; little remained of him by the time he was found. Like his umbrella covering, Seton Yoxall had been taken into the bowels of India.

Mrs. Catherine Pendragon, the second eldest of three sisters born in Battle, Sussex, England, would have enjoyed the opportunity to influence her son John. Unfortunately the chances never occurred. She sweated in the tropical heat and the scorching winds, from pregnancy to miscarriage and unsuccessful or wasted births. And although John Pendragon always viewed her with the natural love of a son for his mother, his meetings with her were largely restricted to mealtimes, when, in any case, he was forbidden to speak.

Seton Yoxall had died just before the rains came; when they did so, Major Nathan Pendragon determined to send his son back to Great Britain for the remainder of his education. It was not only education, or lack of it, that made up his mind; the monsoon heat of India was stretching the boy upwards like a spindly beanshoot under a bell-jar. He was already five feet two inches, the same height as his mother; so thin that he could hide himself, when hunting, behind a single eight-inch palm trunk.

There were regimentally owned carriages, available for the use of the officers and their families; they were more comfortable than the unpadded wagons and springless carts used by the remainder of the men. In one, Major Nathan Pendragon and his son travelled down to Calcutta. It was a lengthy trip, the nights being spent in snake-ridden *dak* bungalows along the route. At the port Major Nathan Pendragon purchased the ticket for a passage on the trading clipper *Southern Horn*. He spoke sternly and at length to her master, and inspected the cabin allocated to John; he then shook the boy's hand, slapped him on the shoulder, and turned and walked away without looking back, even a single time.

There were several other passengers on board the *Southern Horn*; mainly members of the East India Company, but including two military men: a colonel of Skinner's Horse who had been badly wounded, and lost an arm in a battle against the Ghilzai tribesmen, and a private of the Horse Artillery who was being retired after thirty years of foreign service. The colonel bored John Pendragon, insisting on recounting at every opportunity all the problems and difficulties of soldiering for his majesty Shah Shuja-ul-Mulk, and the techniques of punitory expeditions into the Hindu Kush. John Pendragon would politely excuse himself, walking slowly away until he was out of sight of the Colonel, then he would leap up on to the rigging, to clamber the hundred and twenty feet to the look-out barrels above the tops'l yards, where he'd share an hour or two with the friendly seamen on watch.

The voyage to England was not without incident. Off Cape Agulhas, at night, a freak wave over sixty feet high smashed broadside into the *Southern Horn* and rolled her on to her beam ends. It carried away two top-masts, a mile of rigging and five crewmen. She limped, fortunately in better weather, around the Cape of Good Hope and anchored in Saint Helena Bay for refitting. It took the seamen a fortnight, during which time the ship smelt of hot pitch and burning rope, to get her ready for sea again.

* * *

There was ice in the Thames when the *Southern Horn* beat her way up the wide estuary and finally anchored in mid-stream off Greenwich. White slabs, four or five inches thick, bumped and ground against her hull. There was snow on the roofs of the buildings on shore, and on the rising ground beyond the southern banks. Wild geese and skeins of mallards wedged their way across dull skies towards the marshes.

On the next incoming tide twenty of the seamen in a long-boat towed the *Southern Horn* farther upstream to her berth at the London dockside. Young Pendragon hung over the ship's bow and watched fascinated. He'd never seen snow, or ice. More astonishingly still, he had never seen Europeans doing the labouring work of the pallid-faced ruffians on the wharf. They didn't seem to enjoy their work, either; Indian coolies would have been singing. These men grumbled, shouted at each other, went about their tasks sullen, scowling and shivering.

The town! London! It seemed so big, even when seen from the forepeak of the *Southern Horn*. From her look-out on the foremast it was enormous, stretching as far as Pendragon could see, until the buildings were lost in an evil-coloured smoke mist that melted into the grey sky. It made him afraid

30

for the first time in his life; for the first time, he felt alone.

He waited on the *Southern Horn* for five more long days, until one morning a huge red-faced man clumped up the gangplank and shouted for the ship's captain. 'Sir Reginald Spence here,' he boomed. 'I've come for the boy Pendragon.'

Pendragon heard the voice from the depths of his cabin. He hurried on deck.

'Ahhhh,' roared Sir Reginald. 'You must be he, lad. God blast me, look at you, you scalliwag! A bag o' bones and a hank o' hair.' He grabbed at Pendragon and lifted him above his head, holding him out at arm's length and twisting him around as though he were examining a spring lamb in a market place. 'Damned skin and bones! No meat!'

Pendragon wondered if his uncle were a cannibal. He seemed to tower over the boy, his white hair scattering around his shoulders, mutton-chop whiskers stained yellow nearest his nose by snuff or tobacco, the hairs sticking wildly out from florid cheeks. His nose was veined and the colour of a ripe plum, and his hands were like hay forks. God must have envied him his voice; when he spoke, people a hundred feet away turned and listened.

'Food you need, lad,' thundered Pendragon's uncle. 'Good beefsteak, pheasant pie, half a bullock, a dozen hare; washed down with a few shants of Hampshire ale. And a season's riding at the hunt to bring a bit of colour to those parchment cheeks of yours. That's what you need.'

And that was what John Pendragon got, and had, at his uncle's rather decayed country estate near Alresford, in Hampshire. And, as his uncle promised, it did put flesh on Pendragon's bones, and bring warm colour to his face. His hair, bleached by years of tropical sun, darkened to chestnut.

Sir Reginald's wife, Elizabeth, was John Pendragon's aunt; his mother's eldest sister. Having no children of her own, she was delighted with the boy's presence in the old hall, with its half-timbering and ancient wattle and daub construction. But that his aunt Elizabeth was a little insane, and Sir Reginald at least quite odd, young Pendragon had no doubts. They were both happy and noisy people, but life at the old hall was quite incredible after the routine and discipline of a military establishment.

It was considered dawn at whatever time Sir Reginald quit his bed, which was frequently after mid-day. Breakfast was served only when Sir Reginald sat himself at the table; often at five in the afternoon. Lunch followed four hours later, and dinner four hours after that; normally about midnight.

On hunting days, Sir Reginald actually did rise at dawn, rode for three hours and collapsed for the next ten, awakening eventually to refresh himself with a couple of pints of port and begin the day all over again. Work on the estate naturally suffered. Old workers died and were not replaced; ancient oak trees were lopped and sawn, and they too, like the dead workers, were instantly forgotten. Fences drooped and collapsed, hedges grew wild and sagged over the lanes when the wind leant on them. Sir Reginald didn't worry; he knew there were sufficient oak and elm trees left to see him through his old age. The diminishing trees were his capital.

Aunt Elizabeth's insanity was tolerable. She believed herself to be Lord Nelson's mistress, despite the fact that the great seaman had succumbed to his Trafalgar bullet wounds many years before. It all hung on a childhood memory; she had stood with her mother in the streets of Portsmouth and cheered as the victorious admiral drove past in his carriage. This memory alone was the spring from which poured all her subsequent romances. Now she was always dressing herself, powdering and bathing herself, drenching herself in perfumes, brushing or curling her long auburn hair, in preparation for her next secret assignation with her ghostly lover.

'Psssst, Jenny,' she would hiss to her cook. 'If you should by any chance see Sir Reginald looking for me, please do not disclose that I am in the loft above the woodstore.'

'Of course not, my Lady,' the cook would agree, understandingly.

'He's there again,' aunt Elizabeth would say joyfully, blushing like a seventeen year old. 'Straight back from his exploits against the French; his first thoughts for me. Oh, the darling man.' She would lift her skirts, and hurry away across the yard, giggling to herself, her bonnet ribbons fluttering behind her.

* * *

32

After an enjoyable year on the estate, where young John Pendragon, in company with Croaker the warrener, learnt to use ferrets to catch rabbits, snares to trap hare, and to handle an old but pretty flintlock shotgun lent him by uncle Reginald, he received one of the rare letters from his father. It told him that his future education had been arranged, and that he was expected to report to the headmaster of Eton College forthwith.

* * *

There were more shocks to come. Pendragon knew nothing of the Eton educational system; he'd had servants all his life and found no pleasure in acting as general do-everything for boys only a few years older than himself. There was anger, resentment and some violence before Pendragon came to realise that acceptance was less painful than resistance. But in the first year he was a poor scholar. Only one pleasant thing happened; he met another of his aunts, his mother's youngest sister, Georgina.

Aunt Georgina was very much younger than either of her sisters; she had been born late in her mother's life. She was now only twenty-three. She was not merely pretty and vivacious, she was stunningly beautiful. Her hair seemed, at a distance, to be pure silver. It was in fact almost white blonde. Her eyes were green and her lips inviting; her complexion was flawless. Her figure, poise and appearance could silence a complete ballroom at her entry.

Young John Pendragon fell madly in love with her in his twelfth year, on the steps of her London house.

Uncle Reginald and aunt Elizabeth had been invited to spend a month of the summer with friends in Yorkshire. The old hall would be empty. John was already on vacation from Eton and they suggested he might care to spend the next few weeks with another relative, his aunt Georgina, at her home in Park Lane, London. John, remembering his first sights of the great city, was unenthusiastic. He would, he assured his uncle, be quite happy alone in the old hall, just so long as Jenny the cook would be there to prepare food for him and Croaker available for company. Uncle Reginald laughed away the suggestion and punched John hard in his ribs.

33

'Wait until you take a glimpse of the gal, Copper-Nob,' he shouted, 'Knock your eyes clean through the back of your pate. Smartest little filly in England. Got hocks that have turned the head of Prince . . .'

'Don't you dare, Sir Reginald,' interrupted aunt Elizabeth, returning sharply but briefly to reality. 'Especially in front of MY nephew. I will simply not allow it; besides, it is a slanderous lie which borders upon sedition and treason.'

'Good grief!' exclaimed uncle Reginald. 'She'd have me hanged for compliments. Boy, have you ever heard how your aunt trumpets if anyone criticises Horatio Nel . . .'

'Sir Reginald,' warned aunt Elizabeth, furiously. 'You have gone too far.'

'I think I'd like to stay with aunt Georgina,' said John Pendragon hurriedly. It seemed the only way to prevent his uncle and aunt coming to blows at the dinner table.

* * *

Aunt Georgina's house was 39 Park Lane. It was of Georgian design, bow-fronted on the ground and first floor, with a curved balcony giving a viewing area, outside aunt Georgina's bedroom on the third floor. There were servants' quarters in the attic, and the kitchens and larders were in a semi-basement, and extended beneath a small paved garden at the front. The house was built on a corner, and overlooked fashionable Hyde Park.

At the rear was a stable yard, stables and a coachhouse; grooms' and coachmen's rooms were above them.

The décor inside 39 Park Lane was as one would expect in any residence occupied by aunt Georgina Carr. It was elegant and tasteful, the colouring cool and relaxing. She bent not one jot towards the heavier furnishing currently popular, but chose those so light in appearance they seemed to want to float above the rich Persian carpeting. She favoured the works of the modern painters, and was prepared to defend violently the genius of Turner, one of whose paintings graced the wall of her salon. In fact her pet hate was Hazlitt, who had dared to accuse Turner of 'quackery' in his colour mixing.

John Hawkdale Pendragon was delivered by Croaker, uncle Reginald's warrener. They had travelled first by public stage to

Guildford, where they had changed, after a one night stop at the Crescent Inn on Guildford Hill, to another coach which carried them to The Cock in Holborn. From there they took a growler to the Hyde Park address. Croaker was more a liability than an assistance. It was his first trip in a stage coach, his first overnight stop in an inn, and his first visit to London. He was terrified, touching his forelock indiscriminately to anyone who happened to look in his direction.

'I shall walk back, Master John,' he said, twitching like a stoat caught in a gin trap. 'I can't be abiding they noisy smelly pooblic vehicles. Be too dangerous a skippin' and a leapin' on cobbled roadways. I shall walk.'

'But it's fifty-eight miles,' warned John Pendragon.

'I shall cut me a stout wallupin' stick,' said Croaker, looking across Park Lane at some trees bordering Hyde Park. 'An' I shall walk it in two days easy, taking me kip along the hedgerows. There's clean water in the streams, an' no doubt I'll find a field or two of turnips; maybe a rabbit or a hare for supper. Don't 'e worry yourself, Master John.' He banged the brass knocked of 39 Park Lane, so the sound echoed back from some distant part of the interior of the house, then, as he heard footsteps inside, he touched his forelock one last time to John Pendragon and was gone.

It was a crop-haired butler who opened the door. He glanced down his nose at the trunk and carpet bag on the steps, then at John. 'Yes?' said the butler with the tone of a question.

'I'm John Pendragon, aunt Georgina's nephew. Come to stay.'

There was a pattering of soft slippers behind the butler, he stepped quickly aside and John Pendragon found himself confronted by his beautiful aunt. She held her arms wide in welcome, as though they had known each other from childhood, were brother and sister; she wore a flamboyant afternoon dress of cream silk that seemed alive with her movement. The boned corsage exaggerated her slim waist, and was decorated with a fan-shaped piece of material glistening with seed pearls across her breasts. She moved towards him. John Pendragon realised he was standing with his mouth open; he shut it, almost biting his tongue, feeling an unknown warmth slip through his veins.

'John,' she said. 'Dear John. How delightful to have you to stay with me. We will be good friends.'

Never, in the whole time John spent with her, either then, or in subsequent holidays, did she ever refer to him as a child, a boy, a youth, or to his age. He was simply John, or Dear John. She was a young woman of considerable intelligence and charm, as well as beauty.

* * *

Aunt Georgina became Georgina to John Pendragon; she forbade him the title 'aunt', claiming with a shudder it created a picture of a middle-aged woman with thinning hair and bad teeth. She was responsible, though, through the following years for much of his social education.

She lived in luxury on a mysterious pension paid into her bank each month by the German government. Most of her household servants were also German—including the butler, Wolfgang. Her German connections were the one subject she refused to discuss, even when pressed. All John Pendragon ever learnt was that she had travelled to Italy in 1837, and shortly afterwards moved to Bonn, before staying with the court in Brussels, and later in the Duchy of Coburg. She had returned to England in 1839, shortly after the unexpected announcement of Queen Victoria's engagement to Prince Albert of Saxe-Coburg. The engagement announcement surprised a number of intimates of the German Court at the time, as Prince Albert had told William, Prince of Löwenstein, of his intentions to withdraw from the arranged affair. John speculated, asked, but was told no more.

Living at 39 Park Lane was exciting; there were always interesting people visiting. Georgina enjoyed a busy social life, and few days ever passed without either a dinner or luncheon party, a musical evening or an invitation out. John Pendragon learnt his manners, discovered about fine wines, champagnes and brandies, was introduced to fashion and well-tailored clothes, and, of course, to all of Georgina's large circle of friends and acquaintances; titled aristocrats, military men, politicians.

At first he divided his holidays between the Hampshire

estate of uncle Reginald and aunt Elizabeth, but as the pair grew even more strange and disturbed, he found himself spending more and more time in London, until at last he came to realise both he and Georgina considered 39 Park Lane to be his home.

* * *

At fifteen he had little idea of money. An allowance sent to him by his father, now a Colonel, did little more than clothe him in a style agreeable to Georgina, who enjoyed him as an escort now he was almost six feet tall and considered by herself and her lady friends rather handsome. His wardrobe was reasonable; seven coats, which included a morning coat, a frock coat, a dress coat and an overcoat—four of the first and one each of the others, costing £18. He had six pairs of morning and one of evening trousers; a further £9. Four morning waistcoats and also one for evening wear, which cost him £4. There were, of course, his scarves, hats, neckties, gloves, linen and boots, which accounted for an additional £15. The £50 spent on his wardrobe left him little of his allowance, but somehow, in Georgina's company, there seemed no need for money.

John Pendragon's future had never been questioned. It was assumed by Georgina, and by John himself, that he would make a career in the army. At seventeen he left Eton and became a cadet at the Royal Military College at Sandhurst. He enjoyed the college for even the smell was familiar, reminding him of his childhood; the wet chalk on belts and equipment, saddlesoap on leather, mutton grease on gun carriage axles, the odour of percussion caps and gunpowder.

At nineteen he graduated, qualified in all but experience to fight wars on behalf of Her Majesty Queen Victoria. It was natural he would join a cavalry regiment; he considered sailing back out to India to serve with his father but decided, from a career point of view, that he would probably do better in another regiment. Georgina made the final decision.

'It has to be Prince Albert's Own, the 11th Hussars. Such a charming uniform; so well designed, so pretty. And so manly with those red breeches and all that bullion braid. Boring Lord Cardigan spends most of his income on his regiment, and has the best London tailor to make the royal blue jackets. You'll look so handsome at the balls; a fur-trimmed pelisse and a high plumed hat. Not a young lady in London will be able to resist you.'

'They're a good regiment,' agreed John Pendragon. 'But I hear it's not easy to enter. I'm uncertain my allowance will permit me.'

'Pish! I shall make it my gift to you for your twentieth birthday,' insisted Georgina. 'As for an entry to the regiment, Lord Cardigan will have to take you. I doubt if many of his officers have military college experience. Your allowance? I shall write to your mother Catherine, and suggest an immediate increase. Meanwhile, I absolutely insist you let me help you.'

John Pendragon's interview with Lord Cardigan was an indication to him of Georgina's influence. Cardigan made it quite clear he was accepting Pendragon on someone else's orders. Someone else whose orders were unquestionable.

'I hear you are to serve with me,' he said sneeringly. 'Then you'd do damned well to make up your mind now to serve well. Officer or trooper, I stand no slackness or neglect of duty.'

Pendragon was aware of Lord Cardigan's reputation; in the first few months of the man's command, he instigated fifty-four courts-martial, and on one Easter Day had a soldier of the regiment flogged after church, in the very place where the service had just been held. He'd also been accused of fighting a murderous duel with rifled pistols fired by hair triggers. This was considered at the least unsporting.

'Tell me your history,' snapped Lord Cardigan.

Pendragon told him.

'Can you ride a charger?'

'I used to be able to manage a lance, and I have hunted,' said Pendragon.

'A charger isn't a poncing hunter,' snarled Cardigan. 'God blast me! A charger is the finest horse you can buy. It's lightning on four legs. It's a horse which will take a straight line, come hell or high water, through shell or shot. It's strong, and tough, fine bred and courageous. It's got brains, which is a damned sight more than I can say of most of my troopers; the scum, the Iron Duke was right, they enlist for drink. D'you know the most common reason for enlistment?'

'No, my Lord,' apologised Pendragon, surprised at the turn of conversation.

'Because the scum have been jilted by their sweethearts! Well, I take the scum, and I turn them into hussars. The finest hussars in the world. Prince Albert's Own! Damn me, the troopers are in truth Cardigan's Own! And you'll learn too, my lad. I shall expect you to know cavalry drill as well as myself, if that's possible—God help you if it's not. And, no matter how good you think you are as a horseman, I'll prove you different; but you'll end up good, or you'll end up discharged.'

* * *

There was a full year of endless riding, drilling, sabre and lance training, in the barracks square and the training grounds.

Sir Reginald Spence was killed in an accident on the Hampshire estate; he succumbed to an attack of Elm disease. Whilst he was inspecting an ancient tree and estimating its value in terms of pipes of Spanish wine, a large and gnarled branch, weakened by the previous night's storm, broke free and descended violently upon him. By the time Croaker the warrener returned to Sir Reginald's assistance his knightly master was dead. Sir Reginald's legacy to John Pendragon was Dasher Charlie, an Irish horse recently purchased from a racing stud.

Dasher Charlie arrived in London a few days after the end of Pendragon's first year of training. He was an outstanding horse, an ungelded stallion of considerable mettle. Tall, stately, and with all the horsely attributes of good breeding.

Lord Cardigan saw him the hour of his arrival. Pendragon had saddled him for a trial ride.

'Whose is that animal?'

'Mine, my Lord,' answered Pendragon. Cardigan could be a frightening man.

'Let me ride him,' ordered Lord Cardigan. He didn't bother to wait for Pendragon's reply; he swung himself into the saddle, to the astonishment of a guest he'd invited to lunch

39

and was now abandoning. He rode out of the barracks towards the park. He was not seen for three hours. At last he trotted back into the stables, wet with perspiration and breathing heavily. Dasher Charlie was in a similar condition. Pendragon had been waiting with increasing anxiety for his horse's return.

Cardigan dismounted and passed the reins to a groom. He turned to Pendragon with a huge grin on his red and sweating face. 'Damn me. That animal is the finest piece of horseflesh I've ridden for twenty years. Finest without a doubt. Wish I had a thousand like him. Will you sell him? Two hundred guineas.'

'I've just inherited him,' explained Pendragon. 'I'd rather keep him as my charger.'

'Sound man,' growled Cardigan. 'Good sense. He'll be an excellent charger. I'm damned if I'd sell him either, Captain.'

'Not Captain, just . . .' began Pendragon.

'Captain,' said Lord Cardigan, firmly. 'No man less than a Captain deserves a horse like that. What's your name?'

'Pendragon.'

'Well, Captain Pendragon, I don't know what sort of a hussar officer you're making, but I'll tell you one thing for certain; with a horse like that, you can only be a good one.'

*   *   *

The Crimean War began in the hot weather of late June, in Pembroke Lodge, Richmond Park, just a few miles away from London. It began mainly because the Cabinet, who were meeting in the Lodge, had dined too well; most were yawning, some were unashamedly asleep. The Russians and the Turks were already at war. Lord Aberdeen had unwillingly agreed to make vague British troop and fleet movements, that might be construed by the Russians as a possible British intention to take an active part in the campaign. It was a purely political manoeuvre.

Today, however, the Secretary of State for War, the Duke of Newcastle, was quietly reading aloud a despatch, a request from the army stationed near the Crimea for action; he was reading it in such a desultory and monotonous tone of voice that it barely penetrated the dimmed consciousness of well-dined members of the Cabinet.

One man was wide awake; Lord Palmerston. He wanted war. He agreed with the French and their new Emperor Louis Napoleon; fight now. There was a need for war! The British fleet, and a fair-sized proportion of the army, were within striking distance of Russia. They were actually in the Black Sea, waiting!

The Duke of Newcastle droned on.

The Cabinet, still half asleep, nodded an agreement. Later many of them had no idea to what they had agreed.

A despatch consenting to action was sent to Lord Raglan, Commander in Chief of the British Army camping in the swamps on the shores of the Black Sea. He contacted his opposite number in the French forces, Marshal Saint-Arnaud. Together they planned the invasion of the Crimea.

In England there were signs of the escalation towards war. The Coldstream Guards were given permission to lay aside the leather stock that kept their heads erect on parade, and to grow beards. Their fur shakos were replaced by a more practical forage cap. A new muzzle-loading rifle was issued to some regiments. The lancer and cavalry regiments checked and sharpened lances and sabres; young officers crowded into Westley Richard's gun shop at 170 Bond Street, to discuss the choice of new pistols with William Bishop, Richard's congenial gunsmith.

Ships of the line, still carrying sail, but equipped with steam-driven propellers, crowded the British ports and estuaries. Men, horses, supplies were loaded. The movement to Crimea began.

* * *

There was a farewell ball at 39 Park Lane for Captain John Pendragon. Georgina had been planning it for weeks and had hired additional staff for the occasion; the kitchens worked long hours preparing the food for the buffet, and a considerable stock of champagne and clarets had been laid in. Much of the salon and lounge furniture was moved into storage in the stables, giving adequate room for a small orchestra and for the dancing. It was a happy and jovial affair, with John in his best dress uniform, and Georgina in flowing watered silk wearing a tiara of small diamonds in her blonde hair, leading the first of the gallops.

John Pendragon danced until his feet ached, and his blue jacket under the pelisse hung over his left shoulder was damp with perspiration. He took a glass of the champagne, slipped out of the house and strolled across to the trees bordering the park. It was cool, the air fresh and clean after the ballroom. There was no moon, but the night was clear with a million stars overhead. He leant against one of the tree trunks and stared out across the darkness of the park, wondering how long it would be before he rode there again.

There was a rustling beside him. He turned, startled.

'John?' It was a woman's voice.

'Yes,' he said. 'I'm sorry. I can't . . .'

The woman anticipated his question. 'Zara Cashell.'

'Ma'am,' said John Pendragon. She was standing quite close to him and he could recognise her now; Lady Cashell, wife of the Minister for Colonial Affairs, Lord Francis Cashell. He'd met her several times before. She was an attractive woman, a year or two younger than Georgina, with vivid red hair, and an extraordinary pallid complexion.

'Don't Ma'am me, Captain Pendragon. You may call me Zara.' She made a sighing sound. 'It was so close in there; when I saw you come outside for a breath of evening air, I followed your example. Are you looking forward to the war?'

John Pendragon hesitated before he answered. 'Yes, I suppose I am. If only to put into practice all I've been taught.'

'I suppose if young men are trained to kill, then it is only reasonable to allow them to demonstrate their skills somewhere. Do you like to practise *all* that you have learned?' Her voice was teasing.

She slipped her arm through his own. 'There is a chill in the air now. I feel it on my shoulders. Walk me back, please.'

'Of course,' said Pendragon.

'It would be indiscreet for me to remain out with you longer. Though I am more than a little tempted by this handsome hussar officer.'

Pendragon chuckled. 'Handsome is, as . . .'

'Handsome does.' Zara Cashell ended his quotation for him,

then changed the position of her arm, so he was supporting it in a more formal manner as they neared the house. 'I wish to know you better, John. The war will not be a long one. Aberdeen tells me it can be over in a matter of months. I shall look forward to your safe return.'

The ball continued into the early hours of the morning, when at last Pendragon was forced to excuse himself to return to his barracks to make ready for embarkation later that day. There was a brief skirmish of handshakes and good wishes, then Georgina led him into the hall.

'I shall miss you, John.' She was crying now, silently.

John Pendragon stooped and kissed her on the cheek. She dabbed at her tears with a silk kerchief. John Pendragon took hold of it. 'May I have this to carry for my luck? Georgina's tears to remind me of home.'

She smiled at him. 'Of course, dear John. But you must carry it in a charge for me.'

Wolfgang, the butler, was standing at the doorway, Pendragon's fur hat and sabre in his hands. He passed them to Pendragon then waited until he had clipped the sabre to his belt, and straightened the hat before the tall gold-framed mirror. 'The carriage is outside, Captain John,' he said. He reached behind him to the narrow hall table, and handed John Pendragon a small book. 'This is from myself and the staff,' he said gruffly. 'And take great caution, Captain John, for we all love you.'

The book was a bible.

* * *

When Pendragon and the Light Brigade landed at Calamita Bay, they were a thousand strong, but the French, who had embarked their own troops at Marseilles, had brought with them more than men and equipment; they had brought cholera.

It spread rapidly through all the armies.

By the fateful day of the Light Brigade charge at Balaclava, the Brigade was reduced, by illness, to 639 men.

It was a sick war.

Now for Captain John Pendragon, it was over.

3

JOHN PENDRAGON WAS in a poor state of health again by the time he eventually reached London at the end of April, 1855. The journey back from the Crimea had taken three and a half months. There had been delays in Holland, and longer delays at Oostende before suitable arrangements could be made to transport Pendragon, Dasher Charlie, and Pendragon's luggage across the channel. John Pendragon was lame, sick and emaciated; what he had gained in health in the comfort of the sea trip he lost in the harassment of the final miles of his journey.

Had he been fit, it would have been easy to arrange for his baggage to have been brought up by carrier, while he rode Dasher Charlie the last hundred miles from Dover to Georgina's house. As it was, neither Pendragon nor his horse were capable of the ride. Rather than trust Dasher Charlie alone to the dubious care of an independent waggoner, Pendragon stayed a few more days in Dover until he was able to find a conveyance suitable for both himself and the animal. He had discarded his uniform on board the Dutch ship, and was poorly dressed in civilian attire.

The pair arrived in Georgina's stable yard in a hay waggon, having been the subjects of ribald comments from urchins and street traders once they had entered the city. Pendragon was past caring. He was only glad to see the familiar faces of Georgina's groom and coachman.

Pendragon was unlikely ever to forget his welcome. The groom watched the hay waggon rumble its way into his yard with a look of disbelieving horror on his face that such a common vehicle should dare to roll the same paved court as his delicate coaches. He leapt in front of the waggon, waving his arms. 'Stop,' he shouted. 'Get out. This is a private court-yard. Take this thing away at once.' For the first time he noticed Pendragon sitting hunched behind the driver. 'Oh, bless me,' he said, hurrying forward. He turned and shouted again. 'Kurt! Kurt! Hurry man, give me a hand here.'

The coachman ran across to his side rolling his shoulders as though expecting a fight. His eyes widened as he too recognised Pendragon.

'Sir, oh Captain John, whatever? Oh goodness.' He turned, and like the groom began shouting wildly, but in German. Within seconds they had all the servants out of the house.

They helped John Pendragon down from the hay wagon, with much tutting and oo-ing. They were horrorstruck at his appearance, dismayed at the sight of his crutches. The men groaned and the women wept. It was bedlam; made even worse by the waggoner shouting, in a thick Kentish accent, for his payment.

They carried Pendragon into the salon and sat him in one of the satin-covered chaises-longue, disregarding the straw and mud on his clothes and boots. They fussed him. The maids, all of them, ran in different directions, finding him cushions for his back, his arms, feet; the groom—who shouldn't even have been in the house—almost fought the butler, Wolfgang, to fetch him a glass of brandy.

'We read of it, Captain,' said Wolfgang. 'We were afraid for you, and we prayed.'

'We really did, Sir,' squeaked the kitchenmaid. 'All one Sunday in the kitchens.'

'And the next one too,' added the cook.

'You was bleeding heroic, Sir,' said the groom. 'The whole lot of yer. Bless me, I was proud I knowed you, bleeding proud.'

'Watch your tongue,' scolded the housemaid. 'There are ladies here.'

'Was it like they said, Sir? Was it really so terrible?' The kitchenmaid was almost shrieking with excitement, her voice cutting through Pendragon's head. She was kneeling by his feet, looking up into his face, like a child waiting to be told a story.

There was a firm clapping of hands at the doorway, and Georgina's voice, stern as though she were interrupting an orgy. 'What on earth is going on here? My goodness me, what are you all up . . .' She suddenly noticed John Pendragon amongst the crowding servants. Her mouth dropped open. Her cheeks whitened. She swayed as though she were about to faint. 'John?'

Her maid hurried to her. 'Yes, Ma'am. It's Captain John, come back home to us, Ma'am.'

John tried to push himself up from the chaise-longue. Georgina almost ran across to him. 'John,' she gasped. 'Dear, dear John.' She stooped and kissed him, holding his head between her warm hands. She stepped back to look at him. 'John, oh, you're so thin.' She noticed the crutches. 'And these?' She put her hand to her mouth. 'John, oh John, you're wounded. Tell me it isn't too bad. You haven't lost a . . .'

'Please,' John Pendragon smiled a silent request at her. 'I'm well enough. Tired, just tired.'

'Shoo,' said Georgina to the servants. 'All of you, off now. Wolfgang, go and fetch Doctor Ferrier, he must examine Captain John at once. Edeltroud, boil water; as much as you can for a deep bath for the Captain. Emma, make up his bed and see that it is well warmed. And Cook, broth, hot and strong from the fresh beef; lace it with the best port.' The servants scattered, still chattering.

'Wait,' John Pendragon called to the groom. 'My horse, Dasher Charlie, he was my charger at Balaclava. He was wounded too. Please see he's stabled and fed.'

'By my life, Captain,' grinned the groom. 'He'll have the very best treatment there is.' He turned to leave, then stopped. 'Would you be so kind, Captain John, as to allow me to show 'im off to me friends?'

Captain John Pendragon was home at last.

* * *

One of the few things Lord Lucan had been correct about in the Crimea was the forewarning he had given Captain John Pendragon of his welcome in London. For the first few days after his return he was subjected to continuous visits from friends of his own and Georgina; and friends of friends, as though he were a new species of animal on exhibition in the zoological gardens. Dasher Charlie fared no better in the stables and, in fact, the groom could have made himself a small fortune by charging a few coppers for a glimpse of the horse and its Balaclava battle scars. Costers and street traders, their wives and families, nannies and their charges, made a visit to the stables almost a day's outing. There were other wounded soldiers around the metropolis, but Pendragon was the first to return from the heroic Light Brigade charge.

Fortunately, John Pendragon was confined to the house on the orders of Doctor Ferrier. At least this saved him from becoming a public spectacle and being followed everywhere, as happened when those in uniform returned later in the year.

Doctor Ferrier, who was surgeon to many of the Royal household, gave the young man a thorough examination. He was horrified to learn of the state of the hospitals in the Crimea, and furiously angry at the crude surgery used on Pendragon's wounds. Externally the wounds had healed, but the surgeon feared pieces of bone, or even shrapnel might have been left inside; there had been severe damage to the thigh muscles, and to the tendons below the knee. Doctor Ferrier had little confidence in the ability of the Turkish bone-setter, but was forced to admit the man seemed to have done a good job as the leg was at least straight.

However there was nothing much to be done, except to rest John Pendragon until he was strong enough to force himself to use the damaged leg, and rebuild the wasted muscles. As for the future, Doctor Ferrier shook his head at the question; Pendragon would walk, and walk well—even run or swim—but as to riding? Of course, he would be able to canter around the park, and even do a little moderate hunting, but he should forget about strenuous riding, about military riding, when a man might be a full day in the saddle—or sent for weeks, even months, on horseback patrols. There was to be no more army for John Pendragon. The field surgeons had been right.

John Pendragon was disappointed. He'd hoped there'd been a diagnostic error; hoped for a small miracle. Secretly, he'd always believed a few months' rest would see him back with the 11th. Now he was forced to accept the truth. It was unpleasant.

* * *

After a fortnight in the house, when he filled his waking

hours with conversations with Georgina and her friends, and with catching up on his reading and home news, he began short daily walks in the park. At first he used the crutches, but soon discarded them in favour of a stick. A month afterwards he managed with a light cane, although his left leg was still extremely stiff and uncertain, and his knee seized solid at the joint.

One morning he rose early just before dawn, and slipped out into the park wearing only light trousers, a shirt, and soft shoes. He walked across to the section which had been the site of the Crystal Palace before it was moved to Sydenham. There was still a series of stone steps there, and a long terrace. He climbed the steps and stood at the top for a few moments, then suddenly leapt the full six feet from the terrace, forcing himself to take almost all the weight of landing on his left leg. There was terrible pain; he shouted; the knee bent its full distance.

He lay on the ground for several minutes in agony, perspiration streaming from his face. At first he was certain the knee joint had snapped, but as the initial pain passed he tried moving it slightly; the joint pivoted, although still painfully. The lesions which had bound it had parted. He hauled himself back on to his feet, and forced himself to walk all the way back to the house, without using the cane. He never mentioned the incident to Georgina, or Doctor Ferrier, but the sudden increase in the movement of the injured leg caused the surgeon much astonishment.

* * *

The weather was warm with approaching summer, and London, for John Pendragon, had become the most tedious place on earth. He felt frustrated and even guilty as he read the reports of the war in the *Illustrated London News*. Even now, flicking over the pages of the magazine, and studying the artists' sketches of the battle scenes, he could smell the Crimea, the sweat of exhausted men, the gunsmoke and blood and rotting corpses. There were even times when he envied those of his friends who were never to return; at least they had made the supreme sacrifice for their country, while he had done so little.

The days were too long. To shorten them he took to leaving his bed late in the mornings, breakfasting at eleven, then strolling up Oxford Street to meet some of his fellow officers, similarly discharged and equally frustrated, in the coffee shops behind Wigmore Place.

His closest friend was Charles Crighton, an ex-cavalry major, a dandy born thirty years too late, who prided himself on his immaculate cravats and his skill as a gambler, and who still carried three Russian musket balls somewhere inside his chest.

Another was James Lumley, a humorous and slightly portly ex-lieutenant of the Coldstream Guards, who had managed to lose an eye on the point of one of his own guardsmen's bayonets during a skirmish. He cursed his bad luck, but wore a black silk eyepatch embroidered with his regimental crest.

Jack Howard and Cyril Carlton were considered the un-heavenly twins of the Guards and Cavalry Club. They had been brother officers of the Duke of Cambridge's Own, and had been wounded, almost simultaneously, during the battle of Alma. They had shared their training together, their quarters in the Crimea, had their beds side by side in the hospital, and arrived back in England in the same ship. By coincidence, they had been discharged the service in the same hour of the same day. They were seldom seen anywhere apart.

Although grateful for their company, John Pendragon was still bored. He could anticipate the daily conversations; the subjects were inevitable. The current battles, regiments who were involved, the possible battle plans. Then there was some horse racing. Crighton would place a hundred guineas on some impossible outsider; it would win. Lumley's horse, even if it had been the favourite, would trail in only a little ahead of the field of the following race. Had the jockeys been aware of the effect of Lumley placing a bet on their mounts, it is certain they would have arranged for his murder. Howard and Carlton would unknowingly place bets on the same mount, and then spend two hours discussing the coincidence which still seemed strange to them, but which was now accepted by all their acquaintances.

There were scandals. Sir James Howarth was seen leaving a dirty lodging house in Aldwych with a coster girl not more than twelve years old; Sir James was eighty-seven and should have known better.

Crighton swore undying love for Rose Fletcher, a seamstress who worked for Williams and Warrington in Oxford Street. For two whole weeks he rented a room, every afternoon, off the Strand and met Rose there. She lost her job. Only the combined efforts of Howard and Carlton prevented Crighton from marrying the girl, an action which would certainly have resulted in Crighton losing the financial support of his family, and his social position. Rose happily settled for twenty-five pounds and a rail ticket to Birmingham.

John Pendragon met Lady Zara Cashell, as she had promised before his departure for the war.

He was riding now; not mad thrashes along the length of Hyde Park's Rotten Row, but gentle trots along the mile. He was glad to be back on a horse again, and Dasher seemed pleased to feel him up on his back. It was an afternoon when Pendragon had lunched well and felt the need for a little open-air exercise.

The sky was cloudless although, towards the east over the city, there was the usual haze caused by the smoke of the ever busy factory chimneys. Pendragon swung Dasher across the park and rode him at a relaxed trot along Ladies' Mile. It was fairly crowded with horsemen and ladies, and with the carriages and traps of those who were taking advantage of the fine weather. There was the sound of hooves behind Pendragon, and for a moment he expected to hear a shout of welcome from one of the many cavalry officers who exercised their horses on this stretch of the park. Instead, a bay gelding hammered past, its rider side-saddled. The bay was jerked back roughly to match its speed with that of Dasher. A woman smiled at him.

'Captain John Pendragon.'

It was Zara Cashell. She wore the currently fashionable riding habit, which Pendragon always found rather too masculine in its cut to be attractive. On Lady Zara, however, it seemed more feminine than usual.

Pendragon raised his hat, and smiled a greeting.

She was a little breathless from her gallop. 'John Pendragon, I heard you were back, but wounded. I had hoped to

50

meet you before this.' Her cheeks, normally so pale, were flushed by her riding efforts. She was so petite, it seemed impossible she should be able to control as hefty a horse as the bay, which stood only a hand less than Dasher.

Pendragon reigned Dasher to a halt and Zara Cashell swung the bay so she was facing him. She stared at Pendragon. 'A little thinner, perhaps. A little older, but still as handsome.' She paused, then spoke quickly. 'When may we meet? No, I have a suggestion. Cashell is away at present, called to Paris for the signing of some stupid defence agreement. I had planned an evening at the theatre—this evening—the seats are already arranged at Her Majesty's, but I feared they should be wasted. May I be so bold as to suggest you might accompany me? This is little enough notice, so fear no offence at a refusal.'

'I would be delighted,' said Pendragon, surprised at the unexpected and sudden invitation.

Lady Zara smiled. 'And I, too: May we say seven? I shall await you at Grosvenor Square.' As though to deny Pendragon the opportunity of second thoughts, she dug a spur into the side of the bay and at the same time cut it across the rump with her whip. In moments she was out of sight through the grove of trees, leaving Pendragon still stationary on Dasher.

* * *

If Pendragon had any doubts as to the future direction of his friendship with Lady Zara Cashell, they were quickly dispelled in the carriage on the way back to her Grosvenor Square house after the evening's entertainment at Her Majesty's Theatre. Until then, she had been extremely formal, even coldly so, sitting quite two yards away from him in the theatre box, and permitting him only the mimimum amount of personal contact as he escorted her to and from their seats. But this was understandable; there were many acquaintances amongst the audience, and Pendragon was made quite aware she had no wish for them to have even the slightest suspicion of anything other than a respectable friendship with her escort.

In the carriage, however, she sat so close to him he could feel the warmth of her body through their clothing. Her voice was soft, and in a surprisingly low key for a woman; a relaxing voice that Pendragon found seductive and interesting. She was an attractive woman, and it was difficult to believe she was eight years older than himself. Throughout the journey, she questioned him constantly about his experiences in the Crimea, showing great concern at the discomforts of his journey home, but seemingly genuine relief that he was now recovered from his wounds.

At the door of her house, she dismissed Pendragon's carriage and coachman, with a simple, 'It is only a few hundred yards back to Park Lane; Captain Pendragon will wish to take the night air before his return.' The coachman looked at Pendragon, who nodded his agreement.

'No doubt, John, you would care for a brandy before you leave?' she suggested. She led him into the house. 'Forgive me; please give me your coat and hat. I have permitted my servants to bed themselves early. Too large for us, really,' she said waving her hand at the huge rooms with their decorated plaster ceilings and silk panelled walls. 'But accommodation in London is difficult, and we have the estate to maintain in Sussex. Estates! I refuse to live on the Cashell estate; the land is a perpetual swamp, and the manor is quite unbelievably chilly. Cashell likes it for this shooting. Shooting! Two thousand pheasants a season, the man is quite mad. He positively reeks of blood the whole time he's down there.'

Pendragon realised she was introducing small talk, waiting for him to take the initiative. He was standing quite close to her; it was the moment of decision. He took her arms in his hands and pulled her towards him. He knew she would now either freeze in his grip, or respond to his action. She half opened her mouth and bent her head back for his lips, her arms wrapped behind him strongly.

Pendragon could feel the front hoops of her crinoline pressing against him. Her petticoats were deep padding. He kissed her shoulders, tasting the rich perfume of her powder. Her fingertips brushed the soft hair on his neck.

After a few minutes, she pushed herself away from him, looked up at him with a faint smile, and spoke in little more than a whisper. 'You should take me to my bedchamber, John. I'm not a housemaid to be seduced in a drawing-room.' She held his hand and led him up the curving stairway. Her room was already lit; a fire burnt in the grate giving life to the shadows.

Zara stood and looked at him again, her eyes inviting. 'You must help me, John, for I am quite unable to undress myself.'

Later, as they lay naked together on the bed, she wriggled free of his arms and turned her back towards him. She leant down and the warm flesh of her breasts pressed on his hip. She lowered her head and he felt her tongue, hot, against the long blue scar on his thigh. She traced it gently upwards. He heard her say softly: 'And this is for gallantry, John darling.'

4

LONDON WAS FILLING with the wounded. Shops returned almost daily to vomit their degraded passengers into the streets of the city. They came back in no condition to work for any decent kind of living. Once-proud guardsmen earned farthings scribbling ill-drawn chalk sketches on flagstones; ex-artillerymen and troopers gathered cigar ends, collected dog droppings for tanneries, fought for places as crossing sweepers; those who were blind could only beg or pray. Many of the wounded who had survived the hospital conditions of the Crimea died of starvation in London. The 'scum' who had become soldiers became 'scum' again, and lived in disease-infested rookeries in the London slums. Fortunately only the strongest and fittest of them managed to reach the aristocratic areas of the West End; the badly maimed and disfigured, the cruelly warped and twisted, and the dying, embarrassed few people of importance.

* * *

Physically, John Pendragon was now almost completely well again. The good food of Georgina's kitchens had filled out his six-foot frame until Zara teased him that he was becoming podgy. His leg seldom pained him, although he limped. He was exercising regularly, daily. Riding Dasher every afternoon in the park, or taking him over to the open commons beyond Earls Court, where he could meet Zara without the possibility of satisfying the gossips.

Pendragon had not healed so quickly mentally. The sight of a man in uniform was enough to give him the feeling of a schoolchild playing truant from his classes. Both Zara and Georgina did their best to drag him out of himself, but at times he was silent and morose, and no amount of cajoling or encouragement could lift his depression.

By coincidence, one morning Pendragon met Major Fitz-Patrick, the Grenadier Guards officer who had been next to him in the dank ward of the Scutari Military Hospital. Like himself, William FitzPatrick had been discharged as unfit for further military service. The two men discussed their feelings over lunch; perhaps it was the link of their stay together in Scutari, but for the first time since his return Pendragon felt able to talk about his problem.

'You're not alone,' grunted FitzPatrick. He spun a glass between his fingers, watching the shafts of light reflected on the walnut table. 'I think we all feel useless. Cast-off clothing. You'd think they could use us as training officers.'

'I thought of that,' said Pendragon. 'I went along to my old barracks. I didn't even know the officers there. They'd all been seconded in from other regiments. Damned polite and all that, but I think they were glad when I left them. Sorry old man, they said, but this isn't peacetime; even the instructors have to be fitter than ever, pity about the wounds, come and make use of the mess whenever you feel like it. Blasted cheek! They made it sound like charity, as though I might not be able to afford the price of a meal. Fitz, what the hell do they expect us to do?'

FitzPatrick laughed wryly. 'They expect us to do nothing. Or they expect us to do exactly what we are doing; waste whatever time we've got left. There are worse wounded than us, John. Have you been into the City?'

Pendragon shook his head.

'I went,' said FitzPatrick. 'And I regretted it. Scutari was nothing; there are still men dying of their Crimean wounds, but in London, man, let alone in the field hospitals. Some of them have been discharged with their wounds unhealed and still suppurating. God, John, I saw a man of my own regiment; I didn't recognise him of course, but he knew me. Lost both his hands and half of his face. He was polishing harness for a carter with his feet, by heaven. With his damned feet for two pence a day! I gave him what money I was carrying, and the poor devil cried with the eye he'd got left. He'd been a Sergeant Major. I was sick in the gutter. I swore I'd leave England and go anywhere rather than face sights like that again. It might have been one of my orders that made the poor man like that.'

'Leave England?'

'Why not? What can I do here? There are the colonies; there's America. I thought of the fur business, not that I know much about it, but at least there's no shame in making your fortune from it abroad. There's the Hudson Bay Company, the one with the showroom in Oxford Street. I went to see the director. He said there were possibilities for educated men. He said just set yourself up, go and find fur where there is no competition. He gave me a letter to show their agents in Canada. Why don't you come with me? We could work together.'

'Perhaps,' said John Pendragon. 'But don't be insulted, Fitz, if I tell you it will only be as a last resort. I still feel I owe England a debt, and I'm a long way from settling it.'

* * *

Georgina's concern for John Pendragon grew as the weeks passed and he seemed unable to find anything to ease his mind. Her concern was not limited only to his health, but also to his future financial state. The pension he received was so small as to be almost insulting. There was some chance he might eventually inherit the Hampshire estate now the property of his aunt Elizabeth, but that could be years ahead yet. And there was the question of keeping him happily occupied. He seemed to have no hobbies; it was as if the army had meant so much to him, for so long, there was nothing capable of replacing it. She almost wished he could become interested in fossil collecting, or birds' eggs, or geology; anything which would activate his mind and take him out of the city at times.

One evening, at a dinner party, she discussed the problem with Mr. Sidney Herbert, the War Minister. It was nothing new, he assured her. It was normal for men in Pendragon's position. He would get over it in time. The interests would come; in trade or commerce, perhaps.

'Trade or commerce?' said Georgina in horror. 'An ex-officer of Prince Albert's Own, a tradesman?'

Well, perhaps not, agreed Mr. Herbert. But something would surely happen along. If he should hear of anything which might be of interest to a young ex-officer, then he would certainly contact her. He promised.

Georgina fluttered her eyelashes at him, made him feel manly and youthful. She knew he would remember.

* * *

There was an addition to the Park Lane household; Sergeant Henry Cox, ginger-haired, short and square, with a military moustache, stiff and spiked at its ends with pomade.

He arrived early one day and presented himself at the tradesmen's entrance. His voice was gruff and seemed to have a slight Welsh intonation to it, overlaid with Cockney accents. He stood at attention on the top step, with his shoulders pulled back, and his chin tucked so far into his chest that it lowered his voice by half an octave.

'I've got a letter, Ma'am,' he told the housekeeper. 'For a Captain Pendragon, Ma'am. A private letter, Ma'am, from India, Ma'am.'

The housekeeper eyed him from head to toe; there were too many unsavoury ex-military characters around London nowadays, and quite a few of them weren't above thievery for a livelihood. It was the sight of his boots that made her decide he was an honest man; they shone so brightly she could see herself reflected in a toecap. Surely a robber wouldn't bother to keep his boots that clean.

'I'll take it,' she said, holding her hand out for the envelope.

'Sorry, Ma'am, but the sender, he said deliver it personally into Captain Pendragon's hand, Ma'am, and so you see, Ma'am, that's what I've got to do, Ma'am.'

This presented the housekeeper with a problem. To get the letter personally to John Pendragon meant that either Captain John himself had to come through the kitchen quarters to the back door, or that this man should go around to the front door, which was strictly reserved for ladies and gentlemen. She said, 'Wait a minute,' and went inside to discuss the matter with Wolfgang. He returned to the door with her, and also scrutinised the man with the letter.

'Give it here,' he ordered, frowning down at the man.

'Sorry,' said the man. 'Told the lady, it's got to be personal into Captain Pendragon's hand. Him only—no one else.'

'Then you'd better come inside,' said Wolfgang, taking the

only course. 'And see you wipe your feet on the mat. I will ask if he will see you.'

The man, who had been wearing a flat, almost military style of cap, took it off. He scraped his feet first on the iron scraper, although it was a dry day and there was no mud anywhere, and he wiped them thoroughly on the coir mat. He followed Wolfgang into the kitchen, watched carefully every second by the housekeeper. 'Wait here,' said Wolfgang. He went out of the room and returned a couple of minutes later. 'Come.'

The man followed him. At the door of the lounge, Wolfgang stopped him. He knocked softly at the door before entering. John Pendragon was sitting reading a daily newspaper. 'The man,' said Wolfgang, as though the visitor was a bad smell.

'Henry Cox, Sergeant, retired, 5th Bengal European Cavalry, Sir.' He handed John Pendragon the envelope. 'Letter from Colonel Pendragon, Sir. Would you remember me, Sir? Cos' I remember you, Sir, as a boy, Sir.' Henry Cox was standing at attention again.

'Relax, Mister Cox,' Pendragon told him. He read the letter from his father. It was, in fact, more of a reference, telling John that Henry Cox had been a soldier of outstanding ability and honesty; that he was clean living and sober, good with lance or pistol, and to be highly recommended for any position of trust. It asked John to help the ex-Sergeant find a situation in London, if it were possible.

'Course, I was just a lancer in them days, Sir,' said Cox. 'And you was a small lad, begging your pardon, Sir. But I remember you very well.'

'How old are you, Cox?' asked Pendragon. He didn't remember the man. There had been many troopers in the fort at Rhotuck.

'Forty-three years, Sir.'

'When did you go out to India?'

'H'eighteen twenty-seven, Sir. Twenty-nine years' service, Sir. Started as a boy bugler, Sir.'

'No leave?' asked Pendragon.

Cox shook his head and grinned. 'No, Sir. At least, Sir, not English leave. Local leave. Same as your father, Sir, the Colonel.'

'Are you married?'

Cox's face stiffened very slightly. His moustache twitched. 'Was married, Sir. Bengali lady, Sir. Good family background. Three children, Sir. All died in fever epidemic, Sir. Four years ago. Reason I came back for retirement, Sir.'

'I'm sorry,' apologised Pendragon. 'Now, what can we do about you?'

'Can work at anything. Anything honest, Sir.'

Pendragon looked at Cox. The man was clean and tidy, his clothes well pressed. He kept himself well.

'I wonder,' said Pendragon. 'What would you say to being my man? I've been managing without help, but I could use a good man. You wouldn't have to wash linen or press shirts; just suits. Keep my shoes clean, prepare my clothes, help me generally.'

'Live in, Sir?' asked Cox.

'Live in, plus food and thirty pounds a year, for a start.'

'I'd like it, Sir,' said Cox. 'What I don't know, I'll learn fast, Sir. I won't take pay for the first month, Sir. Not 'til I've learnt my job. After that, as you say, Sir.'

Pendragon found Cox's recommendation was unexaggerated.

5

GEORGE PRICE WAS a rough-mannered, burly and tough York-shireman. He needed to be tough as a northerner carrying on a trading business in the East End of London, where anyone from north of Hampstead was considered a foreigner. George Price had begun his business in a small way as an importer of cotton from the southern American states. At first he'd been nothing but a middleman, between shipper and mill, but through use of his shrewd mind, and the placing of a little occasional gold in the right palm, now owned not only ware-houses in England and abroad but also the ships which carried his goods. His imports were no longer solely cotton but in-cluded any merchantable foreign commodity which might be available. It had been suspected, but never proved, that his ships' captains were not above the illegal carrying of slaves, should their holds be empty, their ports of call the right ones, and the winds fast and fair across the Atlantic.

His London warehouse and head office, an enormous slab of a red brick building six storeys high, stood on the north side of the river Thames, downstream of the Fleet sewer and only a half-hour waggon trip from the dock used by his ships.

La Belle Cygne, one of his trading schooners, known to her crew as the 'Dirty Duck', had moored to the wharf the day previously, after a twelve-month round trip to India and Burma. She carried silk, carpets, carved furniture, and four hundred and ninety-one rattan-bound cases of various spices; a cargo worth a small fortune. Her crew paid off with an average amount each of fourteen pounds for the twelve-month voyage.

The soft goods and furniture were unloaded first by the dock's casual labourers; this part of the unloading took a full day, at the end of which the 'Dirty Duck's' holds were bat-tened down again, and half a dozen burly watchmen set to guard her decks throughout the night. Her captain, Peter Jack Roberts, and her first mate, Ted Bratt, stayed on board.

The following morning, at a quarter past six, her holds were opened, and the heavy cases of spice lifted out on slings, and lowered down on to the dockside. They were counted by first mate Bratt, who checked each case against the ship's manifest.

Mr. George Price's warehouse foreman, a lath-thin weed of a man, with a biblical beard and a nervous tick to his jaw, counted the cases again as they were loaded on to one of Mr. Price's wagons for the trip to the warehouse.

The last of the cases were delivered late in the afternoon. The wagoner, who had made eight trips to and from the dock, helped stack the cases in the lower bay of the workshop, and, after feeding, grooming and stabling the horses, went home from work at seven in the evening.

The cases remained unopened for yet another night. Early next day, Mr. Fortnum of the well-known Piccadilly store sent a fast messenger to George Price asking what spices he held available in his warehouses. George Price sent the messenger back immediately with a letter to Mr. Fortnum, inviting him to lunch and to an inspection of his recently arrived cargo. Mr. Fortnum arrived at the warehouse a little after 1 p.m.

Mr. Price had arranged a luncheon at the Green Hand Tavern, east of St. Paul's Cathedral. The men travelled there by Mr. Price's coach rather than soil their shoes in the filthy streets. They passed close to the Cathedral, its railings hung with the baskets of street vendors selling slippers, ornamental grasses, square cakes of green turf for caged larks, oranges, and a thousand sundries. Street urchins washed at the pump, and Mr. Price's carriage was blocked for several minutes by the cart of a wild bird catcher which had shed an iron wheel-rim in the gutter. The food of the Green Hand Tavern was of no great merit, being nothing more than wholesome and plentiful. Its wine, however, was exceptional, imported directly from Burgundy by the owner of the Green Hand Tavern himself; being absolutely pure and undiluted it was something of a London rarity.

The two men returned to the warehouse at three-thirty p.m., feeling in a friendly and comfortable mood. Mr. Price was certain he had the spices Mr. Fortnum would require. Mr. Fortnum was equally certain he would be able to bargain with Mr. Price until a satisfactory costing of the spice was reached.

Mr. Price led his customer into the warehouse and stood beside the stack of cases. He rapped one with his fist. 'Good stuff, Mr. Fortnum. Nothing but the best, and fresh in from India. Certain to please your customers.'

'And that is the most important thing,' said Mr. Fortnum. 'My family's business has been built by selling only the best. May we now examine the contents?'

Mr. Price called over his warehouse foreman. The man arrived, twitching and wincing.

'Have the boxes opened,' ordered Mr. Price. 'The cloves first.'

The foreman signalled two untidy labourers and indicated the pile of boxes. The smaller of the two men clambered up the first stack, and rocked the top box until it slipped. The heavier man below caught it with a grunt, and lowered it to the ground.

The box was marked with a roughly painted yellow cross and a number. Mr. Price looked at his foreman. The man thumbed through a small notebook.

'Er, seven six eight, that's cloves, Sir,' he dithered.

'Then open the damned thing,' said Price, raising his eyebrows at Mr. Fortnum.

The foreman signalled the small labourer again, nodding down at the case. The man pulled out a broad-bladed pocket knife and slashed the rattan bindings. The foreman reached down and lifted the lid. The box contained a lumpy looking sack. The foreman's brow wrinkled. He peered into the sack, then glanced nervously up at Mr. Price. 'It's brick rubble, Sir,' he said.

'Damn and blast all of them,' roared Price. 'Beg your pardon Mr. Fortnum, but we've had more than our share of pilfering in the past. It's those idle scoundrels at the docks.' He turned on his foreman, who cowered away from him as though he expected to be beaten. 'Get down the other boxes of cloves. The three of them.'

'Yes, Sir, the three of them,' stammered the foreman. The labourers were already pulling at the next box. They opened it, and found more rubble. The third of the clove boxes, similarly marked with a large yellow cross, also contained rubble. By this time, Mr. Price was purple with fury.

'The other damned case,' he shouted, pointing at the last of the boxes that should have contained cloves.

His men cut the lid free and jerked it open. It did not contain bricks, or cloves.

It contained the body of a man, neatly folded, jammed down into the case with its head resting on its knees like a corpse in a South American Indian burial jar.

'Oh, dear me,' exclaimed Mr. Fortnum, feeling quite dizzy. He'd had the brief but horrific thought of what could have happened if the boxes hadn't been examined here, but opened in his respectable shop in the presence of a lady customer. 'Oh dear, oh dear.'

'Well,' yelled Mr. Price, his voice almost a scream. 'Get the thing out of the case.'

The foreman reached down and gingerly got hold of the corpse's hair. He pulled. The head lolled backwards.

Mr. Fortnum gave a very feminine scream of horror, and was sick on the cobbles of the yard.

'Holy mother of God,' breathed Mr. Price, who had been brought up a Catholic, but was seldom devout.

The head had almost come away in the foreman's hand. The throat had been cut so deeply that only the spine held it in place. The foreman gasped and let go. The head lolled sideways, the corpse's tongue dropping out of its open mouth, with a ghastly sucking noise.

'Forgive me, Mr. Fortnum,' said Mr. Price, shocked almost to silence. 'I think we had better send for the police.'

* * *

The corpse was collected by half a dozen Metropolitan policemen armed with a handcart and a sheet of tarred canvas. They rolled the body up like a length of carpeting and lashed it with ten feet of hemp rope, then pushed it away from the yard. They asked few questions; it was not their job to interrogate gentlemen. They trundled the corpse half a mile up the Fleet valley, changing places at the cart handles every few hundred yards as the steepness of the incline took their breath away. They turned right beyond Newgate Prison, and hauled the cart into the police station yard in Lower Spire Street. They slid the corpse, narrow end first, off the barrow, and dragged it roughly into one of the stables, then reported to the sergeant.

'Found dead, 'is bleedin' froat cut, Sarge,' volunteered one of the policemen. 'In a h'empty case what was supposed to contain spice, at Price's warehouse.'

'He was stiff as a carpenter's donkey,' said another. 'We had the devil's own job getting him straight. Knees under his chin. Inconvenient for carrying.'

'Murdered,' added a third.

'What's the story?' asked the sergeant, only partially interested. Murders were common this end of London. A dozen a day within half a mile of the station. It wasn't unusual for his men to have two, or even three on their beats during the same tour of night duty. The place was swilling with foreign seamen who carried their money openly, got drunk and almost begged to be croaked.

'I don't tumble it. 'E just turned up in a box, like,' said the first policeman. 'A consignment from h'India—came a couple of days ago h'on one of Price's schooners.' The man peered down at a scrap of paper, and read with difficulty. 'Four 'undred an' nine ... ninety-one cases of spice. Four of which was cloves. Three was empty an' the other was full of dead man. Mr. Price says 'e 'as no idea what 'appened, or from whence the man came.'

'Very well, constable,' said the sergeant. He took the slip of paper from the man. 'Any possessions on the deceased?'

'We ain't cooled him,' said another policeman.

'You ain't looked?' asked the sergeant, his voice disbelieving. 'Not for gold, you ain't looked?'

'No, sergeant,' replied the man. 'Most of us h'is nervous, now, since the inspector 'ad Will Jenks deported for nicking a few guineas off that dead whore in Hooper Street, Lambeth. We prefers to cool 'em in the station, before witnesses.'

'All right,' said the sergeant. 'Where's the dead person?'

'Stable.' The constable jerked his head towards the door.

* * *

The body had been searched and was re-rolled in the canvas, awaiting carriage to the morgue. The contents of the man's pockets, and his possessions, were heaped on the office table in front of the inspector. The sergeant and the most senior of the policemen stood before him.

'That's the lot, Sir,' said the sergeant.

'It'd better be,' warned the inspector. 'What's this?'

'His money, Sir. Twelve guineas, two florins, three pence, one half-penny and four farthings. A total of twelve guineas, four shillings and fourpence ha'penny.'

'I can do my own arithmetic, thank you.' The inspector prodded at a bloodstained bundle of papers with an ebony rule.

'Documents and letters of the dead party,' said the sergeant.

'Have you read them?'

'No, Sir.'

'And these things?'

'His boots, Sir. Looked too good to leave on a stiff. His relatives might care for them.'

'Anything else?'

'This pocket murderer, Sir, by T. Jackson of Maidstone; quite a pretty piece. Careful, Sir, it's loaded. And this knife, Spanish I'd think with a thin blade like that; it was down inside his boot. Oh, and this money belt.'

'Money belt? As well as a purse?' The inspector slid it towards himself. It was stiff with blood. He wrinkled his nose and peeled back the buttoned flap with careful fingers. It seemed empty, then he felt a strip of metal with his finger tips. He eased it out. It was a square of platinum, three inches long, two deep, and thin as vellum. It was impressed with square lettering and a crown with V.R. beneath.

The inspector let a hiss of air escape between his teeth. He pushed himself quickly from his chair and strode from the room. The sergeant and constable followed him, at a near trot. The inspector hurled back the stable door, and crouched beside the corpse. He jerked the canvas sheet from the dead man's face.

'My God,' he growled.

'What's the matter, Sir?' asked the sergeant.

'It's Rambolt, the spy-catcher, you fool,' snarled the inspector. He glowered at the sergeant. 'Well, maybe you wouldn't know him by sight, but I worked with the old blighter for years. Rambolt! Poor old beggar, ending his days like this; from Bow Street Runner to Queen's Secret Agent. Still, he had a long ride for his money.'

The constable looked at the sergeant, his eyes wide. 'By my oath, Rambolt! The Ram a dead 'un. God, England'll never be the same.'

The sergeant nodded. 'Rambolt was the best,' he said.

* * *

'Rambolt's what?' snapped Mr. Sidney Herbert, the War Minister.

'Dead,' said Page Cloverly, his private assistant. He slid the platinum identification plate across the leather-topped desk. 'Throat cut, near the docks.'

'Dead,' echoed Mr. Herbert. He ran his hand over his forehead in a dazed manner. 'Rambolt dead; I thought he was indestructible.'

'We all did,' said Cloverly. 'When a person has been around for so many years, I suppose it's the natural feeling. I remember hearing of him when I was a child. He was a legend. The first time I met him was like meeting a favourite character from a book. He was sixty-nine this year.'

'So old,' sighed Mr. Herbert. 'He should have taken the pension.' He ran a finger up between his heavy eyebrows to the front of his balding head. 'What was he working on?'

'The Woolwich Arsenal explosive theft,' replied Page Cloverly. He was a studious looking man, a sound dresser who looked younger than his forty-eight years. 'Twenty-four tons of gunpowder. No one steals that amount of explosive just to blow safes. If you remember, Rambolt had been working on the Dover case, the one where the two men had been passing on messages to the Russians; the Invasion Secrets case. I think he had a suspicion that all the carp weren't in the net—especially the fattest. He believed the cases were linked. Perhaps the carp turned out to be sharks and killed him.'

'They must have been quick to catch him off his guard,' said Mr. Herbert. 'He was a deadly shot, and he could use that sword cane of his like a French fencing master. He was supposed to have killed a couple of dozen men himself when he was a runner; and several since, I've no doubt.'

'What's to be done?'

'Replacement,' said Sidney Herbert. 'And a damned fast one at that. The cabinet want the explosive back under lock and key as soon as possible. I get questioned at every damned meeting. They imagine it can be used for anything from a modern Guy Fawkes to a working-class rebellion. We've got to replace Rambolt. There are few enough counter agents; Rambolt was invaluable. Someone must be found to take over. It is imperative we find out what he was about.'

'Not quite so simple. Rambolt worked on his own. He wasn't what I'd call a man of letters. His reports were difficult to understand. Taking over will be almost an impossibility unless we know what he was doing. We might get some sort of a clue from a police investigation.'

Mr. Herbert groaned, then said, 'Pah! Damned police. Well named as crushers. The only crimes they ever solve are those where they catch someone red-handed; or those where they can bribe an informant. A thousand unsolved murders every year in the metropolis. The police force isn't a force, it's a farce; Peeler's mob. Each constable only half a grade up from a criminal. At least our own men don't behave like rogues.'

Cloverly coughed, then smiled. 'I believe Rambolt knew the inside of Newgate better than most. I think he served two sentences in his early days, before he joined the Runners.'

'And the Runners were even worse than the police; Rambolt was an exception. A damned good man. No, if we are going to recruit a new man, then I think we should look for something quite different, for someone quite new. New blood, Cloverly.'

Cloverly nodded. 'New ideas could pay off. I most certainly agree, a new sort of man; an educated kind of gentleman. Perhaps a qualified law student; someone with ethics. Someone trustworthy and loyal to her Majesty, but willing to die if needs be.'

'Such as a good army officer,' suggested Sidney Herbert. 'An educated army officer. No, dammit; an ex-army officer! One who'd still like to serve, but can't. By God, that's it! An educated and well-bred ex-army officer.'

'If an officer was *that* enthusiastic, then in all probability he'd remain with his regiment,' warned Cloverly.

Sidney Herbert looked up at him, and raised a finger. 'Unless,' he said, quietly, 'unless the man happened to have been wounded. Not too seriously mind you, but enough for him not to be able to serve. Now, if there was such a man; there is such a man! Yes, I do believe there might be exactly the man.'

Cloverly looked curious. 'Who?'

'Pendragon,' said Sidney Herbert. 'Captain John Pendragon; if he'll consent to do it.'

6

GEORGINA WAS HORRIFIED; her green eyes flashed. 'A spy? That man Herbert is a fool, he insults us both.' She shook her silver blonde hair like a wild horse tossing its mane.

John Pendragon leant back in the quilted chair, and crossed his knees. He laughed. 'Not a spy, Georgina. A counter agent if you like, but hardly a spy. It's a Royal post. The possibilities amuse me, and I shall feel useful.'

'But chasing criminals, even though they may be foreign, is common police work. It's, well, worse than being a tradesman, or a dentist.'

Pendragon laughed again. Georgina was always prettiest when she was angry. 'I haven't made up my mind yet. But I don't think Mr. Herbert is a fool; nor Page Cloverly. And I don't think the offer is intended as an insult. They're asking me for help. As they say, the idea is something quite new. Until now, this kind of thing has always been done by ex-Runners, or the new police; Herbert doesn't think they're up to it. The foreign powers make use of diplomats, their travelling aristocracy. A man with the background of a Runner can hardly compete. Cloverly called it a modern and distinctive form of investigation.'

Georgina was determined to remain shocked. 'John, you can't really be interested in so preposterous a suggestion, no matter its name.'

'I'm interested in anything which might occupy my time,' confessed John Pendragon. 'Sitting around in coffee houses, going to the races, pleasurising, it becomes tedious. Besides, I must confess the thought of tracking down those responsible for Rambolt's death does have a certain appeal.'

'Rambolt!' Georgina said the name as though it were a curse. 'That man! Rambolt the spy-catcher. He was nothing more than a common footpad. I think he worked for the publicity he received in the low and vulgar press; for commission he received from street reciters and ballad singers. He was a patterer's hero.'

'Perhaps,' agreed Pendragon. 'But he did good work for the government. There is also the fact that Sidney Herbert offers me what he calls suitable remuneration for gentlemanly service.'

'Like a common workman. John dear, you don't need money so badly.'

'I need some,' said John Pendragon, firmly. 'I seem to have lived on your kindness since I was a child: my allowance was never enough. I believe you mentioned my circumstances to Mr. Herbert. I'm grateful to you, but you can hardly blame Herbert for trying to assist.'

Georgina was now even more furious. 'Circumstances! You make it sound as though I told him you were a pauper; not just a wounded officer. I had in mind a post of some responsibility, perhaps in an embassy, or as equerry. Not *this* . . .'

Pendragon stood, put his hands behind his back, and walked across to the window that overlooked the park. Georgina watched him. He was an attractive young man, and his limp was endearing and masculine. She sighed, pressed her lips together, and allowed them to relax to a slight smile.

'Good,' said Pendragon. He jerked Dasher Charlie to a position of great danger?'

'Not so dangerous as angering you, Georgina,' grinned Pendragon, turning to face her.

* * *

The Crimean War was now grinding into its final stages with no obvious signs of victory for either the Russians or the allied sides.

Lord Raglan was dead; from cholera or perhaps a broken heart. Exactly forty years after the day he had lost his arm at the battle of Waterloo, he stood in an advanced trench under heavy fire and watched a bombardment of Russian grapeshot cut long swathes through his infantry as they prepared a massive attack on the redoubts defending the city of Sebastopol. A French attack, following a misunderstood signal, led to even greater calamity. To support them Lord Raglan was forced to signal the advance into fire that was later described as a 'massive volcano'. After the battle, and the allies' terrible retreat, the Russians flew a derisive black flag, and then fired into the wounded on the battlefield. Raglan never recovered from his sadness and shock at that bitter day.

Between March and August, 1855, the Russians lost eighty-one thousand men, killed or wounded, around the besieged city of Sebastopol. They became desperate. On August 16th the battle began afresh. The Russians attacked; through lack of information they charged headlong into a withering concentration of allied fire. They turned to run, but a second wave of their own men carried them forward into the guns again. It was the beginning of the end. Sixty-nine Russian officers and twenty-three thousand more of their men died.

The Russians clung to Sebastopol as though the whole result of the war depended on them holding the city. They knew only a miracle could save their entire army; they hoped it would be a miracle directed, perhaps politically, by the Czar himself.

7

IT WAS THURSDAY morning. Pendragon awakened at a reason-
ably early hour and rang the servants' bell for Cox. The man
was at his door within seconds, already neatly dressed with
his usual military smartness. He knocked softly and waited
outside until Pendragon called him.

'Come in, Cox.'

'Sir?' he asked from beside the door.

'I think we should ride this morning,' said Pendragon. 'After
breakfast.'

'Of course, Sir,' answered Cox, taking the word 'we' in the
Royal sense, and moving towards the tall mahogany hunting
wardrobe to lay out Pendragon's breeches and riding boots. 'I
will have the groom saddle your horse, Sir.'

'Saddle two of the beasts,' said Pendragon. 'I want you with
me.' He paused and stretched himself, then leant over the
basin on the marble-topped wash-stand and poured out the
jug of cold water. He swilled the water over his head and
neck. Cox had stropped his razor the previous evening. It lay
ready and opened on a towel beside the soap and the badger-
hair lather brush. Pendragon spoke over his shoulder. 'Are you
inclined to a little possible adventure, Cox?' He began lather-
ing his face.

'Yes, Sir,' replied the man.

Pendragon picked up the razor and felt the keen edge with
his thumb. 'Then we shall talk as we ride.'

* * *

Hyde Park was almost deserted as most people were still
breakfasting; some two hundred yards ahead of Pendragon
and Cox there was a solitary rider having trouble with a
sprightly chestnut mare who seemed to dislike long grass and
prefer the cinder track of Rotten Row. Pendragon held back

and kept Dasher Charlie down to a gentle walk. Cox rode
Georgina's shining black gelding with the assurance of a man
who had spent almost a lifetime in the saddle, but kept himself a discreet couple of yards behind Pendragon. Pendragon
waved him alongside and when he caught up, rested forward
on his saddle, and told him of Mr. Sidney Herbert's request.

'Well, Cox?'

'Very interesting, Sir,' answered the man. 'It would please
me to help, Sir. Done a bit of inquiring, I have, of a regimental
nature, of course, Sir. Would enjoy the opportunity, Sir.' He
smiled happily.

'Good,' said Pendragon. He jerked Dasher Charlie to a
smart canter, and took a line across the park that would bring
them to Tyburn before they swung right to return to the Park
Lane house.

* * *

Pendragon washed again and changed into his morning
clothes before calling for Cox to have the light carriage prepared in an hour's time, at eleven o'clock, for the two men to
make their trip down to Mr. Price's warehouse. To Pendragon
it seemed the best place to begin, if there was to be any
beginning at all. The information he had been given on Rambolt's death was only sketchy, but he didn't want to go to the
police; Mr. Herbert had thought it unwise, as he wished to
keep Pendragon's identity secret for as long as possible.
Price's warehouse offered the only chance of furtherance of
the investigation.

Pendragon had thought of visiting Rambolt's home with a
view to searching for any possible written information, notes
or papers; but was surprised to learn from Page Cloverly that
neither he nor Mr. Herbert had any idea where the dead agent
had lived. He came and went like a ghost; whence, or to
where, no one knew. He reported only when there was something of importance to relate, or when certain expenses
needed to be met. His salary had been paid into a bank twice
a year.

* * *

Oxford Street was busy, and with so many coaches about, it

took an age to reach Holborn. Cox waved his whip and shouted at the hansom cab drivers who seemed to think prior right of way was theirs for the cost of the licence. Pedestrians wove their way through the traffic, the women shoppers lifting their wide skirts above their ankles as they crossed the roadway with its surface layered with filth and horse droppings. The weather was extraordinarily hot, and the refuse on the road and in the gutters was stinking. The pavement was little better for the pedestrians; London seemed to be a city of streets sellers. They crowded every sidewalk with their wares, making the streets noisy with their shrill cries.

'Here, laddie, watch out!' Cox shouted a warning, and rapped his whip stock against the side of an omnibus drawing across the road to drop its fares nearer the kerb. The driver looked down from his high seat and swore at Cox. Cox flicked his whip end at the nearest of the two horses, causing them to shy away towards the road centre and give room for Cox's carriage to pass on the inside.

'You snotty-faced oaf,' roared the furious driver as Cox drew away.

There was another hold-up in Holborn, where labourers were levelling cobbles outside the old timbered houses which somehow miraculously survived on the right-hand side of the road. The carriage horses were nervous for a few seconds as the labourers thumped heavy wooden rammers down on to the square granite sets, but then settled to wait until space was cleared to allow traffic to pass again. In the crush, a cab wheel scraped the side of Pendragon's carriage, and Cox waved his whip again and shouted angrily. The bearded cabbie, who had no teeth and who seemed drunk even though it was only 1 p.m., whipped his own horse savagely, driving it up on to the pavement, where he jumped down from his seat, passed the reins to an urchin who had been running barefoot alongside him, and disappeared inside the doorway of a scruffy ale house.

There was a public hanging taking place outside Newgate jail, and to avoid the crowds of spectators Cox took the carriage north, then turned right and right again, to take them past the Oxford Arms, in Warwick Lane, with its seventeenth-century galleries, and then turned left towards St. Paul's. The traffic was lighter now, mainly goods carts carrying market wares. They moved slowly on thick-spoked wheels, and Cox was able to overtake them before turning right down the hill towards the docks and Mr. Price's warehouse.

In the warehouse yard he dismounted, held open the carriage door and stood at attention waiting for Pendragon to climb out. He tied the horses to a rail and followed Pendragon up to Mr. Price's office.

'Can I be of any assistance, Sir?' asked an elderly clerk in the dimly lit office.

'Mr. Price,' said Pendragon, 'if you please. An official matter.'

'Of course, one moment please Sir,' said the man at Pendragon's tone of authority. He hurried through a door and returned a second later. 'Please come inside, Sir. Your man can wait here,' he added, looking at Cox. Cox glared at him.

'You may come in with me,' said Pendragon to Cox. Cox gave the clerk a superior look.

Mr. Price stood as they entered, leaning forward over his desk and holding his hand towards Pendragon. Pendragon shook it. The room smelt of sweat and stale cigar smoke. 'Please be seated,' said Price, indicating a chair before his desk. 'Now what can I do for you?'

It was a new experience for Pendragon and he wasn't certain how to introduce himself. After a second of hesitation, he said, 'My name's Pendragon. I represent certain interested persons in the Government, who are concerned with the corpse discovered in a shipment of yours.'

Mr. Price looked surprised. 'I'm sorry. I thought you were a customer. You will be from the police?' He seemed puzzled. Pendragon, in his impeccable dress and with his upright military bearing, was an unusual policeman.

'No, not the police,' said Pendragon. 'The Government. Should you care to view it, I hold an authority from the Minister of War, Mr. Herbert.' His tone forbade argument.

'Well,' said Mr. Price. 'I am surprised. Naturally, there is little help I can offer. The dead man was simply found within a case that had held spices. Three other cases were pilfered and empty. Pilfering of this nature takes place from time to time at the ports; it is not unusual, only aggravating and

75

costly.'

'The corpse, however, was unusual,' said Pendragon.

'Of course,' said Mr. Price in a hurt tone. 'We don't make a habit of shipping dead men into the warehouse.'

'Tell me,' asked Pendragon. 'The shipment; four hundred and ninety odd cases. Where was it from?'

'India, Burma, Ceylon; different cases, different spices. Quite a normal shipment.'

'Carried on your own ship?'

'*La Belle Cygne*,' Price answered. 'A 'good sound vessel, about twenty years old. Her master has been with me a long time, as has her mate. Good men, both of them. The cargo is checked in the go-downs in the foreign ports, loaded by my own seamen, and unloaded over here straight on to my own wagons.'

There was a window behind Mr. Price, and the sunlight beating in created a halo around the man, making it difficult for Pendragon to see his face. He moved his chair slightly to the side. Price noticed and apologised. 'I'm surprised a seemingly ordinary murder—well, one of only many in this part of London—should attract the attention of the Government.'

'It runs a little deeper than an ordinary murder,' said Pendragon. He avoided giving Price more information. Rambolt's death was as yet unpublicised. At this stage, there was no way of knowing whether Price himself was involved, although it seemed unlikely he would allow the corpse to be discovered on his premises if this was the case. 'May I count on your co-operation?'

Price clasped his hands together. 'Of course, Mr. Pendragon. I will be very willing to help; but what can I do?'

'Show me the warehouse, the cases, let me speak with your labourers and the waggoners.'

* * *

Mr. Price waved his hand at four empty spice cases, standing in a row against one of the warehouse walls. The warehouse was ill-lit, but dry. There were a few rat droppings around the empty boxes. Mister Price saw Pendragon glance at them and shrugged his shoulders. 'Rats! Warehouses are always full of them. They can eat away a month's profit overnight. I use one of the Brill Place rat-catchers; almost exclusively, otherwise I'd be overrun. These are the cases, Mr. Pendragon.'

'Captain,' corrected Cox, from beside him, as though Price had said 'Mr.' quite long enough.

'Captain? A military man? I do apologise, Captain Pendragon.'

Pendragon frowned briefly at Cox, but Cox had the same look on his face as a training sergeant at Sandhurst who was permitted to rebuke his superior officers so long as they were under his care. Pendragon tilted one of the cases and looked inside.

'It should have contained cloves,' said Price. 'There was only rubble. In those sacks over there.' He pointed at a heap of rubbish a few feet away.

Pendragon looked into a second case. It was obviously the one which had contained the body of Rambolt. There was a thick layer of blood at the bottom, now dried, and the sides were heavily splattered and smeared a deep crimson. Rambolt must have been pressed inside the box, even as he died, for the blood to flow so freely. Pendragon sniffed at the box. There was a curious over-rich smell about it, more cloying than blood and more pungent than spice. He repeated his sniffing with the remaining empty boxes. Cox watched him, then did the same thing. Pendragon finally examined the sacks of rubble. There was nothing special about them; the rubble could have come from any of a hundred London building sites, and the sacks were the common sorts to be found in all of the vegetable markets.

'How do you know what the cases contain?' asked Pendragon. 'By those yellow crosses?'

'The crosses mean nothing. Just marks probably put on by Indian merchants. I know the contents by the numbers,' Price told him. 'Here, this number, seven hundred and sixty-eight. That's cloves. Seven hundred and sixty-nine is dried root of ginger, and so on. We use a number system as it's easier for writing into the ship's manifest; fewer mistakes than with names. Sailors can count, and know numbers, but they're seldom good at their letters.'

'You say the cases are only handled by your men,' said

Pendragon. 'What happens to them on board your ships?'

'Nothing,' answered Price. 'They're loaded into the holds abroad, and are then securely battened down until they arrive here at the port of London. Of course, the holds are opened if we take in extra cargoes on the route, but always under the eyes of a ship's officer. We keep a close watch on all our employees, Mr., er, Captain Pendragon. One finds honesty a scarcity in these times.'

'What time of the day did the cases reach this warehouse?'

'The last, by early evening. They were all stacked, the warehouse locked, and several of my guards posted about the area.'

'And there was no chance or opportunity for them to be opened during the night?'

Price shook his head vigorously. 'None of that, I assure you. We had much pilfering when the warehouse was first built; this is the area for those sort of games. My guards are rather special, men of some reputation, one might say. There are six night guards. The head guard is a man named MacLevan, known around here as the eye-taker. Two thieves he caught in the warehouse just a week after he commenced his job were both handed over to the police, blinded. How it happened is not known. MacLevan claimed it must have been accidental during the fight which ensued, and, of course, the criminals made no charges. It has made MacLevan a rather effective head guard. The remainder are all ex-prize fighters, except Tobin, who was a Royal Parks gamekeeper.'

'Can I speak to them?' asked Pendragon.

'To MacLevan, yes; the others don't arrive here until seven, unless you care to wait.'

'MacLevan will do for a start,' said Pendragon, wondering just how fearsome the man was going to prove.

Price turned and shouted across the yard, in his broad Yorkshire accent. 'Mac! MacLevan, come here, man!' It was the tone of voice one might use to shout for some moronic ghoul.

A narrow door opened in an opposite wall and a burly man appeared, blinking in the afternoon sunlight of the warehouse yard. He saw Mr. Price and hurried across.

'Aye, Mr. Price,' he said. The man was a Scot, wild and

78

rough looking. Although broad shouldered he was shorter and lighter than Pendragon had expected.

'This is Captain Pendragon, MacLevan,' said Price. 'He wants to ask you about the stolen cloves.'

'And the dead man,' added Pendragon. 'What do you know of him?'

MacLevan's eyes narrowed, as though Pendragon was accusing him of the crime. 'I know nothing,' he said sulkily. 'Only there was a great kauch over a pifferin'.'

'Try and speak the Queen's English, man,' ordered Price. He turned to Pendragon. 'The man has been down from Scotland but two years. The Clearances, you'll remember. He doesn't find the English tongue easy.'

MacLevan stared down at the ground, avoiding Pendragon's eyes. He thought for some time. 'A lot of noise about only a little,' he said at last. 'One dead man is nothing. The spices were not taken from here. Nothing is now stolen from this warehouse. There's none about here as would be so frawfu'; brave. They've learnt.'

'You've no ideas, then, man?' asked Pendragon. The watchman's sullen attitude was making him angry.

'I'm paid English gold, to stop the stealin' frae this place. And that I do. What goes on elsewhere is no business of mine.'

Pendragon grunted. 'Tell him to go,' he told Price. Price waved MacLevan away. Pendragon waited until he was out of earshot. 'A difficult man. Not exactly forthcoming, was he?'

Price nodded. 'But a good watchman. He's quite right. I get no stealing on these premises while he's around. Worth every penny of the pound a week I pay him.'

Cox spoke for the first time since their arrival in the yard. He'd followed them around silently, just watching and listening. 'Captain, Sir, perhaps a word or so with the waggoners who carried the cases from the docks.'

'Yes,' agreed Pendragon. There was a chance they might have noticed something. 'How many waggoners do you have?'

'A dozen on wage,' said Price. 'And a handful I can get whenever I need them.'

'And they all carried the shipment from the dock?'

Price laughed. 'All? Goodness me, no, Captain Pendragon.

That would be the way to bankruptcy. One waggoner would do this job, several trips to the boat and back. No, heavens above, the others are mainly used for deliveries. Waggoners are cheap, I could run a hundred, but horses and wagons are expensive. A single horse costs twice as much as a man, in London. There's none of your free grass for them around here.' Price began walking back towards his office. He indicated that Pendragon and Cox should follow him. 'I don't know which of the waggoners carried the spices, but my pay clerk will have a record. They're paid daily. If you pay a waggoner weekly, he doesn't come back to work the next day; he's in the gutter drunk, then he starves for the next six days.' He reached the office door and pushed it open, stepping aside to allow Pendragon and Cox to pass him. He followed them inside.

The clerk was scribbling in some ledger, but glanced up as they entered. As he saw Mr. Price he slid from his high stool and nodded his head.

'Which waggoner carried that last shipment of spice up from *La Belle Cygne?*' asked Price.

The clerk pursed his lips and rubbed his hands together nervously. He furrowed his brow, reached into a pigeon-hole above his desk and pulled out a narrow account book. He read down a page, following spidery writing with a yellow fingernail. 'Ah,' he said. 'It was a Mr. Tom Grindle, Mr. Price.' He held the book sideways for Price to read the entry.

'Yes, Grindle,' repeated Price. 'He's quite reliable. Been working for me for about five years. As I remember, he's quite a good sort of man as waggoners go.'

'I'd like to speak to him,' said Pendragon.

'Of course.' Price turned to the clerk again. Fetch Grindle for me, will you?'

The clerk answered with a shake of his head. 'I'm sorry, Mr. Price, but he hasn't been in. It's unusual, I grant you, but I took on one of the casual workers to replace him until his return.'

'Then where is he?' asked Price.

The clerk shook his head again. 'I believe he's ill. That's what the other waggoners inform me. They said a consumption. I told them to tell him boil two handfuls of sorrel in a pint of whey, strain it and drink it three times a day. Very good for consumption.'

'Where does this man Grindle have his room?' asked Pendragon.

'But a mile east of here.' The clerk flicked through the pages of the ledger. 'Here, I have it. Bowman Street, Whitechapel. But no number, though finding him shouldn't be too difficult.'

'Thank you,' said Pendragon. 'And my thanks for your assistance, Mr. Price. No doubt if I need more information, you will help me again?'

'Delighted, Captain Pendragon.' He bowed Pendragon and Cox from the room.

* * *

Cox unhitched the horses, and pulled them around so they faced out of the warehouse yard. 'Whoa, there.' He steadied them, let the reins rest and opened the carriage door for Pendragon. 'Can't say I have much time for merchants, Captain, Sir,' he said quietly, preventing his voice from carrying across the open area. 'Men of a devious nature; no doubt due to them always seeking a profit, Sir. And I can't say I found his employees much better. Especially his Scots watchman; might make a fierce soldier, if he could take discipline, but wild men such as he shouldn't be let prowl loose in a city. Gallows bait, he is, Sir.'

'You're probably right, Cox,' agreed Pendragon, climbing into the carriage and settling himself back in the leather seat.

'Don't give away nothing, do they, merchants, Sir? Not even a bucket of water for the horses. Where would you like to be going, Sir?'

Pendragon pulled out his hunter and flicked open the case. It was nearly five o'clock. 'Whitechapel, I think, Cox. We'll take a trip to see waggoner Tom Grindle.'

Cox cracked his whip above the horses' ears.

* * *

On the journey, John Pendragon went over the details of his visit to the warehouse. Not a lot had come to light; not enough. Price was obviously quite certain the theft of the oriental spices, and the murder, had taken place outside his warehouse; his tough guard seemed to confirm the view, unless MacLevan was himself responsible for both theft and killing.

But Rambolt? Rambolt wasn't interested in common theft! Rumour had it he wouldn't arrest an ordinary thief, even if he saw him stealing, unless it was a government secret being taken. It was the way Rambolt operated. His friends were the rogues and thugs of London. He came and went in their territories, a welcome figure; something of a Robin Hood, a common folk's hero.

The spice boxes! Pendragon pondered on them. They hadn't smelt of cloves. They'd smelt of the damp brick dust and sacking, but behind that odour was another, the warm and sweet scent which Pendragon felt he should know from the past, but one which wasn't to be readily named. He moved over to the front seat, and turned so he could talk with Cox.

'What did you make of those cases, Cox?'

Cox glanced down at Pendragon. 'Spice cases, Sir? I was surprised they could get a dead man into one of them; they must have jumped on him to make him fit. Otherwise, well, Sir, they were spice cases, like plenty I've seen in India, Sir.'

'I was thinking of the smell in them,' said Pendragon.

'Ah yes, Sir, the smell.' Cox furrowed his brow and thought hard. 'Well, if you was to ask me, Sir, they smelt like a coolies' doss-house. Incense and op ... opium, Sir. Damn me!'

'Of course; opium!' Pendragon banged his fist down on his knee. 'I knew I should recognise the smell.' There'd been opium in Turkey, during the war. Some of the more foolish of the soldiery had smoked it; that and hashish. It made them even more foolish, and eventually it was deemed a flogging offence.

'If there were four cases of it, Sir,' observed Cox, 'it would be worth a large amount of gold, Sir. Four cases of opium is an amazing lot of the drug, Captain.'

Enough ransom for the Royal Household, thought Pendragon. More than enough! Four cases like that, each capable of holding two hundred pounds' weight of the drug, might be ransom for two Royal Households; even a nation! No wonder Rambolt had been involved. Or payment for explosives! An interesting and dangerous combination, and in such quantities the inference was certainly of some threat of national proportions.

* * *

The streets were narrower now, and the buildings on either side dulled the evening sun, making an early dusk. The road itself was dirtier, dung and mud packed into a rough surface, so deep it was impossible to tell where road and cracked pavements met. There were still a few noises—street markets and steet sellers, as there were all around London, but here Pendragon could see the wares were of a poorer quality, the vegetables unwashed, and the street vendors' cries edged with the whine of poverty. He felt it was like moving from a coloured to a sepia print. Clothes, especially on the women, were drab and dark. Men, no doubt having just finished their day's work, if they were lucky enough to have any, stood in groups on street corners, or sat with coarse china beer mugs in their hands at wooden tables outside the plentiful ale bars. Hordes of poorly clad children swarmed everywhere; whatever else the poor might lack, it was not offspring. They ran behind Pendragon's carriage trying to steal themselves rides on the rear axle; but they found themselves unlucky, for the top surface of the iron axle was studded with sharp spikes to discourage such antics. A little farther along the road another group of children tried running alongside the carriage, to spit at its occupant. Cox caught the first a smart crack across his backside with the long carriage whip, and the others ran off laughing and cat-calling.

'Not the best of places for a gentleman, Sir,' apologised Cox.

'Not the best for any human being,' Pendragon said, softly. He remembered his own childhood, both in India and on the Hampshire estate. It was a memory all full of fields, and open spaces. Sunlight and the smell of fresh-cut hay; game pie, buttermilk, and a full stomach every day. He shook his head slowly, and felt a little guilty.

Just before they reached Bowman Street the light became so poor that, for safety, Cox was forced to stop the carriage and light the oil lamps. They guttered and smoked for a few seconds until he adjusted the wicks, then shone yellow beams forward. It was chillier now, and Pendragon regretted travelling without an overcoat. He turned up his collar, and tilted his tall hat forward, so that he could sink farther into the seats of the carriage.

On the odd street stalls the costers had lit flares or oil dips above their barrows, and there were a few gas lamps alight along the main road. The side streets were near dark, except for the glow from shuttered windows spilling slim beams of light through cracks in the woodwork. There were open doors, people silhouetted as they sat or crouched on their doorsteps. The brightest areas surrounded the beer houses, the gin bars, the inns and taverns, lit by huge gas lamps advertising their trade. They were already crowded with noisy drinkers.

Cox leant down from his seat, and pointed towards a street sign. 'Bowman Street, Captain, Sir.' He tightened the reins and pulled the horses to a halt.

Pendragon looked at the street for a time; it was uninviting. Washing, hung out to dry, stretched across the street's width at several levels for as far as he could see in the poor light. There were heaps of disgusting refuse piled in the centre. A drunk man or perhaps a woman was slumped against a metal post. A group of men examining a fighting cockerel argued beneath the washing lines.

Pendragon heard Cox say to himself, 'What a damned hole.' He looked at him and saw he was staring in through a window as yet unshuttered.

'Ask those men where we might find Grindle,' Pendragon told Cox. Cox, who jerked as though he were waking from a dream, nodded, and shouted down the narrow street.

'Hey there! You lot with the cockerel. Which one of you knows where Tom Grindle might be?'

There was silence for a few moments. Cox noticed one or two of the men sliding away into the darkness, as though he was some threat to them.

'What did you ask?' called a voice.

'Grindle,' shouted Cox, again. 'Tom Grindle, the waggoner. Where does he live?'

'Who wants Tom?' asked one of the men. 'If you're crushers, then nommus yer arses out of 'ere, for we can do without you.'

There was a growl of assent from the small crowd. Some of the doors in the alley opened as inhabitants looked out, curious.

'We're not police,' Cox assured them. 'Just private gentlemen.'

'H'aristocrats,' snarled another voice. 'The rich hooks it bleedin' all. Go an' play in yer own street.'

'An' throw us yet gold before you leaves,' shouted an unseen woman with a voice as sharp as a freshly ground knife. There was laughter.

Pendragon stood up in the carriage so the men could see him. 'There's a coin for Tom Grindle, if he's around. And another for the man who leads me to him.'

The men of the crowd muttered, then one of them walked forward towards the carriage. He looked at Cox and Pendragon carefully.

'They don't look like crushers,' he said over his shoulder. 'We don't like the Bobbys around here, Mister,' he told Pendragon. 'You got work for Tom Grindle?'

'Not work, but I'm prepared to pay him for assistance,' Pendragon told him.

'Then I'll take you to his missus,' said the man. He looked at Cox. 'Not you, coachman. You stop there. You put a foot down off that carriage, and you're done for.' Pendragon climbed down and stood by the man, who walked around him, looking him over. 'All right, Mister, you'd best follow me.'

Pendragon followed. The man led him into the narrow street. The group with the cockerel said nothing, but split apart and moved back against the wall as the two men passed, then joined again to follow behind them, the bird squawking angrily.

* * *

After a hundred yards, with Pendragon forced to pick a way between debris and garbage, the man stopped in front of an unpainted wooden door. 'Here,' he said. He kicked the door with his studded boot. There was no answer, so he kicked again harder. The door shook. There was an angry shout from inside.

'Lay off, will yer.'

The door opened and a thin woman, her hair like larded rats' tails, stuck out her head cautiously.

'It's me, Harry Oranges.' The man who had led Pendragon identified himself. 'I got a gent here says he's got a bit of coin for your Tom.'

The woman leant farther out of the door and peered at Pendragon. 'If you've got coin, you gives it to me,' she said. 'Not my old man, Mister. Else he'd be cuttin' it to do a tightner at the bloody ale house, wouldn't he, Harry?'

'He might, and perhaps he might not,' replied the man, softening his gruff tone of voice now he was talking to the woman.

'I want to speak with him,' said Pendragon. 'A matter of great importance.'

'Huh!' The woman gave a small artificial laugh. 'Get him! Of great importance.' She mimicked Pendragon's intonation. 'Well, Mister, if it's that bloody important, you best find him yourself, 'cos that's more than I've been able to do for two days and three nights. He's bleedin' well scarpered, an' me with nine kids, Mister, and not a flatch to me name. Now where's that coin?'

Pendragon felt in his waistcoat pocket, where he kept loose change, and passed the woman a half guinea. She almost snatched it from him, then examined it in the light of the doorway. Her mouth dropped open. She looked at Pendragon incredulously.

'God,' she said. 'You *are* a real gentleman. Bless you, Mister.' She tightened her fist around the coin as though it were about to disappear. 'I'm sorry, Mister, I really don't know where he is. He just didn't come home from work. Maybe he's gone for good, I don't know.'

'It's possible I may call here again,' said Pendragon.

'If he comes back, can I give him a name?'

Pendragon shook his head. 'My name is of no consequence.'

The woman looked at the coin in her hand again. 'Well, you're a generous gentleman. You're welcome to come here again. Anytime, Sir.' She stepped back, and closed the door.

The man who had led Pendragon to the house shrugged his shoulders. 'I thought he was away,' he said. 'Haven't seen him myself the past day or so. But waggoners is like that; they come and they goes with the work. Like as not he'll be back tomorrow after tripping to Watford or someplace. Unless, 'course, he's bedding around a bit.'

'He's got a woman, ain't he? Name of Dilly Gowan, or Groan or somethin',' said a man in the crowd who'd followed them.

'Shut your teeth you bloody tresseno,' hissed another man. 'His missus 'as probably still got her ear to the latch-hole.'

The man began leading Pendragon back up the street; now Pendragon had proved he was not the police he was friendlier. 'I heard he's got a bit of fancy, and maybe her name is Dilly, but I don't know where.'

The man who'd given the girl's name spoke again beside Pendragon's shoulder. 'If I was lookin' for Tom Grindle right now, and I thought he was with 'is petticoat, then I'd do a bit of askin' at Dirty Dick's, or the gin shops around there.'

They reached the end of the street, and Pendragon could see Cox looking anxiously in his direction. He waved his arm to show he was all right, then gave the man who'd led him a couple of shilling pieces. The man nodded his head in thanks. The group of men stood watching as Pendragon climbed into the carriage, and Cox turned it around and whipped the horses away as though he were glad to see the last of the place.

* * *

'I shouldn't have done that, Captain, Sir,' called Cox, as they drove towards the city. 'Left you alone in that alley. Would never have forgiven myself, Sir, if anything had happened, Sir.'

Pendragon laughed. 'Forget about it. They were quite friendly once they decided I wasn't a policeman. Do you know Dirty Dick's tavern?'

'Heard of the place,' replied Cox. 'It's, er, not quite the inn for gentlemen, if you'll pardon me, Sir. Quite low, I'm informed. Notorious I believe is the expression, Sir.'

'Well, that's where I'd like to be taken now,' smiled Pendragon.

'As you will, Captain, Sir,' replied Cox, in the tone of voice that indicated his disapproval.

* * *

Dirty Dick's was an old inn. Its half-timbering stood only because, at some past time, a heavy brick building had been constructed next to it, making use of its side walls and holding it upright. The same thing had happened on the inn's other side, and Dirty Dick's was now supported like a drunken man between two of his sober friends.

There was more light here on the edge of the city, and Dirty Dick's gas lamps themselves illuminated a good hundred yards of street. There were drunkards littering the pavement and leaning slumped against each other nearer the doors. A man, crying with delirium tremens, was flopping in the gutter like a stranded whale. Sawdust, kicked from inside the tavern, made the uneven flagstones yellow in the glare of the strong lamps. In a neighbouring doorway a prostitute, her petticoats and skirts pulled over her shoulders, entertained a customer, while three feet away her woman friend argued with another man, shouting and cursing him for a miserly blaggard.

Cox was obviously loath to stop the carriage, and Pendragon had to lean forward and tap him on the shoulder as a reminder. Cox pulled on the carriage brake when the horses had halted. 'Yes,' Cox agreed. 'That could be the place, Sir.' He said it as though Dirty Dick's was one of a hundred in a row, and he'd found his possible goal by accident.

' 'Ere,' screamed the arguing prostitute from across the road. Her voice echoed off the buildings. 'You up on the 'orse carriage.' Cox looked over at the woman with distaste. 'Yes you, Pie Face. Tell this 'Arry what a lady costs in the east of London. Not a bloody frippeny piece, I'll tell yer! A short time is a shillin'. Ain't that right, Pie Face?'

'I'm sorry, Captain Pendragon, Sir,' apologised Cox, his cheeks a deepening colour in the street lighting. 'I did happen to mention this wasn't the place for gentlemen, Sir.'

Pendragon laughed. 'Gentlemen aren't necessarily ignorant of life, Cox. Nor of words; though I must say I find the price of goods astonishing. See if you can call a lad to mind the carriage.'

'Yes, Sir.' Cox stood on his seat, put his hands, cupped,

around his mouth and shouted: 'Horse! Horse carriage!' He had to shout a third time before two street boys appeared from a black alley, racing each other towards them with their bare feet slapping on the paving stones.

'Me, Gov,' yelled the first to reach them, half turning to strike out at the second boy. 'I was first, Guv. Let me watch 'em, Sir.'

Cox frowned at the first boy. 'All right, lad.' He jerked hard on the brake again to make certain the carriage couldn't move. 'What's your name?'

'Nick,' said the boy, grinning now he knew he had the job. 'I'm a good watcher, Sir.'

'You sit down there, Nick,' ordered Cox, indicating the edge of the high pavement. 'Hold these.' He tossed the boy the reins. 'Don't let them go before I get back with my master. And don't let anyone touch the carriage, or heaven help you. Payment when we see a good job done.'

'Yes, Sir,' beamed the boy.

'And no sleeping,' warned Cox. 'I know you now, lad, and if you don't do a good job of guarding, then I'll find you and redden your backside.'

The boy laughed, used to such warnings.

Cox waited until Pendragon had joined him on the pavement, then looked across the road at the inn. 'Well, Sir, I hope you're not to be shocked,' he said.

He led the way over the road.

A drunken man lurched towards them. 'Got a penny for a wounded Crimean soldier, Sir?'

'What regiment?' snapped Cox.

'Oh,' slurred the drunk, surprised at the question. 'Well, it must have been the, er, Royal Rifles.'

'Poor try.' Cox stepped past the beggar, keeping himself between the drunken man and John Pendragon. 'They're serving in India, my lad, not the Crimea. See what I mean, Captain, Sir, around here they lie, steal, without even a thought.'

'Darlin',' called the occupied prostitute in the doorway. 'If you wait just half a minute, I'll be free. Hurry up,' she squeaked at her nerveless customer. 'You've 'ad your lot.'

Cox reached the inn door before John Pendragon. He hesitated, then pushed it open a few inches and peered inside. 'It's very crowded, Sir,' he said.

'Never mind, we're here for information, not to enjoy ourselves.'

Cox pushed the door wider. As it opened, the room belched a stench of unwashed bodies, stale beer and cheap tobacco. The air was thick with smoke from pipes, cigars and the lamps, several of which were burning oil and not gas. There was a lot of noise, much of it coming from a tipsy group of men and women beside the door who were singing.

'Watch your pockets, Sir,' warned Cox as Pendragon pushed his way inside. Cox followed, keeping as close behind Pendragon as was possible without tripping him.

Pendragon found himself wedged between two men slopping beer from their tankards and shouting a conversation at each other. He turned sideways, forcing himself past, and one of the men cursed him. There were no empty tables, and no seats. Pendragon fought his way to the long bar.

'Yes?' shouted a burly barman, wiping the edge of a tankard with a dirty rag.

Pendragon looked at Cox. 'Would you like a drink?'

'I shouldn't be drinking with you, Sir.'

'Nonsense. A mug of ale?'

'Thank you, Sir.'

'Two good ales,' called Pendragon to the barman.

The man reached below the bar and slid pewter tankards across to Pendragon. They had obviously been filled before, ready for an order.

'Not those,' Cox told him curtly. 'You just fill fresh ones, not them from the slops tray.'

The barman smiled, and replaced the tankards beneath the bar. He filled two more from a barrel on a shelf, and passed them to Pendragon.

'I was brought up around here, Sir,' Cox told Pendragon. 'I know a fair number of their tricks.' He lifted his tankard. 'Your health, Captain, Sir.'

'And yours, Cox.' The beer was warm, and bitter. Pendragon grimaced, then leant over the bar and signalled the barman. 'I'm looking for a Tom Grindle. A waggoner. I believe he comes in here.'

'Perhaps,' replied the barman. 'There's many as do, and

many as don't.'

'He's got a lady friend, a Miss Dilly Gowan, or some name like that.'

'There are a lot of lively ladies in here,' said the barman. 'Look around you. Shouldn't be a bit surprised if they all came if yer shouted Dilly.' He wiped his nose on the cleaning rag and sniffed loudly.

'It's worth two guineas to find Tom Grindle.'

'Is it now?' The barman leant towards Pendragon, resting his thick forearms on the sticky bar top. 'Well then, it must be important. Two guineas is a good reward. What did this Grindle do? Rob yer bleedin' bank?' His tone became aggressive. 'Listen here. This is a bar, see. I sells beer and good liquor, and nothing else, see. If you wants to know something, ask them.' He waved his arm towards the customers. 'If you wants to buy another drink, then ask me.' He turned his back on Pendragon, and began finding work for himself amongst the casks at the back of the bar.

There was a group of men sitting around a dead fireplace at the far end of the room; half a dozen of them. By their dress, they were costers. Their clothes were a little better, flashier, than those of labourers, and they wore coloured scarves round their necks. Pendragon went across to them. As he arrived, they stopped talking amongst themselves and stared up at him.

'I'm sorry to disturb your drinking,' said Pendragon. 'I'm looking for a man ...'

'Then yer in the wrong place, Mister,' interrupted one of the men. The others laughed. 'Try yer own end of London.'

'He's a waggoner,' continued Pendragon, ignoring the jibe. 'Name of Tom Grindle. He's got a lady friend around here, a Miss Dilly Gowan. I'll give two guineas for his whereabouts.' He noticed a couple of the men glance quickly at each other.

'Now why should a gentleman like you be wanting this Tom Grindle?' asked the man who'd made the first remark.

'I need to talk with him. An urgent matter.'

The man turned back to face his friends. 'Funny, very funny. The more gold yer have, the more urgent everything is.' He looked up at Pendragon. 'We don't know a Tom Grindle, do we, lads?' The other men shook their heads.

91

As Pendragon began to walk back towards the bar, a thin-faced woman with dark ringlets falling each side of her over-painted face pulled at his arm. 'I was listening, Mister,' she said, her voice rough with gin and tobacco smoke. 'Suppose this Dilly woman wanted to find you, where would she look?'

'She would look nowhere,' said Pendragon, disengaging himself from the woman's grasp. 'Though I would be prepared to meet her if you can show her to me.'

The girl raised her painted eyebrows. 'My, we are mysterious, and haughty.' Her eyes flickered across the room in the direction of the group of costers. 'I like it, and I like you, Mister.' She spoke gaily and loudly. ' 'Ere, take a look at this.' She pulled at the top of her square-cut dress, completely exposing one of her breasts; white and pale veined. 'Give us your hand, Mister, and you can have a free feel.' Pendragon began moving away. 'Don't go,' said the girl, the pitch of her voice rising. 'Let me finish me patter, Mister. You name it, I does it. And if you can't name it, then be sure I do that as well. And for a haughty dandy, dearie me, I'd make a very special effort to please.'

'Leave the gentleman alone,' warned Cox. 'He doesn't find his pleasures with your kind.'

'Doesn't he,' said the girl, loudly and indignantly. She pouted at Cox. 'What does he like?' She reached down and gathered her skirts, lifting them as high as her bodice. She wore no undergarments. 'Doesn't he like this then? Scared of the naughty pox, is he?' Her voice was a shriek. 'Don't you fancy a look at my pussy-cat, Mister?' She pulled her skirts higher, pushing her naked stomach and thighs towards Pendragon. There was a boisterous cheer from an audience watching them. 'Go on, your Majesty,' she jeered. 'Try and find yourself a royal whore.' She began dancing a drunken jig, men around the bar clapping in time to her steps.

Pendragon and Cox left.

* * *

The air outside seemed clear and sharp after the atmosphere of the bar. Cox shook his head, furiously. 'I told you, Sir. I warned you. It ain't no good, Sir, a gentleman like yourself going around asking questions in places like that.'

'Questioning is the quickest way to get answers.' Pendragon was determined not be put off by Cox. 'Try a near-by gin shop, that's where one of the men in Bowman Street suggested. Well, Cox, where's the nearest gin shop?'

'Oh, God, Sir!' Cox groaned. 'One thing about officers, if you'll forgive me, Sir, is when they makes up their minds, nothing changes them, Sir. But if Miss Carr should know what you were about, Sir . . .'

'We must avoid speaking of it to her, Cox,' warned Pendragon. 'Miss Carr knows a little of this matter, but not all. And also, Cox, tell no one else of this new business of mine.'

'No, Sir,' said Cox, miserably. He looked along the road. There was another batch of lights a hundred yards away. He pointed. 'That's probably one, Sir.'

'Ah, yes.' Pendragon began walking quickly towards it. There were footsteps behind them.

'Mister,' said a voice.

Pendragon turned. It was one of the men from the group of costers. 'Yes?'

'You was askin' for Tom Grindle.'

'Yes.'

'Well, I knows where he is. He's in a penny gaff, down there.' The man pointed to a narrow alley, two buildings away from Dirty Dick's. 'I seen him go there half an hour past.'

'You'd better take us,' Pendragon told him.

The man led Pendragon and Cox into the alley. It was quite dark, but there were some lights in the distance. The man was hurrying.

Cox opened his mouth to ask the man to go more slowly, but didn't manage a word. Someone in the darkness kicked hard at his shins, sweeping his legs away from beneath him. He shouted a warning at John Pendragon. The warning was seconds too late.

Hands grabbed at Pendragon's shoulders. He reacted quickly, twisting himself free. Something hard hit him across the side of his neck. A heavy fist smashed into his temple, making flashes of bright light rocket across his eyes, blinding him. More hands grabbed at him. Someone stuck a walking stick between his legs and he stumbled to his knees. Booted feet kicked at him.

There were no sounds other than the heavy breathing and grunts of their assailants, and the thud of blows they rained on the two men. Pendragon and Cox fought back, but were heavily outnumbered. Pendragon felt an unshaven face pressing near to his own, and butted at it. The owner of the face swore. Pendragon was forced down by the weight of the men; he smelt their breath, foul and ale ridden. A hand grabbed at Pendragon's hair. A voice hissed gruffly, 'Keep away. Bleeding well keep away from Tom Grindle. Lay off him, d'you hear or we'll kill you.' The hand smashed Pendragon's head back on to the cobbles several times, then the men were gone, their boots hammering away down the alley.

* * *

Pendragon heard Cox groan. He pushed himself on to his knees dizzily, and felt around until he found the man's body. 'Cox?'

'Oh, damn me,' moaned Cox, sitting up in the darkness.

Pendragon examined himself. He didn't seem too damaged, just badly bruised. His head ached and it hurt him to breathe, but his ribs seemed unbroken by the men's kicks. He could feel his cheekbone swelling beneath his right eye, and his upper lip was split.

'Damn me,' groaned Cox again. 'Captain? Captain Pendragon, Sir?'

'I'm here.'

'Are you all right, Sir?'

'Slightly battered,' replied Pendragon, now standing, but unsteady.

'Can you walk, Sir?'

'Yes, of course, Cox.' Pendragon felt angry. Robbery of this nature was common enough in London. He should have been prepared for the attack instead of making it easy for their assailants.

The two men walked slowly back to the light of the main road. Pendragon's clothes were torn and dusty, and Cox's no better.

'Oh God, Sir,' said Cox, looking at Pendragon. 'The other servants'll never forgive me, Sir.'

'Nonsense.' Pendragon began brushing at his coat. He

94

jerked his cravat into place and pulled at his collar. 'I believe we've both had quite enough for one day. We'll make our way back to Park Lane, Cox.' He felt exhausted and dirty.

'Yes, Sir,' agreed Cox, He helped Pendragon straighten his clothing. 'Have you got your purse, Sir?' he asked, anxiously.

Pendragon put his hand in his hip pocket. 'Gone! I suppose one of them couldn't resist the opportunity.'

'We should report the matter to the police, Captain,' suggested Cox.

'And that would be a fine beginning for my career as a Queen's Agent.' Pendragon snorted angrily. 'The ten guineas in my purse is little cost for the lesson I've learnt tonight, Cox. Perhaps I should even thank those rogues. If nothing else, they've shown me my ineptness at this work. I could have been the shortest-lived agent on record.'

In the carriage, Pendragon thought over the day's events. So far there were only two things that could be worked on; the opium, and Grindle. He began to doubt the wisdom of his own appointment. Rambolt had been a good man for the job; he could mix with London's underworld, and no doubt enjoyed a thousand personal friends who would pass on information to him. Why this theory of Sidney Herbert that the new agent should be a gentleman? Perhaps Sidney Herbert was wrong! Pendragon tried to picture himself as Rambolt, dressed in dirty uncouth clothing, sitting in some dark corner of an ale bar, a nondescript figure that heard and saw everything; the mind of a logician clicking every minute piece of information into place as it arrived. The thoughts of Rambolt frustrated him. He couldn't be an imitator. He'd make mistakes, just as he'd made some today, but he'd never repeat them. What was it old Croaker the Hampshire warrener had said to him once in his thick Hampshire accent? 'That there ferret, lad. Yun watch 'ee an' learn. See 'is nose a twitch. Now he's a gone down the hole after that bunny. If he bain't there, ferret come out sharp without a wastin' 'is time. But that animal is a lookin' everywhere. A lookin' and a smellin'. Won't be a grain of chalk he don't notice, won't be an inch of burrow he won't cover. Rare things is ferrets.'

Rare indeed, thought Pendragon, for a ferret was what he must be. Grindle was somewhere, perhaps he'd been within a hundred yards of him tonight. He had to be found; found, and quickly. The link between the opium and explosives had to be discovered. Pendragon could only guess at the urgency. There were terrifying possibilities.

8

PENDRAGON'S VISITORS ARRIVED at 39 Park Lane a little after one o'clock in the morning. Pendragon had been in bed for an hour, having managed to avoid meeting Georgina on his return, and then taking his supper in the privacy of his own room. He'd bathed his face in cold water for half an hour and much of the swelling had already gone, but he knew he would have to think of some convincing excuse for his brightly hued eye in the morning. Sleep was an impossibility. Though tired, his mind tossed ideas back and forth, jumbled them and sorted them. He had the uncomfortable feeling he was lying above a keg of gunpowder and someone had lit a short fuse.

The housemaid, only a little while in her bed after her chores and not yet asleep, wearily answered the thundering knocks at the front entrance with curling papers in her hair, and wrapped in her black outdoor coat with its thin fur collar.

Two women stood in the porch. The housemaid couldn't see them clearly in the poor light, but she could smell and recognise the cheap perfume that rolled towards her like waves breaking on hot sands.

'Yes?' asked the housemaid, sharply.

'We wants to see a Captain Pendragon,' answered one of the women, her voice rough as a holystone.

'The Captain's a-bed,' said the housemaid, uncertain as to the correct action to take next, if any. 'You'd better call again in the morning.' The women hardly seemed to be the kind the housemaid expected the Captain to invite to his address, but until she learned more she thought she should at least remain civil.

'The morning ain't no good,' rasped the woman. 'We wants to see 'im now.'

'Can I be of assistance?' Wolfgang stood behind the housemaid and spoke from the darkness of the hall.

'Blimey,' exclaimed the woman. She leant closer towards the door, trying to see Wolfgang's face. 'You can help, duckie, by telling Captain Pendragon as how two ladies wish to see him. And no lip, mind, because we happen to be quality ladies.'

The housemaid frowned. 'I haven't met *any* ladies who called on gentlemen in the middle of the night. Nor any as felt the need to label themselves.'

'Well, you 'ave now, dearie. If this Captain Pendragon is in, then you'd better tell him if you wants to keep your position. It's a very urgent matter, dearie.'

'If you'll wait for a while, I'll get the Captain's gentleman to see if he's awake,' said Wolfgang, not at all happy with the situation. He wondered if he should slip out the back door and tell the groom to see if he could find a policeman to remove the two women as quietly as possible. He decided against the action only because he doubted if Captain John would be personally interested in them, and therefore there had to be a special reason for their late night visit.

He climbed the three flights of steep stairs to Cox's room. He could hear snores inside. He knocked softly, then opened the door. He could see Henry Cox lying on his back in the bed. The curtains were open, and soft moonlight just enabled him to make out the form of the sleeping man. He reached down to shake him, and found himself hurtling backwards across the room, as Henry Cox awakened, quickly and violently.

Cox hurled himself on to the astonished butler, with a loud, 'Got you, you villain!'

Wolfgang struggled. 'It's me, Wolfgang. I had to wake you. Someone is downstairs to see Captain Pendragon.'

'Oh,' Cox sounded almost disappointed. He pushed himself away from Wolfgang, and then helped him to his feet. 'Sorry. Got rather into the habit of sleeping lightly, I have. Dacoits; thuggee. Ain't wise to come creeping into an Indian army man's quarters at night.'

Wolfgang pulled his jacket around himself and rubbed at a bruised shoulder. 'I knocked, but you were snoring, so I come in.' He was so apologetic that for a moment Cox wondered if he had actually caught a thief redhanded. 'There are two women,' continued Wolfgang. 'Not very pleasant women, and of a certain occupation, I would think. They ask for Captain Pendragon.'

* * *

The women were still standing on the doorstep, being obviously guarded by Wolfgang and the housemaid, when Pendragon came down the stairs. He went straight into the salon, where Wolfgang had lit the gaslights. 'You'd better bring them in here,' he told Cox. 'But ask them to keep their voices down; the rest of the household are still asleep, and I want them to remain so.'

Cox disappeared, and Pendragon could hear him talking softly in the hall; he returned with the women. He brought them into the room and stood by the door, hesitant.

Pendragon recognised one of the women, the black-haired and noisy prostitute from the tap room of Dirty Dick's. He was surprised, but kept his face emotionless. 'I presume you followed us back here,' he said.

'Followed you?' The woman laughed. 'I give up followin' gentlemen when I was thirteen. Here, Ducks, 'ave your wallet back.' She handed him the slim calf-leather purse. 'Don't bother to look, Captain. Your ten guineas is all there. It was your name and address I was wanting.' She laughed. 'I lifted your gear when I did me little dance, it never fails. Used to earn a good livin' just like that, only with drunken sailors, not gentlemen, Captain.'

'You're very smart,' smiled Pendragon.

'A little smarter than you, Captain. I see they give you a nasty fist in the glim.' She made the observation without sympathy. 'But you was lucky, Captain. You was really askin' to be served out. They was Tom Grindle's mates, or some of them. I heard you speakin' to them, which was why I come over. If you wants to know something, Captain, you should always ask one of the likes of me; you don't ask half a dozen coster lads with a barrel of beer in their guts. That way is bound to be trouble. And, 'course, we didn't know you. Your wallet took care of that. A hussar officer ain't likely to be a rascal now, is he? Bit of a lark, my little act, wasn't it? Weren't too unhappy was yer, Captain?'

Pendragon smiled. 'Not too much. So you do know where Tom Grindle is.'

'Yeah. He's with 'er.' She looked at the other woman, who had so far remained silent.

'In me room, Sir,' said the second woman, speaking so softly Pendragon barely heard her. She was a little older than the black-haired woman, thin-faced and with matchstick arms and legs. 'He's awful sick, Sir.'

'Dying, maybe, poor bleeder,' said the first woman, in a matter-of-fact manner.

Pendragon felt uncomfortable. 'I was told he had consumption, by the clerk at the warehouse.'

The thin-faced woman began sobbing.

'He's her man, she's Dilly Gowan,' explained the first. 'He's married to someone else of course, but been her steady man for a long time. It ain't the consumption; someone done for 'im with a blade. Tried to kill 'im, the poor soul. That's why them coster mates of his wanted to muzzle you; they fancied you as one of them as did it and maybe wanted to finish the job. But I thought, well, if you was a Captain, and you really did live 'ere in Park Lane, then you was a right gent, and only around for helping.'

'He's a good man, my Tom,' wept the thin-faced woman. 'He ain't ponced on me, and he ain't complained. A woman's got to make her crust where she can nowadays, and he ain't said nothing. Kept his real wife and kids as best as he could. Now they gone and done for him.'

'Who?' asked Pendragon, gently.

The first woman shook her black ringlets firmly. 'She don't remember. If you can get him to a doctor, or to an 'ospital; an' if you can see Dilly all right until Tom can be back to his waggoning, then he'll maybe tell you.'

'I'll come back with you now.' Pendragon rang the servants' bell, knowing that Cox, Wolfgang and the housemaid would be waiting below until the women left. 'How did you get here?'

'Shank's mare,' said the first woman. 'How bloody else does the like of us get anywhere, 'cept when we're with a toff? Or

100

on a coster's cart, an' there ain't many of them around at this time of night.'

Cox opened the door. 'Sir?'

'Wake the coachman, Cox. Give him my apologies, but tell him I want the large carriage, the berlin. Fast as he can. He can drive us. I shall go up to my room and dress, and in the meantime ask Wolfgang to arrange something for these ladies; biscuits, and some hot chocolate.'

'Shall I ask the housemaid to stay here with them, Sir?' asked Cox.

Pendragon looked at the two women. 'What on earth for?' he said.

* * *

The roads were quite deserted now, except for huddled figures in doorways, where urchins and London's itinerant unemployed and beggars curled themselves under sacking, rags or newspapers, to get their poor night's rest. Moths skittered, dazed and stupid, around the gas lamps in the still air; thin, starving cats hunted vermin and searched for garbage in the gutters. The horses' hooves on granite cobbles sounded sharply hollow in the dark ravines of the streets, and exaggerated the loneliness of London night.

For the first time in London, Pendragon was armed. Tucked into his waistband, and uncomfortable with its bulk, was the second of the pair of pistols given to him, before he left for the Crimea, by Georgina. The brother pistol, unless it was now a souvenir of some Russian soldier or peasant farmer, lay in the long valley of death amongst the litter of war. The pistols had never been intended to be carried concealed, and Pendragon determined to visit Bill Bishop as soon as possible to buy something more suitable. For the moment, however, the heavy double-barrelled pistol was a comforting companion.

The first part of the journey had been completed mostly in silence once the black-haired woman had said: 'Head for Dirty Dick's.'

Tom Grindle, the waggoner who was lying wounded, had, said his mistress, told her nothing; Pendragon suspected she was lying. All she claimed to know was that he had been attacked and stabbed, and without money for medical help would certainly die. There was little she could do; even on a good night the number of customers she might hope to find would not pay a quarter of the money required to seek the assistance of a good doctor. Pendragon, when she heard of his questioning in Dirty Dick's, seemed her only hope.

The black-haired woman, who called herself Antoinette, although it was unlikely to have been the name given to her by her parents, broke the silence to direct the coachman along the Commercial Road, then right into Cannnon Street and across The Highway to Wapping Lane. Just before the London Docks she told him to halt the carriage.

'Down there,' she said to Pendragon, pointing to the opening to a small mews. 'We won't take in the carriage. Too noisy this hour of night. S'only twenty yards, Captain.'

The coachman unclipped a carriage lamp and handed it to Cox. The lamp's beam shone down the mews, rolling back dark shadows, and making doorways jerk and sway in the light. Pendragon and Cox followed the women into the yard; Pendragon kept his hand on the butt of his pistol, as an insurance against a repeated attack.

At a narrow door the waggoner's mistress poked her finger through a crack in the twisted woodwork, and lifted a latch. The door swung open. They followed her up a flight of uneven pine stairs that groaned and creaked. At the top was another warped door. She opened it: it led to a small room, about twelve feet square. There were no windows, and no fireplace. Pendragon wondered how they heated the place in winter; it was obvious they worried little about ventilation in summer. The room stank of mouldering cloth and wood rot. There was a rough country-style armchair next to a table made from a tea-case. Against one of the walls was a six-drawer chest, crudely whitewashed. A rope, held to the walls by blacksmith's cob nails, stretched across one corner of the room and served as a wardrobe; there were several petticoats draped over the line, and a man's jacket, bloodstained dark and slashed across one side of the front. With a bed in the farthest corner, there was little room left to move. A piece of church candle guttered in a cracked saucer on the packing-case table.

The woman hurried across the room to the bed. A heavy-

102

built man lay unmoving on a palliasse of straw. 'Tom, 'ere Tom, it's me. Dilly, Tom. Your Dilly. Come with help, Tom. With a gentleman to save you.'

The man on the bed turned his eyes slightly, looking in the direction of the door and the group of people standing watching him. Pendragon moved to the woman's side. He avoided getting too close to the bed; it was unpleasantly reminiscent of those in the Scutari Hospital and seemed likely to be even more louse-ridden.

'You ain't gone, 'ave you Tom? You ain't gone?'

'I ain't gone,' whispered the man. 'Though I'm comin' round to thinking it ain't such a bad idea, Dilly.'

'Tom, oh Tom, don't say that.'

'Who's he?' asked Tom Grindle. He stared at Pendragon.

'I'm Captain Pendragon. What happened, Tom? Tell me, and I'll get a doctor to you fast.'

Tom Grindle moaned. 'Doctor now, or I says nothing.' He shut his eyes.

Pendragon turned to Cox. 'Go; take the coachman and carriage, and bring back a doctor.' He turned to the prostitute: 'Do you know where we can find one near here?'

'None as'll welcome a night call,' replied Antoinette. 'But maybe with two men with me, we can persuade one to come back. I'll take them. Can I tell 'im he'll be well paid, Captain Pendragon?'

Pendragon nodded. Cox led the woman from the room, and Pendragon heard the stairs creaking again.

The lips of the man on the bed moved. 'Who are you? A policeman, or a priest?'

'Neither,' said Pendragon. How could he explain convincingly to a dying man? He looked at Dilly Gowan. 'Do I have a promise for secrecy?'

'Yes, Captain.'

Pendragon leant closer to the man. 'You know of Rambolt?' The man's head moved slightly. 'Well Rambolt's dead. Killed. I take his place.'

The woman turned her head and looked at Pendragon disbelievingly. 'I ain't heard of Rambolt dyin'.'

'It's the truth,' said Pendragon. 'I'll swear it, if it will make you happier. Now, what happened to you?'

The man slowly eased his head around on his sacking pillow and opened his eyes, staring straight at Pendragon. 'Two men. Three nights ago, after I finished work. I was walking here. They followed me, I suppose in the mews, they scuffled me; they was yellers.'

Pendragon didn't understand the man. 'Yellers?'

The woman, Dilly, answered. 'Chinese. We 'as a lot around the docks.'

'They done me,' breathed the man. 'They 'ad knives; one 'ad an axe too. They near 'ad me then, but one didn't fancy his work. The other one, though, he gets his bleedin' blade in; then they runs off when I shouts, and me mates and Dilly found me.'

'Do you know why?'

'Tell him, Tom, oh for God's sake tell him. You won't pass him to the crushers will you, Captain?'

'No,' said Pendragon. 'No more than Rambolt would have done.'

'All right,' said the man. His voice was getting hoarser, and more inaudable. 'I sold a load, didn't I? Come to an arrangement for ten guineas of gold coin. Promise you won't turn me in, Sir?'

'I won't mention it to the police,' promised Pendragon.

The man nodded, almost imperceptibly. 'Well, I had these cases to carry. A full shipment for Price. I was drinkin', one day last week, when this gentleman come over. You, lad, he says, you want to earn yourself a bit? He was foreign, a big man with a beard, but a right toff. I thought he meant a bit of extra carryin' on the side; you know, slip a case of his in with Price's, an' cart it from the dock. I says, yes; what and for how much? He says all you got to do is stop your waggon in the ward of the Waterloo Tavern, in Dock Street, on the way back with a load; just leave it there for a full ten minutes while you slips inside and has an ale.' Pendragon leant closer as Grindle continued. 'Can you get the job of carrying the spice cases off the *Belle Cygne*? If you mean the "Dirty Duck", I says, then yes. But I tumbled him, and reckoned he wanted to split a case and slide a few pounds of some stuff out; then I thinks, an arsehole to Price, he's a miserly bastard and don't pay a waggoner but farthings. What if I gets caught?, I says to this toff. You won't, he promised; all you done is stop for a wet, and who's to blame if a bit of your load is missing it could 'ave been stole anywhere. So, for ten guineas in gold, I says yes.

'I tell you, 'e says, I'll be waiting near the dock, and I'll give you the eye when you got the load I wants.' The man paused and licked his lips. Dilly Gowan reached under the bed and brought out a short dumpy bottle. She held it to the man's mouth, and he drank thirstily. She wiped a dribble from his chin when he'd finished drinking. The man swallowed, then spoke again. 'Well, I'm working, see, on that cargo from the "Dirty Duck", an' I see this toff, with two Chinese, with another waggon near the wharf. I puts me own waggon ready for loadin', then I walks across making like I was interested in his horses, and I says to him, 'ere, what you want a bleedin' waggon for? You ain't stealing me whole load are yer? No, he says, what we takes you won't miss; now go an' wait, and when you sees me lift me arm, you'll know that's the bit I wants.'

The man was obviously becoming exhausted with his talking, and Pendragon hoped he would have the strength to complete the story. Grindle shut his eyes for a couple of minutes before he spoke again. 'I done three loads, an' I sees his signal. I waits until the dock workers 'ave finished with me waggon, then I takes it up out of the dock. I sees the foreign toff and the Chinese a followin' me, but I pretends I don't know 'em. Like the toff says, I goes into the Waterloo Tavern, and I asks for an ale. Just then, in comes the toff and he comes right next to me an' slips ten pieces in me pocket. I counts 'em still inside, and has a quick looksee so's I know it's gold and not brass. Then I gives him a nod. Ten minutes, lad, he says; not a second less. He gets himself a brandy and sits by the door, and I reckons his Chinese is doing the dirty work, while he keeps 'is 'ands clean. Oh, Christ, Sir, how long that doctor goin' to be? My bellows is sliced to hell.'

'Not long,' Pendragon said. 'They'll be as quick as they can. Any time now, I expect.'

'I hope they ain't too long. Well, after I was in the Waterloo for a few minutes, in rushes one of the Chinese, an' he jabbers at the toff. The yeller was right upset about something, and the toff gets upset, too. They both hurries outside. I goes over to the window an' has a butcher's. I sees the other Chinese climbing off the back of me waggon, an' then they all jumps on their own cart, and whips hell out of the horses and fair gallops out of the yard. I waits a bit, then I delivers the load to the warehouse, and goes on an' finished me day's work.'

'And someone attacked you as you came home?'

'Bleeders!' The wounded man groaned. 'Out in the alley. Didn't give me a fair chance to use me fists or I'd 'ave showed 'em. One got behind me, was a-going for me throat. I sees his arm come round, with the knife all glinting. I twists meself, but he gets it into me chest. I seen his arm, with a drawing on it, sailors calls it a tattoo, a snake it were, a green snake. But I wouldn't know the Chinese, 'cus they all looks alike as fleas on a dog's back.'

Dilly Gowan looked at Pendragon, pleading with her eyes. 'That's all he knows, Sir. Honest. Nothing more. That's his tale, just as how he told me. Don't inform on him, Sir. He'd be deported for certain; he could die in them rotten hulks on the river, Sir.'

'I'll say nothing. My word as an officer.'

The latch on the lower door clattered, then the stairs groaned their warning. The room door opened and Cox appeared, accompanied by the black-haired Antoinette and a shrunken man who walked bent forward as though his grey beard was fastened into his waistcoat buttons.

'A doctor, Captain, Sir,' said Cox. 'I don't know what he's like, but he was all we could get, Sir.'

'Sauce, damned sauce. I don't care for your impudent man, Sir,' the doctor wheezed at Pendragon. 'Who's sick, then? Is she sick? They all are: syphilis!'

'The man in the bed,' Pendragon told him, sharply. 'And doctor him well, or you'll answer to me.'

'And will I now?' said the doctor. He leant over the bed, and adjusted his spectacles, peering down at the wounded man's face. 'Stick out your tongue, man. Say ninety-nine.'

'It's his chest,' explained Dilly Gowan. 'Look.' She pulled down the bed covers. Grindle was bandaged with bloodstained rags, from under his armpits to his waist.

'Then unwrap him, woman,' ordered the doctor, curtly. 'I

can't heal flesh through a layer of old clothing.'

Pendragon turned to Cox. 'I think a little guard duty is required. There's every possibility the villains who attacked Grindle will return to finish their murderous work. Are you prepared to stay here with the man?'

'More than prepared, Captain,' said Cox. He thrust his hand into his topcoat pocket and pulled out a heavy studded brass knuckle. 'After our earlier encounter, Sir, I took the liberty of arming myself. It might not look much of a weapon, but with this on I can punch through an oak barrel. I'll look after the man, and God help anyone who threatens him while I'm here.'

'Good.' Pendragon spoke to Antoinette. 'Early tomorrow morning, if Tom Grindle is fit to move, I'll see he's taken where those devils won't find him.'

'I've got a sister in Islington, Sir,' suggested Cox. 'She takes in lodgers. There'll be a safe room for him there. I'll take him over first thing by growler.'

'Excellent,' said Pendragon. 'And then come back to Park Lane.' He felt inside his coat, then handed several coins to Antoinette. 'Here, something for your trouble. And this will pay him.' He nodded towards the man who was cleaning Grindle's wounds. He deliberately avoided using the title doctor as it was unlikely the man had any true medical qualifications. 'I'll see to Grindle's keep until he's fit enough to work again.'

Antoinette smiled gratefully. 'You're a good man, Captain. Tom Grindle is much in your debt, but he's the sort as don't forget favours, as is Dilly and me.' She winked at Pendragon. 'An' if you're ever short of company, or well, you know what I means, anything, come and ask for me.'

'One day I might,' replied Pendragon. He couldn't be insulted by the woman's suggestion. She was offering him the only thing she could.

As Pendragon walked out to the berlin waiting by the end of the mews, exhaustion seemed to settle on him like a heavy winter cloak. A few moments after he had settled himself in the seat, and the coachman whipped the horses to a brisk trot, he was asleep.

9

NEXT MORNING IT was raining, a warm drizzle that greened the dusty leaves in the park and made a quagmire of the filth on the roads. Wheels of the elegant West End carriages were splattered to polished axle-hub height. Pendragon sat puzzling at the mother-of-pearl inlaid writing desk in the Park Lane study, and jotted notes on perfumed sheets of Georgina's hand-made writing paper. He glanced up, catching sight of himself in the oval giltwood framed mirror above the desk, and was startled by his appearance. His eyes were puffy and the right side of his face was bruised deep yellow. His upper lip, still a little swollen, gave him an arrogant sneer. He grimaced at himself. Damn Page Cloverly and Sidney Herbert; they'd recruited him for the work, but given him only the sketchiest notion of how it was to be performed.

'Investigate,' they'd said, as though everyone knew everything about investigation. 'Use logic—a man of your education and background should find no difficulty.' No difficulty in what, Pendragon wondered. It was like trying to climb a ladder with too many of the rungs missing to allow further progress.

Page Cloverly had been a little more helpful than Herbert. When the interview with the Minister was over, Cloverly had taken him into his own office and shown him previous reports Rambolt had submitted.

'You see,' he said. 'If nothing else, Rambolt gave us records to file, not that his English was particularly good, but it was adequate. If I were you, Pendragon, I'd keep a record of everything that ever happened connected with my cases. Keep referring back to them; cross reference everything. Check statements against statements. I wish I could help you more, but I'm at the wrong end of the business. I only see the end product; the last furlong of the race.'

Education was all right, thought Pendragon, but he couldn't see what use his Eton study of subjects such as Euclid and Livy might be to investigation. So far, the work of the investigation seemed to be a matter of following up each stage as it presented itself. If he were to draw the stages, instead of writing them as notes, they should join, cross and link together like roads on a map; their direction should always be forward. Those swinging away from the main route should be avoided or abandoned once they made their direction clear. Others of even the slightest relevance should be closely examined. Investigation seemed to be like forward planning of a battle campaign, on strange territory; an adaptation of military intelligence. He hoped it would be so.

He studied the notes he had made so far, each under their own separate headings. 'Report of Rambolt's death. Interview with Herbert. Stolen explosives. Revolution? Grand theft? Sabotage? Arson? Trip to warehouse ... opium. Opium plus explosives. Grindle's story. The foreign "toff" and the Chinese. Chinamen and opium.'

Who was the foreign gentleman, wondered Pendragon. What nationality? And Rambolt; how did his death fit in? The Waterloo Tavern! There was no point in putting Rambolt's body into a spice-case if he'd been killed elsewhere; the amount of blood in the case indicated he was killed immediately prior to being placed there. The agitated Chinamen at the Tavern! Rambolt must have been watching them take out the contents of the cases; somehow they'd seen him, and killed him. It hadn't been part of their plan, or they'd have shown less concern. The attack on Tom Grindle was to eliminate a witness who would obviously tell all he knew, to escape the probability of the hangman's noose when the body was discovered. And the only identifying feature on one of the Chinese was a green serpent tattoo'd on his arm.

The foreign 'toff'? Pendragon tried to guess the nationality; it wasn't easy. The current most likely nationality was Russian; Russian, that was, if you discounted the unrest in India, China and Egypt. Of course, the man could be almost any nationality, in the employ of another. It could be a German intrigue, or French; although international relationships were supposedly good with both these countries, interests were clashing in Africa, and again in China, and could easily be sparked into open dispute. Pendragon shook his head slowly. All he could do for the moment was to follow the only path; that leading to the Chinaman with the tattoo.

* * *

The rain had stopped by ten a.m.; the clouds broke, lifted, then cleared. The sun dried the footpaths and made the road surfaces steam, filling the humid atmosphere with the stench of horse dung.

Pendragon took his breakfast late with Georgina on the balcony outside her room. At that height, there was a slight breeze, the air fresher and more pleasant. As he sat facing her, Georgina frowned and leant forward to examine his bruised face.

'It would appear,' she said coldly, 'you have taken up the vulgar sport of prize fighting.'

'I can assure you no,' said Pendragon. He tried smiling, but the movement of his face made him wince. He spoke more cautiously. 'I had an argument with Dasher's head. I leant forward as he reared.'

'Huh!' Georgina made a disbelieving sound. 'It doesn't improve your looks, John. I doubt if Lady Zara will find you presently attractive.' She frowned again. 'Will the marks be gone by the end of the month? I do hope so, for I am planning a small party.'

'They'll be gone,' Pendragon assured her. 'I promise to be a credit to your household.'

'I'd rather you were a credit to me, and didn't seduce all my friends.'

'Not exactly all, Georgina.' Pendragon laughed.

Georgina smiled. 'No, not all. But certianly all of those who could be described as presentable. Sometimes you make me feel like a procuress.' She giggled. 'I envy you. You, and your friends Crighton, Lumley, Carlton; even FitzPatrick. Gay blades about town! One day women will be as emancipated. You have no idea how much I sometimes long to be free enough to wander where I will, to stroll out alone in the evenings, explore the streets, without rousing comment or objection.'

'You are emancipated, Georgina,' Pendragon assured her.

'Oh, more than most, perhaps. I love and live how I will, within limits of current decency. But decency is confining; like corsetry, like work. Work is such a bore.'

'For months now, you've been telling me work is a virtue.'

'Only for the lower orders,' said Georgina. 'For gentlemen, and particularly for ladies, work is a bore.'

'On the contrary, I'm finding my work quite interesting; it's like exploration, always new ground. There are no experts in the subject, and no reference books. I have to learn as I go along. I believe the French have advanced methods and perhaps one day I shall study those, but . . .'

'There you are,' interrupted Georgina with a grimace. 'Being quite boring, already. Let us talk of something pleasant, something to aid not disrupt my digestion.'

'Just one more boring thing before we do,' said Pendragon. 'Of all your friends, can you suggest one with a knowledge of China? Someone who might be able to give me some information about the Chinese habits and customs.'

'Darling,' Georgina smiled, and looked superior. 'A curious, but nevertheless quite a simple problem. The stout and obnoxious Colonel Hangshaw. I believe he was stationed in China for many years.'

'Hangshaw? The Royal Marine Light Infantry officer?'

'That very Hangshaw, darling. In fact I often thank God there are no more than one of his name in my acquaintance.'

* * *

Colonel Hangshaw's house stood in its own gardens, a little north of Regent's Park. Pendragon walked part of the way for exercise, then caught a hansom cab for the last mile. He told the driver to wait for him in the gravelled driveway.

Colonel Hangshaw, completely bald, flabby-faced and some sixty-five years of age, was resting in his library surrounded by stuffed animal heads and trophies. He was awake, but only just.

A three-quarter empty port decanter rested on a table beside his chair. He stood ponderously as Pendragon was shown inside.

'Ah, Sir,' he said loudly, his voice reminding Pendragon of

the late Sir Reginald Spence. 'I've heard of you, Captain. A brave hero, I'm told by your dear aunt, the beautiful Miss Carr.'

'You flatter me, Colonel.' Pendragon bowed.

'Damn you for your humility, come and have a seat; your aunt would have it you attacked the Russian guns at Balaclava singlehanded.'

'She exaggerates,' smiled Pendragon. 'There were a number of others with me, all of them braver men.' He wondered what Hangshaw was making of his rather battered appearance but either the Colonel was short-sighted or chose completely to ignore Pendragon's bruises.

'That's as may be, as we both well know, Captain,' growled Hangshaw. 'Port? Of course! Help yourself; damned stuff is supposed to be a twenty-eight, but it tastes like fifty-four bilge water. Well, Sir, what purpose brings you here?'

'I've come about China. Information. I'm told you're an expert.'

'Whoever told you was damned right. I know as much about China as any man. Spent twenty years of my life stationed there; stinking hole of a place, it is. Dirty brown rivers, and flat plains of mud and rice paddies. Towns are creeping with everything horrible ever created. Don't make one decent drink in the whole country. Rice wine, pah! Tastes like stallion piss. Smells like it, too.'

'I wanted to know about tattoos.'

'By God! Tattoos. I've seen some, Captain. Some not fit for viewing by gentlemen. Hah! Saw one once, on a woman. Young ensign found her in a market. Brought her into the mess as a curiosity. We stripped her off, on the table, at dinner. She was covered from head to toe in tattoos.' He roared with laughter at the memory. 'When we tickled her backside with a stiff bit of a cane, the cloud of butterflies on her back almost lifted her from the ground.'

'It's a curious form of personal decoration,' said Pendragon, understanding Georgina's dislike of Hangshaw.

'Curious? It's barbaric—typical of the people. Primitives, all of them.'

'Do they all tattoo themselves?'

'No, not all of them. Do it with a needle and paint. Prick

112

their skins and rub in the colour. Family thing sometimes; sign of their clans.'

'Clans?'

'Well, whatever they call clans; societies, triads. Part family, part religion, part politics. Nasty things. Cause a lot of trouble. We beat the devil out of them in 'forty-two; you remember, Captain? The Opium War! I was in Kweichow. Too damned far inland for Royal Marine infantry. Should have kept us near the coast. Went to Kweichow to save the Engineers. Did a good bit of fighting and subdued the whole territory. Not much stops a Royal Marine, Captain. Seen a man get a hundred lashes for dirty equipment in the morning; die like a hero in a battle in the afternoon. Prefer fighting in the morning myself. Fighting in the afternoon gives a man indigestion.'

'What do the societies, the triads, do?'

'Do? They damned well tattoo themselves! Something to do with their Buddha. Got lots of silly names for themselves. The White Lotus Society, the Hung League, the Celestial Bamboo Sect, the Eight Diagrams. And they give their leaders important-sounding titles. King of Red Heaven, Great King of Mankind. Pah, a lot of nonsense, and a lot of trouble! Always fighting the Manchu administration. There's trouble now with some local oaf named Hung Hsiu-Ch'uan. Blasted primitive. Mark my words, Captain, we'll have more war in China. We should be building up a force there now, as a punitive measure. Nip the whole damned lot in the bud, as it were. Hang their leader; quarter him. Make a good job of it; shoot a couple of thousand of the insurgents, and whip the rest.'

'Do they hate us? The British?'

'Hate us? Of course they hate us. Sworn enemies of all foreigners. Damned cheek. They're the blasted foreigners; trying to get us out of the country! Damn me, it's *our* country! We won it fairly and squarely. It's British territory, every damned inch of it won with good British blood. Caught one once.'

'A society member?'

'Yes, damn the man. He crept into the barracks on a moonless night. He was quite insane; came in dressed in priest's robes. He had an axe and a curved sword. Killed the two guards on the gate; just lopped off their heads, clean as a

113

whistle. Then he walked into the barrack room and killed another eight before anyone woke up. We chased him up on to the fort wall, and he just stood there challenging us to fire. Said the bullets wouldn't harm him. Soon proved him wrong Got a marksman to put a crease along his topknot. When he came around, I'd got him nailed spreadeagled, naked, to the outside of the stockade. Thought we'd make an example of him. Slit his guts open and stuffed in a couple of handfuls of maggots from the carcass of a dead dog; rough-stitched him up again, and left him there for a full week before he died. He made a very effective example; we didn't have another attack of that nature afterwards. Bullets wouldn't harm him! Huh, blasted witchcraft! Poppycock!'

'So these triad societies are sworn to fight us? And they identify themselves with tattoos?'

'Yes, to both your questions, Captain. They'd be shot of us if they could, though God knows they can't rule themselves. We do them a favour. The tattoos? They're anything their primitive minds find attractive. Might be an ant tattoo'd between the thumb and forefinger of one hand, or perhaps a lotus flower on their wrist, or a dragon climbing up their arm. They like dragons; typical. All the members of a society have the same tattoo.'

'And would they use drugs? Opium?'

'What primitive doesn't? Take the working classes of this country; gin is their drug. The dervishes chew hashish, and Chinamen smoke opium. Or else they use it as currency to buy arms to fight us. In the damned end it gets smoked.'

'Opium is used as currency?' The thought startled Pendragon.

'With so many divisions in the country, it's the only common currency,' said Hangshaw. 'With a lump of opium in his pocket, a man can trade from Kwangtung to Hopeh. It's more acceptable and a lot more desirable than gold. If we offered Chinese native troops opium instead of British silver as an inducement to sign on, we'd have every able-bodied man in every province in our China army.'

'So if someone gave London's Chinese eight hundred pounds of opium, what would you think, Colonel?'

'I'd think the feller was mad,' growled Hangshaw. 'They'd

cut a throat for an ounce of the stuff at the right time. Huh! Eight hundred pounds of the stuff; there isn't that much in the whole of the Western provinces. Eight hundred pounds of opium would buy you a War Lord, and the whole of his damned fighting force.'

* * *

'Eight hundred pounds of opium would buy you a War Lord, and the whole of his damned fighting force.' The words echoed and re-echoed in Pendragon's mind. Buy you a War Lord! Could there be such a thing as a War Lord amongst England's Chinese population? If there was, would the opium give him the necessary power to recruit an army; an army of mercenaries willing to fight and die on English soil for some European power? Could a War Lord draw his men from amongst the triads who were already sworn to fight against the British? It was a terrifying possibility. How many men? And the gunpowder stolen from the arsenal; twenty-four tons of the finest grade. Twenty-four tons would be enough to arm every rifleman, and to mount all the cannon in a full regiment for a major battle. Pendragon wiped sweat from the palms of his hands.

He paid off his cabbie in Hanover Square and walked through to Bond Street. It was crowded with private carriages, being a popular shopping area with the ladies, and there was little room on the pavements; even two ladies walking side by side in their crinolines occupied a good nine feet! Their footmen, hurrying along loaded with boxes of shopping, trying not to lose sight of their mistresses and yet remain courteous to other fashionable ladies, made progress slow.

Westley Richards' gun shop contained its usual complement of officers, who seemed to treat it more as a club than a business establishment. This, though, was largely the responsibility of the eccentric Bill Bishop, the enormous and friendly manager who was always immaculately dressed in a swallow-tailed coat and a wide-brimmed top hat, as though he were about to receive an immediate summons to Buckingham Palace. His only concession to his trade was the spotless white apron he wore over his coat, which reached almost to his ankles.

As Pendragon entered, Bishop excused himself from a small group of very young men who were discussing the merits of a saw-handled pistol, of a pretty but rather impractical design.

He raised his tall hat to Pendragon, and bowed slightly. 'Don't tell me, Sir. I recognise you as a past customer. You would be a cavalry gentleman. Yes, a gentleman of the Hussars. The 11th. A Captain. I have it, Sir. You are Captain Pendragon of Prince Albert's Own. You have an excellent pair of my pistols; infidel killers. Double barrels; yes, jove, ten-bores! Real man stoppers. I trust they are serving you well, Sir?'

Pendragon smiled. 'Right as usual, Bishop. God, what a memory. I fear, though, one of your pistols was lost in battle.'

'The 11th,' said Bishop. 'Ah, yes. I learnt with sorrow of the action. Many good customers, and many of my pieces of work have been lost. Not that my work matters, it can always be replaced; but the good young officers . . .' he sighed. 'However, I am most glad, Sir, to see that you at least are safe and sound. I presume you would like the pair complete again?'

'Not exactly; well, not at this moment. I want a little advice on a new weapon, something I can carry concealed in my normal dress. Not too bulky, but reliable.'

Bishop locked his fingers across his chest and revolved his thumbs, an indication that he was giving the matter deep consideration. He pursed his lips as though about to let Pendragon into some hitherto-undisclosed secret. 'Might I wonder if Captain Pendragon is a man of tradition, or progress?'

'Progress,' said Pendragon curtly. Buying from Bishop was like attending a demonstration of French mime. Normally it would be entertaining. Today he had too much on his mind.

'Aha,' said Bishop, looking satisfied. 'Then, Captain, I have something rather interesting. Captain Pendragon will no doubt be familiar with a number of weapons with revolving cylinders?'

'I know of them,' agreed Pendragon.

'Well, Captain, I have one such rather special little weapon. It is foreign, I admit, but I assure you it has been well checked and finished in my own workshops.' Bishop went to a drawer and came back with a roll of green baize. He held it lovingly in his left hand, and rolled back the fold with his right. 'So,' he said, as though it were a consignment of diamonds for the Hatton Garden jewellers. 'A little beauty, Captain.' He unfolded the last layer of felt. 'D'you see? The best of two worlds, Captain. A Beaumont-Adams revolver, made under licence by Dandy of Liege. The advantages of British design, with the novelty of a European bore. Point two-seven-six; very unusual, but very useful. Reliable, and quite lethal at a reasonable range. The smaller bore allows considerable reduction in weight, and thus the weapon weighs ounces rather than pounds.'

The pistol was certainly one of the prettiest Pendragon had seen. The maker's name was inlaid in gold along the top strap, the grips were polished ivory and the butt cap and trigger guard were of silver chased with hunting scenes. The frame and cylinder were engraved, rather inappropriately thought Pendragon, with stags. He raised his eyebrows at Bishop.

'You are going to say, Captain Pendragon, that this is a ladies' weapon, and the engraving is rather overdone. And I am going to disagree with you, even though you are a customer. Please come down to my range.'

Pendragon spent a further half an hour in Westley Richards, practising with the pistol, learning how to dismantle and clean its intricate mechanism. Then, with the weapon in its fitted case under his arm, he walked down Bond Street to Piccadilly and found a free cab for the last mile back to Park Lane. There was another visitor at the house when he arrived, Page Cloverly, but although Pendragon apologised for his absence it was obvious neither Page Cloverly nor Georgina considered the waiting tedious.

'I was passing this way,' explained Page Cloverly. 'Thought I should kill a couple of birds with the one stone, and drop in your warrant.' He handed Pendragon a small buff envelope, and turned to Georgina. 'I'm afraid I must confess to a lie, or, at least, to the inference of a lie. Of the two birds I mentioned, only one was business. The second was the opportunity to meet you. I have heard much spoken of you by Mr. Herbert.'

Georgina blushed. 'Mr. Herbert is known to be prone to a certain amount of exaggeration.'

'Nonsense,' exclaimed Page Cloverly. 'If anything, he under-represents. I have heard him say you are a woman of considerable good looks. Miss Carr, that is certainly under-representation.'

Pendragon chuckled. 'I feel as though I should leave, and make a second entrance.' He glanced quickly at Georgina, wondering if Cloverly's obvious flattery was disturbing her, but he saw she was enjoying the man's attention. He opened the envelope Cloverly had given him. It contained an oblong of platinum inscribed with a crown and initials, and his own name. At the top corner was a number, and at the bottom an inscribed signature of Mr. Sidney Herbert and his title War Minister. On the reverse were a few words of authority demanding assistance and recognition for Pendragon should he so require.

'It looks the sort of thing I should wear around my neck on a collar,' said Pendragon.

Cloverly laughed. 'In truth, I believe originally that was so. The first agents had an uncommon habit of losing everything they owned. Now it is a matter of tradition. Wear it where you will, but guard it well. Rambolt kept his in a moneybelt; others, I believe, sew it into seams, or slot it into the sides of their boots.'

'May I look?' asked Georgina. Pendragon passed it to her. 'It is of rather common metal,' she observed. 'Can the Crown not afford gold for its officials?'

'Afford, yes,' answered Page Cloverly. 'But platinum has many of the qualities of gold, without the value; therefore should it be found, then it may possibly be returned. If it were gold it would certainly be smelted. Mind you, nothing lost in London is ever returned. I've heard it said, and believe it, that even were a lion lost from the Prince's botanical gardens it would never be returned, but would find its way to the stew-pots of a Holborn eating house.'

'The thought repulses, but fails to surprise me,' smiled Georgina.

'And how goes your investigation?' Page Cloverly asked Pendragon.

Pendragon tried to speak convincingly. 'Swiftly. But it is assuming quite alarming proportions.' He avoided greater explanation in front of Georgina, and hoped Page Cloverly would understand and not press for more details.

He was relieved when Cloverly simply nodded and said: 'As we expected, regrettably.'

'He has become a ruffian, Mr. Cloverly,' said Georgina. She smiled coquettishly. 'Perhaps it is your company, Sir, for he tells me tales not even a twelve-year-old maidservant would believe. His eye, you will note, is of a startling yellow hue. He informed me he collided with his charger's head whilst taking the air in the park. His charger's head! He has ridden since his childhood. Were he not able to avoid a horse's head, he would hardly have been a hussar. He has been struck upon his eye! Probably by a common fist, for the action is hardly that of any gentleman of my acquaintance. Duelling scars, or wounds of honourable battle, I can endure, even admire. But the bruises of low assault are not becoming to a gentleman.'

Page Cloverly laughed. 'Then I shall tell you something, my dear lady. Yesterday I was with His Highness, Prince Albert. Whilst Mr. Herbert was making his report to Her Majesty the Queen, I enjoyed the pleasant company of the Prince himself. He was sorry to learn of the death of Rambolt, but I informed him of the appointment of one of the officers of his regiment. I told him Captain Pendragon's name, and I must say I was surprised to find he already knew of him. He was absolutely delighted with the appointment, and has expressed his earnest desire to meet the Captain at the earliest opportunity. So, Miss Carr, although I admit that in the course of his duty Captain Pendragon will undoubtedly mix with strange company, his commission is of the most honourable in the land.'

'You say he knew me by name?' asked Pendragon, astonished.

'Quite by name,' said Page Cloverly. 'He remembered even the date of your joining Lord Cardigan. He was aware also that you had survived the Crimean action.'

'Well I'm damned,' breathed Pendragon.

'I should not consider myself damned to be known by Prince Albert,' commented Georgina. 'I would consider it merely an example of the thoroughness of his Germanic mind. It is quite probable he can name all the officers of his regiment. He is a man of considerable intelligence.' Pendragon could detect just the slightest hint in her voice which he recognised as a warning that the forbidden subject was being raised.

* * *

No sooner had Page Cloverly left than, much to Pendragon's relief, Cox appeared. It pleased Pendragon to note that although the man looked tired he had taken the trouble to change and shave before presenting himself.

'How went it then?' asked Pendragon.

'Well, Sir, you might say I took a prisoner.'

'Took a prisoner? Grindle was attacked?'

'Not attacked again, Sir, but I think you should come and look at the catch.' Cox spoke as though he'd snaffled some Dacoit who'd been caught wandering in the barracks compound.

Pendragon followed him to the kitchen. He was surprised to see Antoinette, the prostitute who had led him to Grindle, standing surrounded by the kitchen staff. As she saw Pendragon, she grinned and dragged from behind her a small ragged boy. The boy twisted himself free and stood glowering angrily.

'Our prisoner,' said Cox formally. 'Miss Antoinette was kind enough to come along and give me a hand with him. He's as slippery as an eel, and I didn't want to lose him when I delivered Tom Grindle to my sister's this morning.'

'Grindle's all right?' asked Pendragon.

'He'll live, thanks to you, Captain,' answered Antoinette.

'My sister'll see him well cared for, Sir,' said Cox.

Pendragon looked at the boy. He was grubby and unwashed, with dirty yellow hair hanging in stringy curls below his jacket collar. He wasn't wearing a shirt or vest, and had on a pair of ragged moleskin trousers several sizes too large around the waist, folded back on themselves in a big tuck across his thin middle. He wore large boots that almost slid from his feet as he moved, making him shuffle rather than walk. He stared up at Pendragon, bristling like a captured wildcat and unblinking. Antoinette shook him by the shoulder. 'Well then,' she ordered, 'tell the Captain who you are.'

'I'm Ted,' growled the boy. 'Ted Blower.'

'Are you now?' said Pendragon. He wondered why Cox should have bothered him with so young a lad, who was most likely only a common sneak thief.

'Like I said, he's an eel, Captain,' warned Cox. 'He led me a chase and a half before I caught him, and then only because he had it away on his toes into a blind alley where he couldn't shin over a high wall.'

'It weren't so,' grumbled the boy. 'You got me 'cus I lost me boots an' stopped to pick 'em up.'

Antoinette shook him again. 'You young villain, don't argue with your betters. Scruffy little bastard he is, Captain; crawlin' with fleas. Look at him.' She pushed him forward. 'His bleeding bones rattle. One of Tom's mates saw him hanging around the day after Tom got done over. He was keepin' himself to himself in the courtyard, grubbin' the garbage; not that it would do him much good around there. He was watchin' Tom Grindle's room. Weren't you, eh?'

'Well, you knows why,' said the boy. 'You tell him then.'

'He must have thought everyone except Grindle was out this morning, Captain,' said Cox. 'Miss Antoinette had gone to buy a little milk. I was still in the room and Dolly Gowan was dressing Grindle. This lad slipped the catch and came in. I grabbed him, but he got free, dodged Miss Antoinette on the stairs and was away.' Cox looked around the crowded kitchen. 'Can we go to the study, Captain? We have to tell you something private.'

'If you wish.' Pendragon led them up the stairs. Behind him he could hear the boy's boots clumping on the woodwork.

Once in the study, Cox closed the door firmly behind them. 'You'll forgive me, Captain, but Miss Antoinette knows your private business. With what the boy said, she put two and two together.'

'But honest to God, Captain, I swears me silence, and I means it. A thousand tortures wouldn't drag a word of it from me mouth.'

'I hope not,' said Pendragon grimly. 'Well, what more happened?'

'Well, Captain . . .' Cox began to speak but was interrupted by Antoinette.

'Mr. Cox wanted to hand him over to the police; as well he

121

didn't. I told him we don't hand over lads to the crushers down our way. Not likely, Captain. What, and have 'em transported for trying to steal something to keep 'emselves alive? No thank you! We just grabs 'em, and one of the men takes them on his back, and they get a good strappin'. They learns better that way not to steal from such as theirselves. But this lad, Ted, he starts a patterin' and a shouting about murder, and how he's going to find the murderer and see him Ketched at Newgate. Got a villainous mind has this lad; shouts as how he'll hang on the murderer's feet while he's a swinging. So we takes him up to Dolly's room and I give him a bowl of soup. Mr. Cox says to him, Lad, you better start talking fast and sure, else there'll be no skin on your arse for a month.'

Cox blushed. 'I was angry, Captain, having to chase him so far. But Captain, then he said he was Rambolt's lad.'

Pendragon leant forward, suddenly more interested. 'Rambolt's boy?'

'So he swears.'

Pendragon looked down at the boy and stared at him hard. 'Is that the truth, boy?'

'Yes, Mister.'

Antoinette banged the boy on the shoulder. 'Captain, Ted. I told you, you calls him Captain, or else it's sauce.'

'Yes, Captain,' said the boy.

Pendragon squatted so he was level with the boy's face. 'Rambolt's son?'

The boy shook his head. 'Strike me, Captain, no! I ain't his son, just his lad. I run for him, see. Done his messages. Done a bit of watchin' for him. He give me fourpence a day an' a bed, an' grub.'

'And what do you know about Rambolt?'

'Well, I know he's croaked, Mister.' Antoinette shook him, angrily. 'Captain,' he added sullenly. He brushed his hair from his face with a thin-fingered hand.

'And how do you know that?'

'Cus I seen it done, didn't I?'

'You'd better tell me,' ordered Pendragon, sternly. He pulled a chair from behind him and sat on it, facing the boy.

'Well,' the boy hesitated for a moment. 'He was watchin'. That was his job, spy-watchin' and talking. I don't know who, 'cus most times he never says much to me, just tells me watch that man and tell me where he goes and who he sees, and I does it. Well, I was following the Ram, so's I was always at hand if he wanted me. He goes right down to the docks, and stands there, like a statue he was when he was standin', in a hut by the dock gate. He was just lookin' for near a whole morning and some of the afternoon, too. Then, sudden, he's out and following an empty waggon up White's Lane. There was three men on the empty waggon, one of them as looks like he shouldn't be there but had been better placed in a carriage. The other two, they was yellow lascar men, or some such foreigners. I keeps well back like I been taught, and then they reaches the Waterloo Tavern in Dock Street. There's a coachin' yard there an' they stops their waggon just inside the yard. Rambolt, he does a scuttle and gets into a doorway an' watches.'

'You go on, tell 'im,' prodded Antoinette.

'I seen one of the men, a big man with a beard, the one that's wearin' fancy clothes, he goes an' looks at another waggon what's come up from the docks, and is in the yard. He points at some boxes, and he says something to these lascar men, then he hoofs it inside the Waterloo. I keeps well back an' watches as well. I sees the two men go over to the other waggon, and they cuts the top off a case and lifts out stuff, then they puts it in their own cart, and they put a sack or something in the case and ties it back down. They does this some more times, a taking of stuff, and a putting of other stuff back; what it was, I don't have no way of telling. Then I sees Rambolt moving. I don't think he was going to interfere with them, not collar them nor nothing, but I think he was goin' in to the Waterloo to look after the fancy gent. He gets right by one of the foreigners, h'Indians or whatever, Frenchies maybe, and he's a looking the other way, like he's just passing. I seen this foreigner glance at him, and I hears him shout something and pull out a big blade. It was as big as I ever saw, and it shone in the sun. He slings his arm around Rambolt's neck, and his slits his gizzard from ear to ear. Next, he's got the Ram bundled into a box, quick as a black rat in a sewer. I knows the Ram is done for, 'cus his legs is kicking and twitching, and he ain't shouted. I runs, doesn't I? I'm going to yell murder and fetch the crushers 'cus they done the Ram, and I thinks I'll see them swing for it, at least.'

'Then how did you find Tom Grindle?' asked Pendragon.

The boy fidgeted. 'Well, I guesses, if I tells the crushers, sure as certain they'll not believe me. They'll set me up before the magistrates, and I'll be found a vagrant. Best I'll get is a month on the treadmills; worse could be the hulks in the River Thames where I hears they gets their liberties with boys like me, an' then I'd see a penal colony and never be back in London; not for ever as I know. So I don't go to the crushers, I sits and does a bit more thinking, like Rambolt taught me. I thinks, well, I seen them taking stuff off a waggon, and the waggon must be going somewhere an' maybe the waggoner would see where they went. Like as not the waggoner had struck a bargain; many does I know of. I goes back, and I asks the dock gates who's unloaded that day, and they say, well, Price unloaded from a ship, and so did King's, and a few others. Just cases I says, not other things. Well, the dock guard, he tells me. Taylor's done cases, and so did Price. I asks for their warehouses and goes along. I don't see the waggon in Taylor's warehouse, so I does a quick mile the other way, and gets to Price's. Sure, there's the waggon, and there's the waggoner grooming down 'is animals. I just waits until he's finished, and I tails him home.'

'And you saw him attacked, too?'

'In the alley,' said the boy. 'By the same ones as croaked Rambolt. Only the waggoner was lucky. He had time to shout, and the man with the blade missed his neck. The waggoner got his chin down and turned, and the knife sliced his chest. Next thing, there's men everywhere and the one with the blade has scarpered. I thinks again, and says to meself, if I speak with that waggoner, he'll tell me what I should do. I waited some more, and I had a sleep under a bit of sacking in the alley corner, and I tries to see him this morning. He catched me.'

'Mr. Cox told you he was a slippery customer,' said Antoinette. 'Old for his years, ain't the boy, Captain? That's what our life does for you.'

'How long were you with Rambolt?' asked Pendragon.

The boy frowned. 'I suppose about four year. Since I was

about eight. I was on the loose, an' he picked me up. He didn't beat me but seldom, and he give me good food. Meat and bread sometimes. And he kept a dry kip. Before him, I was scrapin' sausage skins an' putting them in brine, and that ain't good work because the brine can hurt your hands an' arms terrible; almost as bad as climbing for a sweep.'

'Tell me,' said Pendragon, his face softening. 'Where did Rambolt live? I heard tell he lived nowhere.'

The boy grinned for the first time. 'That was his plan. Rambolt used to say he was like a flea. He told me never eat long in one place, or you'll get scratched. We was never anywhere more than one or two weeks. He had carpet bags, and they was our home; leastwise, they held all his things. One day, we'd up and move, next we'd settle. A few days later, on again. Sometimes here, sometimes there. Battersea once; Blackfriars another time: like a flea! We lived all over London, and once we even went to Dover and I saw the sea. He was a good geezer was Rambolt.'

'Where are his bags?' asked Pendragon.

'I should say they'd be where he was,' answered the boy. 'The last place. Only like as not I'll never see them, as they'll be taken for rent. He was in a gaff in Cow Cross Street, only a tobacco spit from Smithfield.'

Pendragon stared at the boy, and the boy stared back.

Pendragon felt in his waistcoat pocket and pulled out the thin oblong of platinum. 'You ever seen one of these, Ted?'

'Yes, same as the Ram's.'

'Then you know what it is?'

'Rambolt used to say it was 'is ...' the boy searched for a word, 'his credentials.'

'A Queen's warrant,' said Pendragon.

'Lawks!' exclaimed Antoinette.

'Well lad, will you do a bit of work for me, as you did for Rambolt?'

Ted Blower smiled again. 'Would we be a catchin' them as did for the Ram?'

'I hope so,' said Pendragon.

'Then I'll work for you.' The boy paused. 'I'll need food, regular like, and a place for bed, and a wage of around ...'

'Steady, steady,' grinned Pendragon. 'I want you to take me

to Rambolt's room when you've eaten and been cleaned up. You'll take regular meals in future in the kitchens. Later we'll find a bed for you in the stables. As far as wages are concerned, I'll decide what you're worth.'

Antoinette punched the boy's arm roughly. 'You don't know your luck, lad. Now you just behave yourself or you'll answer to me.'

'But more likely to me, son,' threatened Cox.

* * *

When Antoinette had left, after again promising eternal secrecy, and young Ted Blower was having a strip-down in the stable yard. Pendragon paced the conservatory, his hands clasped behind his back. He was feeling satisfied. The boy was another firm rung on the ladder; a lucky catch. The lead to Rambolt's room was manna. Thank God he'd left Cox to guard Grindle. Things were moving steadily forward.

'Damn!' Pendragon swore. The movement might be too slow to prevent whatever calamities the villains were planning. Their noticing of Rambolt would have warned them the authorities had knowledge of at least some part of their plotting; Pendragon realised it might already be too late.

10

RAMBOLT'S GAFF, AS the boy called it, was in a galleried tenement in Cow Cross Street, only a couple of hundred yards north of the Smithfield meat market with its packed cattle yards. It was a stinking area, with almost every building connected in some way with the meat trade. Cattle were brought in from the surrounding country districts, herded through the filthy streets to the market pens, auctioned and taken to the near-by slaughter houses, then butchered. The hides were scraped and treated in the local tanneries; the bones, hooves and horns, boiled down for glue; the offal sorted, and the intestines cleaned out for tripes and sausage skins. There was no waste, even the excreta and the contents of stomachs and bowels were piled outside the abattoirs for collection and subsequent use as manure in the market gardens. Smithfield could be smelt from two miles away in warm weather.

Rambolt's lodging was in one of the buildings nicknamed rookeries, because of the landlord's ability to cram as many as a hundred people into a structure containing as few as ten separate rooms. In one extreme case the police reported as many as thirty people sleeping in a single room measuring as little as ten by twenty feet. To sleep communally cost one and a half pence a night. There were no sanitary arrangements in some lodgings; in others, refuse chutes, simply slides of rough wood open at the top, carried refuse and excrement down from floor to floor through the centres of the rooms, and deposited it in open sewers or cess pits in the cellars. Fumes from the sewage rose up the chutes, and drifted evilly throughout the dwellings.

There was no lighting and little ventilation. The original glass in the windows had long been broken and replaced with tarred paper, the inhabitants preferring warmth to the glow of moonlight. There were only two house rules; pay in advance, and look out for yourself.

The Ram had hired a room of his own, and paid weekly for the privilege of a padlock on his door. The boy, Ted, led Pendragon and Cox up the steep and broken flights of stairs in the daytime darkness, with the ease of a farm cat hunting the barns at night. On a small landing, where it was possible to see because of a break in the roof tiling, he stopped and pointed at a narrow door. 'It's here. Only the Ram kept the key, and I never had one.'

Cox felt the lock, rattling it in the hasp. 'You'll like me to open it, Captain, Sir?'

'Please,' answered Pendragon. He was having difficulty preventing himself from vomiting at the stench.

' 'Ere, you'll cop it,' the boy commented.

Cox kicked hard at the door, getting the whole weight of his body on to his foot. The door splintered near the hammered iron hinges. He grunted, and kicked again, then barged it with his shoulder, and the door shattered inwards. 'Done, Captain.' Cox stepped aside.

The room was some seven feet by five, and unlike those below had a skylight of cracked and dirty glass wedged open by a piece of wood. There was a narrow box bed to one side, and a heap of bedclothes in a corner. The only other items of furniture were a greasy pine table beneath the window, and a three-legged stool. Two carpet bags rested on the table, and a long black cloak hung on a peg on the wall.

Pendragon stepped into the room and lifted one of the carpet bags. As he did so, there was a sound from the entrance, and a man's voice said, 'What the 'ell you lot up to?'

Cox answered him. 'Collecting personal belongings.'

'You ain't no right. This room is hired private.'

'Your tenant's left. We're collecting his baggage.'

'If a tenant leaves baggage, it belongs to the landlord if there's rent owing.'

'Well, is there, man?' Cox made his voice aggressive and military.

'No,' admitted the landlord, sensing trouble for himself if he persisted.

'Then here's a shilling to mend the door, now buzz off,' ordered Cox. 'And more trouble from you, and the state of this filthy hovel will be reported to the Sanitary Commission.'

'And a fat lot they'd do,' growled the landlord insolently.

Cox grabbed at him, spun him by his shoulder, and booted him hard on the backside. 'Consider that a warning. Now hop it, fast.'

The man muttered angrily, but moved a few steps down the stairway, and stood in the darkness.

Pendragon tipped the contents of the first carpet bag on to the table. It was mostly clothing, clean and neatly folded. There were two sets of cutlery, a thick wallet, a flask of gunpowder and a few dozen lead bullets. He put the clothing on to the bed, and tipped out the second bag. There was more clothing, a pair of thick slippers, a notebook, a cased pen and ink bottle, two books in popular and cheap editions, and a heavy leather sack. Pendragon untied the neck of the sack; it contained five-guinea pieces in gold, perhaps thirty of them; Pendragon didn't count, but passed them to Cox, who hefted the sack and dropped it into his pocket.

The boy kept silent, but his eyes never let Pendragon. Pendragon opened the wallet. It contained only receipts, bills from grocers, a rail ticket.

Pendragon put the wallet, books and notebook into his topcoat pocket. 'Have a search through the clothing,' he told Cox.

Cox rummaged and examined the pockets, shook out vests and socks. There was nothing more.

'We'll leave,' said Pendragon, glad the search was completed. Even here, in the attic with the window open the smell was distressing him; the atmosphere nauseous and heavy.

'Here, what about . . .' began the landlord, who had found sufficient courage to return to the small landing.

'You can keep the clothing and the belongings,' Pendragon told him. 'Your tenant has no further use for them, and I'm certain we have none.'

'And think yourself damned lucky,' added Cox, 'I've no time for vultures, and you're the worst I've ever met.'

* * *

The sunlight in the street was blinding after the darkness of the hallways of the building. Pendragon hesitated at the door, shielding his eyes. Cow Cross Street was crowded; two market porters pushed past shouting for passage, sides of beef across their backs.

'Here what the . . .!' exclaimed Cox, stumbling against Pendragon. 'Here, lad. Damn me!' Young Ted Blower was off through the mass of people, weaving amongst them, running as fast as he could, dodging like a hare at a coursing. He was out of sight before either of the two men could react.

Pendragon straightened himself. 'Let him go,' he said. 'He's done what he considers to be his duty. I doubt if he knows more that would help us.'

'Help us, Captain, Sir? The young blighter's just helped himself! That gold coin you passed me, Captain, he lifted it clean from my pocket.'

* * *

'Copious bits of paper', was how Page Cloverly had referred to Rambolt's official reports. Pendragon was in no doubt they had been scribbled on pages torn from the notebook he was now examining. No wonder Herbert and Cloverly found them difficult to understand. In several obvious cases, the pages had been ripped out hurriedly, leaving the first letters of words still in the fold of the book. Rambolt's age showed in his writing; words which began bold faded to thin lines, as though the writer lacked the strength to finish them. He obviously neglected to clean his nib point, and dropped blots or smudged letters. In most places, minute splatters of ink surrounded the lettering where the nib point seemed to have managed to cross itself, or the pen had turned to Rambolt's old hand. The book smelled of the coarse, rope-wrapped plug tobacco steeped in rum that sailors were fond of chewing, and which Rambolt must have carried at times in the same pocket as the notebook. Pendragon was surprised at the amount of information so small an item provided of its previous owner.

Pendragon could see Rambolt was not methodical in his use of the book; he ignored the ruled lines, and wrote diagonally, even sideways on the pages. His lettering sloped back and forth and even his spelling of small words was inconsistent. The pages, torn out for his reports, were from any part of the book. And his rough jottings must have been simply memory joggings which he no doubt used when writing the final report for his superiors.

The carriage taking Pendragon and Cox back to Park Lane bounced on a rutted section of roadway, jolting Cox against Pendragon. Cox apologised and wedged himself more securely in the corner.

'By the way, Captain, Sir, I wonder if you are finding anything of use to your investigation?'

'A little, perhaps,' mused Pendragon. 'There are odd notes in here.'

'I was doing a lot of thinking last night, Captain; keeping myself awake. That opium stuff, it worries me, Captain. Eight hundred pounds of it! Well, I remembered the farm workers use it to keep their kids quiet while they earn their livings in the fields, and I thought to myself, what if it were all put into London's water supply? All that opium! It could send the whole of London to sleep for a week, and we'd all be at anyone mercy. A diabolical plan that would be.'

Pendragon laughed. 'Diabolical, yes. Practical? Hardly! Half of London's population takes its water from streams or the river, and if they can survive the sickness the foul water can cause, then a little opium would never hurt them. No, Cox, this opium, I've decided, is payment for some mischief; remember the explosives?'

'I don't forget when you tell me, Captain, and I'm unlikely to forget twenty-four tons of gun-powder; that would be five hundred and seventy-six barrels. I'd have hated to be one of the guards who was on duty when it was taken; chances are they haven't seen daylight since, except for their flogging.'

'Suppose you were an enemy of England, Cox, what would you do with twenty-four tons of explosives?'

Cox thought for a few moments. 'I think I'd blow up the Government, Captain; God forgive me! I'd blow up police stations as well, and the barracks.'

'For what purpose, Cox? A new Government could be formed within hours! It's seldom you have many of your policemen actually in their stations, and most of our troops are abroad. Our standing army here, at the moment, is fairly small and mostly in training. You would create a nuisance, but little else.'

131

'You're right, Captain,' agreed Cox, rather sadly. 'I'd make a poor officer. I haven't the wit for it, have I?'

'One thing I learnt as an officer, Cox, was never to do my thinking when I'm tired; that's when you make mistakes. I did my thinking this morning. If I had twenty-four tons of explosives, and a reasonable army of men, and I wanted to cause the biggest amount of troubles to our armies overseas, Cox, I'd blow up ships.'

'Ships, Captain?'

'Yes, ships. Cox. Think of the Crimean army, Cox, and how we rely on the Royal Navy. If it weren't for them, the whole of the Crimea would be Russian by now.'

'But our lads, Sir . . .'

'I know, Cox. The soldiers do the fighting, at least, most of it on the land. But they can't fight without guns, without horses, without food and supplies. And they can't fight without reinforcements. If you sank ships, Cox, and if they were loaded with supplies for our troops, then you could control the Crimea within months.'

'No wonder I was only a damned sergeant, Captain,' groaned Cox. 'I never thought of any of that. And, by God, twenty-four tons of explosives placed right could destroy a lot of ships.'

'A fleet,' said Pendragon.

Cox nodded.

The carriage slowed, and Cox glanced out of the window to find they had arrived in Park Lane. He twisted the doorcatch, jumping out as the carriage stopped. He stood and waited as Pendragon climbed down.

'We shall see what this notebook tells us later,' said Pendragon. He looked up towards the house entrance. 'Well, I'm blessed!'

Cox followed his surprised gaze. The boy, Ted Blower, was sitting on the wall beside the entrance gate, swinging his legs and trying to look as casual as possible. When he was certain the two men had seen him, he jumped down and strolled cockily across to them. He handed Pendragon the sack of coins.

'You damned scamp,' exploded Cox, his moustache bristling.

'Didn't never even take one of 'em, Captain,' grinned the boy, glancing at the small sack Pendragon was holding. 'Tell the truth, I never even had no time to look inside, though I knows the feel of gold if I ain't owned none.'

'What on earth have you done to yourself?' asked Pendragon, peering at the boy. Blood was running down both the boy's arms, and was dripping from his fingers. His trousers were even more torn than before, and there were splashes of blood on the lower parts of his legs, and dribbles showing on his ankles above his boots.

Cox grabbed at the boy's arm and pulled back the sleeve. 'God Almighty, Captain! Look at him.' There were a series of deep puncture wounds up the boy's arm, from wrist to elbow. Cox pulled up the other sleeve, the wounds were identical.

'It's nothing, Captain,' grinned the boy, cheerfully. 'Just that your coachman keeps his axle-spikes sharper than most.'

'You rode on the axle? On the spikes?'

'You damned little idiot,' said Cox. 'What the hell did you want to do that for?'

'I 'ad to show you, didn't I? I 'ad to let you see why Rambolt used me and not other ones. Else you wouldn't take me on permanent, an' I don't fancy meself a h'unemployed. Well, I showed you I can work for you like I done for 'im.'

'I suppose you've more than proved your point,' said Pendragon. He looked at Cox and raised his eyebrows. 'And what shall we do with him then?'

Cox looked fierce. 'I should think what I ought to do, Captain, is take him in the coachyard, and larrup some sense into him. Though like as not there's no chance of sense where there's obviously no feeling.' He put his hand on the boy's shoulder. 'Come along, Ted lad, best we excuse ourselves from the Captain and I'll see what we can do about those wounds of yours. And, blow me, if the Captain doesn't employ you, then I'll have you myself as a future trooper.' He smiled down at the boy.

'There are indications he'd make a good one,' agreed Pendragon, watching Henry Cox with the boy, and remembering his own early childhood in the care of Sergeant Major Bowers. Cox and Bowers were similar in many ways; tough on the outside, as hard as nails in the battles, but soft at heart. 'He'd better be signed on with us, Cox. He'd make a terrible foe if he joined the enemy.'

* * *

Pendragon dined alone; he was glad of the opportunity to study Rambolt's notebook even as he ate. Wolfgang, sensing Pendragon's engrossment, served the meal in silence. Pendragon read and re-read the untidy writing, much of which was as indecipherable as Egyptian hieroglyphs. It was as though Rambolt abbreviated everything. There was one name, though; written sideways down the margin of the centre page. It was almost certainly misspelt, but it was recognisable; Selo Mikhailovich.

Pendragon knew of the man.

* * *

Selo Mikhailovich! Pendragon and the Russian had never been formally introduced, but Georgina had pointed him out at the New Year ball of Sir Hubert Pennick, the Whig Member of Parliament. It had been three years before at Knightsbridge House, but the picture of the man remained in Pendragon's mind; Milhailovich had been drunk, or appeared to be so, laughing boisterously and making loud and coarse comments about some of the ladies to a group of officers from one of the Highland Regiments. Georgina had overheard him, and had been furious.

'That man is a pig,' she told Pendragon. 'The remarks he is making would lead him to Westminster Fields if the officers were true gentlemen. They're afraid of him, and his reputation. Look at him, swilling in drink.'

'Who is he?' Pendragon had asked.

'That object,' said Georgina contemptuously, 'is Count Selo Mikhailovich. He claims to be cousin of the Czar of Russia. He behaves more as the relative of a wild boar. His growth has obviously been to his body, and not to his brains. Russia produces giants, not gentlemen.'

Mikhailovich, bearded and with his jet-black hair long and swept back over his high collar, was at least six feet five in height and twice the breadth of any of the officers standing beside him. 'What does he do over here?'

'Do?' Georgina gave an artificial laugh. 'Do? He arrived at no one's invitation, and has embarrassed the court into accepting him through his blood relationship. He seems to have money enough to frequent all the gaming rooms, and houses of ill-repute, as and when the mood takes him. Do? I have heard he lost four thousand pounds in one throw at dice at a gambling house. And there is little doubt he ruined Sarah Ashley.'

'The late Lord Ashley's daughter?'

'She was foolish enough to accept an invitation to dine with him. He raped her, poor child, in a private room in the restaurant. Her brother called him out the following day; the boy was seventeen, and had as much idea how to use a sword as I have myself. Mikhailovich didn't even bother to take off his coat when they met on Hampstead Heath; he killed him, I'd told, within ten seconds of them raising their swords. Regrettably he was able to claim both diplomatic immunity and provocation. The man is a murdering rogue.'

Yes, thought Pendragon, staring at the name in Rambolt's notebook, there could be only one Selo Mikhailovich, and his name in the book must surely indicate his involvement.

* * *

'Ah, John.' Georgina swept into the dining-room, stopped and pirouetted so her dress billowed and swung above her neat flat-heeled slippers. 'Do I look fine enough?'

Pendragon closed the notebook and smiled at her. 'Georgina, I have never known a day when you did not look fine enough; though I've been led to understand that to show one's ankles in such a manner in male company is to invite seduction.'

Georgina giggled, and shook back her silver-blonde hair. 'It is rather my intention, John. I must confess. I am expecting a certain gentleman; your friend, or rather business acquaintance, Mr. Page Cloverly. He is taking me out to dine. I wish to dazzle him a little, John, I find him a gentleman much to my liking. He is kind, entertaining and of an amusing humour.'

'It's time you settled down, Georgina. Mr. Cloverly is a single gentleman of good breeding, and respectable. You could do far worse.'

'Tish! Of settling down I have no intention. To settle is to become aged. He shall be an entertainment. I am quite bored with old men, and have suffered too much of their company lately; that horrid work of yours, John, has deprived me of a valued escort. In truth, I confess I have had to seek out Clarendon. And the night before last, I accompanied Grenville. They are both positively ancient, and both smoke those dreadful Burmese cheroots. Granville plucked at his moustache all through dinner and was quite revolting. I kept expecting him to scratch himself, and the anticipation made me quite distressed and nervous.'

Pendragon laughed. 'I doubt if Page Cloverly plucks his moustache, but I admit to the odd delicate scratch myself, although in privacy.'

There was a knock at the door. 'Oh my goodness,' gasped Georgina. She looked at the ormolu and tortoiseshell clock on the gilded wall table. 'Eight o'clock exactly. Mr. Cloverly is punctual to the minute. Do I look well? My cheeks are not red?'

'Georgina, you look perfect, as ever.'

Wolfgang appeared at the salon door. 'Mr. Cloverly, Madam.'

'Ah, Miss Carr,' Page Cloverly bowed his shoulders towards Georgina. 'And John; how are you? Miss Carr, you look quite charming. Seeing you again is like a return to spring from the overburdening heat of summer.'

'Mr. Cloverly,' Georgina smiled sweetly, 'you should not make so free with your compliments in company.'

'Although,' said Pendragon grinning, 'no doubt she appreciates them. Georgina, I must ask you a favour. It is simply that I would like to borrow Mr. Cloverly for some ten minutes; I promise no longer.'

'You and your wretched business again, no doubt,' pouted Georgina. 'Just this once.'

'A beautiful woman, Miss Carr,' commented Page Cloverly, when she had left them alone. 'And very well connected. Now what do you wish to talk about?'

Pendragon told Cloverly of his discoveries relating to the death of Rambolt, and the smuggling of the opium. He finished with his suspicions of the involvement of Count Mikhailovich.

'Fair work,' complimented Page Cloverly. 'And quickly done. I'm inclined to agree with you about Selo Mikhailovich. He's been floating around for a few years now, and far too often in the company of people who should know better. There was a move to ask him to leave when the war began, but he swore a love of the country and, I suspect, oiled a few palms, and has managed to remain. He lives at Duke House in Cambridge Square. I've been there, as a matter of fact. He enjoys the rather outdated style of decoration. It's like a Pharaoh's tomb. The old King George would have been en-raptured. He gambles; it's like an illness with the man. He spends every night in the gaming rooms.'

'At the moment,' said Pendragon, 'you must realise, much is supposition. I'm guessing at Mikhailovich's involvement. His name may have been in the notebook only as a suspect; per-haps for an entirely different line of Rambolt's investigation. I am much more concerned with the whereabouts of both the explosives and the opium. If I can discover their hiding place, then they can be recovered and at least any imminent danger is removed. Mikhailovich may well be the leader but could equally as well be merely the tip of the iceberg. However, if I get proof of his guilt, we can arrange his arrest.'

'Arrange his arrest? My dear fellow!' Cloverly was incredu-lous. 'Arrest a Russian Count while peace is at the moment being negotiated by our overseas diplomats? You and I may well have our suspicions of the Russians' true intentions, but the Cabinet will have none of us beginning the war afresh. We have it reliably that Sebastopol is being held merely as a token; the Russians will withdraw at a politically convenient time, despite what our Crimean commanders think. The pair of us may know there are plots within plots, and the Russian wolf plans to turn its jaws against Europe, but expect no help, John; none from the army, and less from the police. Arrange the man's arrest? Even though we had proof that he were to make an attempt upon the life of our dear Queen tomorrow, he could not be simply arrested.'

'Then even if he is guilty, he will go free? The explosives, and the opium? Is their recovery all of my work?' Pendragon was puzzled.

'All of it? By the dear Lord, no! It must be completed. Every one of those who plot against the country must be eliminated.'

'I agree, but how?'

Page Cloverly leant towards Pendragon. 'Rambolt had the answer, dear fellow; enemies of the state simply disappeared. To where? I have no knowledge, nor want of such. And therefore, John, this is what is expected of you; by myself, by Sidney Herbert, by Her Majesty's Government, and no doubt certainly by Her Majesty Queen Victoria, if she were to learn of the matter. You, John Pendragon, must remove the Queen's enemies. If he is guilty then commence with Count Selo Mikhailovich. In which case I suggest you do it secretly, with discretion, and in a manner which in no way involves Her Majesty's Government, nor which causes international embarrassment to the Crown.' He paused briefly, then almost hissed the words: 'But kill him.'

11

KILL MIKHAILOVICH IF he is guilty! It had been an order, and a strangely brutal one from Page Cloverly who was always so perfect a gentleman. Kill the Queen's enemies, dispose of them with discretion. Page Cloverly had been almost casual. Pendragon was disturbed by the realisation that Cloverly and Sidney Herbert expected him to be an executioner without argument; and it was plainly accepted by them as a normal part of a Queen's Agent's work.

There was quite a difference between killing men in the blaze and heat of battle and executing them in some cold-blooded manner in their civilian life. Pendragon felt it was like being invited to inspect a prison, and arriving to find you were required to act as hangman at the prison's gallows.

If I find Mikhailovich is the guilty man, he wondered, can I kill him even then? Can I simply point a gun at his head and pull the trigger? Can I poison him, or cut him down with a sabre?

If it were a question of honour, then the answer was yes. Or if it were a question of Georgina's honour or reputation; in those cases, he would have no hesitation. Had he been Sarah Ashley's brother or her beau, then the Russian's death, even the thought of it, would have given him the greatest satisfaction. And if the Russian was threatening the realm? Threatening the safety of his beloved Queen Victoria? Dammit! That was exactly what the man *was* doing; or could be doing. It was a question of honour; a matter of the protection of the country. Cloverly was right. If Mikhailovich was guilty, then he should be killed, for he was even more of a foe than the enemy soldiers who could be met on a battlefield; at least they wore their colours proudly and openly.

Pendragon knew now he could kill the Queen's enemies, whether they were foreign, or simply traitors. He knew he would be able to kill them coldly and without feeling. It was far more justifiable than the senseless slaughter of thousands in the Crimea. But the feeling was frightening and gave him a strange uneasiness, a prickling at the nape of his neck, as though he had stared in a mirror and found a different face reflected. It was a face which he realised he would have to learn to recognise, and accept.

*   *   *

The house was empty but for the servants, and most of those had gone to bed early as their mistress was out. It was an airless night, with heavy storm clouds gathering to the west. Pendragon went upstairs to his room, undressed and slipped on a cool silk robe. The gaslight to the side of the bed hissed, and Pendragon settled himself at the bedside table and studied Rambolt's notebook again. Somewhere it contained information; he was sure of it.

He turned the pages again slowly, carefully examining each of them, reading every word.

'Nothing!' An hour later he closed the notebook. Surely Rambolt couldn't have relied on memory alone? Pendragon picked up the notebook again and idly rapped it on the table top. He tossed it down angrily. His fingers were sticky and he felt in his gown pocket for his kerchief. He paused, lifted his hand and smelt his finger-tips; beeswax. Beeswax? He lifted the book again. The edge of the thin leather binding was sticky with the sweet-smelling wax. Pendragon frowned, it was not the normal custom for a bookbinder to use a material so easily softened by heat. He ran a thumbnail under the edge of the leather and rolled it back.

'I'm damned!' The leather was sealed by the wax only around the edges; inside, flat against the stiffening of the cover, was a strip of fine paper. Pendragon peeled back more of the leather until he could slide the paper free; it was covered with numbers. There were hundreds of them, written in script so fine and minute Pendragon had difficulty reading them. He put down the list and went over to his wardrobe. He reached inside and found his military telescope, then un-screwed the front lens. He returned with it and sat, studying the writing carefully, close to the gas light. The figures were in groups of three, with fine lines drawn vertically between the groups.

'98 4 3/ 119 1 12/'. The numbers covered both sides of the thin sheet of paper.

It was obviously Rambolt's code, but seen as it was, it seemed at first to be the code of a mathematician. Pendragon bit his lip. Rambolt was supposed to have lacked a formal education, although he could read and write. The code was unlikely to be mathematics, far more likely to be something relatively simple. The numbers might just be letters of the alphabet. Pendragon tried several combinations without success, reversing the alphabet, splitting it into sections; it didn't work.

A prayer? Perhaps it was a code based on a prayer; there were too many. Guessing, he tried with the most frequently used; the Lord's Prayer. A failure.

Rambolt's books! Of course! Pendragon damned himself again for not realising sooner; a book code! He'd used them himself while at school for passing secret notes to friends. Unless you knew the book, the code was safe except from an expert with days to spend on the deciphering; particularly safe from one's schoolmasters.

Rambolt's two books were a poor library. One was a collection of poems by some unknown and not very talented workman poet, the other was by Dickens, *The Cricket on the Hearth*, in a red linen binding. The code could be from either, but Pendragon realised if he were correct, then it was probable Rambolt varied his codes from book to book, and perhaps even mixed them at times. As he was more familiar with Dickens, he began with that one.

Ninety-eight would be the page number. He opened the book. Four; the line. He counted downwards. Three; the letter. The letter was 't'. Pendragon jotted it down, and began the second number 119 1 12. The letter was 'h'. After several minutes Pendragon sat back on his bed feeling satisfied. In front of him was a complete word; it had no significance as yet, but at this moment it gave him great satisfaction. It was 'There'.

* * *

It was four hours' work, without even a short break. Pendragon heard Georgina return and go to her room. Outside, the night sounds of London died away until only the odd sound of hooves, or the squeal of a distant carriage brake disturbed the silence. At last, there were no more numbers.

There is no doubt it is Wan Hei of the Green Serpents. It is my belief the powder is in his emporium. He will act no more until he receives the payment which is due. Payment is in shipment on *Belle Cygne* and will be the drug opium. Distribution will follow payment to societies in Liverpool, Southampton, Portsmouth, Bristol, Falmouth. Date of Night of Fire probable Queen's fleet inspection at Falmouth. They will concentrate on line ships and dock installations, but I fear assassination attempt. All ports will be fired at same time. Crucial period late August. M must be watched at all times. I can act only when opium arrives.

Pendragon grunted. There were no more numbers, no more hidden slips of paper. Rambolt had been killed before he could make his promised move. Damn them! The Queen, and Prince Albert, when were they due to make their annual inspection? Pendragon hurried down to the study and found the *London Illustrated News* with its list of Royal engagements. He brought it back to the bedroom and thumbed through the pages. He felt his throat dry with sudden panic. The date of the Royal inspection was set for the twenty-eighth of August; just ten days' time. If the explosives were to reach all the ports in time for use on that date, then they must leave London, if they had not already done so, within the next twenty-four hours; thirty-six hours at the most!

Pendragon bit his lip. His eyes smarted with the last few hours of concentration in the poor light. He read the report again, searching for more information. Wan Hei must be the triad leader, the so-called War Lord; he must own the emporium where the powder and opium were possibly stored. The place would be in London, but exactly where? Most likely the East End, near the docks, where most of London's Chinese population were concentrated. And 'M'? It must mean Mikhailovich! Damn them and their plotting. The Night of Fire reference made Pendragon feel uncomfortable as he realised how close his guess at their intentions had been; the ships of the line, and the port installations. The death of the Queen Victoria and the chaos and destruction to supply lines, would undoubtedly be followed by concentrated attacks in every overseas colony.

God knows how many British soldiers would die in the Crimea, India, Africa, Egypt. The territories would be lost for ever. The Russians would sweep the British Crimean troops into the sea. The Chinese and Indians could rebel without fear of immediate reprisal; reject British rule. In Africa and Egypt there were German and French interests who would be happy to step into any gap left by the departure or elimination of Britons.

Dear God, breathed Pendragon. This was no small plot to disrupt England internally. This was aimed at her complete destruction; destruction of the Throne, the country, the Empire. If successful, England could not survive.

What sort of an army could this man Wan Hei raise? This sort of destruction needed more men than would be found in a single society in London. There were Chinese in all of the British ports; thousands of them! Bound together by payments to their clans, and with a hidden but united desire to remove the British from the soil of their native China, they were a considerable army, quite adequate to the requirements.

Pendragon swore silently as he remembered how close he'd been earlier in the evening to telling Page Cloverly he was no longer interested once Cloverly had suggested possible murder. Had he backed down, and found later that his action had caused such tragedy and catastrophe to Britain, he could never have lived with himself.

A day and a half! Pendragon jerked the bedside bell-pull to call for Cox.

* * *

Cox, as usual, arrived even at this late hour looking as though he had been dressed and awake awaiting Pendragon's summons.

'The matter is most urgent,' Pendragon told him. 'We'll see now if young Ted is worth his salt. Has he slept yet?'

143

'Four hours, I should think, Captain,' said Cox. 'Though I've noticed he has the knack of sleeping anywhere, at any time, when he's nothing to occupy him.'

'Fetch him to the study,' ordered Pendragon. 'I think we need him now as he's never been needed before. Let's hope he learnt something from his late master.'

*   *   *

The boy was still sleepy when Cox led him into the study. He stood there, his eyes still a little blurred, with an old length of sacking he was obviously using as bedding still wrapped around his shoulders.

'I'm sorry to drag you from your rest,' apologised Pendragon, who had hurriedly dressed.

'It's all right, Captain,' said the boy. 'The hour don't matter. Often I've earned a crust at a later time than this.'

'I've urgent work for you, Ted. Urgent and very important. The kind of work you say you know. I want some information about a man; the man who may have been responsible for killing Rambolt.'

The boy's eyes brightened. 'The geezer what done the Ram? 'Struth, Captain, ain't no time what I wouldn't work to see that one kicking on a length of hemp. What d'you want of me?'

'Duke House, Cambridge Square. Do you know it?'

'A bit norf of 'ere,' the boy nodded. 'I knows the Square, I'll soon find the 'ouse.'

'There's a man living there. I've reason to believe he may be the leader of the ones who killed Rambolt, and the chief planner of a lot that threatens the Queen and the country.'

'The Queen?' Cox looked at Pendragon, his eyes wide.

'Both their Majesties,' continued Pendragon. 'You go there, Ted. It's late, but you may get a chance to see the man to-night. If not now, then first thing in the morning. I only want you to identify him. If you see him, and recognise him as the man with the Chinese at the inn, then come back here as quick as you can and tell me.'

'It's done, Captain,' grinned the boy. ' 'Ere...' He handed the piece of sacking to Cox.

'You take care, lad,' warned Cox. 'No breaking and entering; just keeping a sharp eye open.'

'You could bet yer life.' The boy shouted the words as he ran from the room. Cox shook his head at Pendragon.

* * *

There were three hours of darkness left. Pendragon did not return to his own room, but sat thinking in the armchair in the study. A little after dawn when he heard the maids begin their day's work in the kitchens, he rang for them, and when the housemaid appeared he asked for an early breakfast. By the brief look of disapproval on the girl's face he realised she was under the impression he must have been out all night and had recently returned home.

He had been drinking his tea only a few minutes when Wolfgang appeared with Ted Blower. The boy looked flushed and was breathless; he had obviously been running.

Wolfgang was apologetic. 'He insisted, Captain John. Said you had told him and it was urgent.'

'Quite so, thank you,' said Pendragon. 'You can leave him with me.' He waited until Wolfgang had left, but before he could begin to question Ted the boy burst into excited chatter.

'I seen 'im. I seen 'im, Captain, that man. The very one as did for the Ram. I seen 'is face and near as bloomin' touched 'im. Near touched 'im, I did.'

'So early this morning? Are you absolutely certain?'

'H'absolutely, Captain. I thought I'd seen 'im even earlier in the basement area, but then the lights was dimmed and I wasn't so certain. Then, first crack of sun this mornin', I sees 'im across the stable yard. I watched him a talkin' to the coachman, an' then I seen 'im waitin' while the coach was readied. Sure as sure, it was 'im. Big man as I ever did see. Big, and with a black beaver. Cor, a giant! I'd never forget 'im, Captain.'

'Are you too tired for more work?'

'Tired, Captain? I ain't tired. Ain't many lads gets as much shut eye as me. Is it more work to 'ang that man?'

'In a way, Ted. I want to find a place called Wan Hei's Emporium. Can you remember that? Wan Hei's Emporium.'

'I don't need to remember it, I knows the name already. I heard tell of it, they call it One Eye's. Times a lad can get carryin' work there, I've been told. I knows roughly where it

145

is, and I can soon find it with a bit of askin'.'

'When you do, Ted, watch the place for a couple of hours. See if there are many Chinese working there. And remember exactly how it's situated; where the main doors are, and if there's a rear entrance, or any low windows. But take care, and be back here by noon.'

'Would the Chinese be the ones who slit the Ram's gizzard, Captain?'

'Probably, yes.'

'Then, I'll be extra careful,' promised the boy. 'On account as 'ow I don't want mine in a like state.'

'Good lad. Now go and tell Cook I say you've to have the biggest breakfast you can eat, before you go.'

The boy's eyes shone. 'Thanks, Captain.'

* * *

So the mysterious foreigner was Mikhailovich after all. It had all been too easy, thought Pendragon. Every rung on the ladder complete; a simple matter of climbing it steadily. Once he knew the exact whereabouts of Wan Hei's Emporium, it was a matter of planning the final action.

He thought of Mikhailovich and felt his anger growing inside. A little more proof was all he needed, but how to get it within the next few urgent hours was the problem. Was Mikhailovich working alone? It was possible there were other Russians involved; even probable. And, unspeakably, there could be British traitors in the plot.

There might be proof of Mikhailovich's certain guilt in the Russian's house. Pendragon smiled grimly; first a Queen's Secret Agent, then a thief to steal at dead of night into some stranger's house to rob him of papers, and finally a murderer. Sidney Herbert had a warped sense of duty to feel it was a position for an ex-officer!

If Pendragon had been correct in his estimation of the time required to get explosives to the other parts there were thirty hours left, providing the powder hadn't gone already. Thirty hours to get the proof; thirty hours to get incriminating evidence and take what action was necessary. Suppose he was wrong, and the time less? Perhaps Mikhailovich should be dealt with first, and the proof sought afterwards; there was much

146

at stake, and one life was little against the cost of a nation.

Once Ted returned, Pendragon finally decided, the boy must go again to the Emporium accompanied by Henry Cox. They must keep watch together. At any sign of the departure of a large consignment of goods, young Blower would act as a runner to inform Pendragon. Meanwhile, Pendragon must visit Sidney Herbert and explain the seriousness of the situation to him. Damn it, it was more than unreasonable to expect two men and a boy to tackle perhaps twenty Chinese. He could deal personally with Mikhailovich later. The Royal Navy were the answer! If he could convince Sidney Herbert there was good cause to involve the major service, then the Chinese could be allowed to take the consignment downriver, out of the port of London. They could be seized once they were clear of the city and into the estuary. Half a dozen well armed Royal Marines would do the job with ease. Sidney Herbert must see that as the most sensible course of action.

* * *

Ted Blower had not returned by lunchtime.

* * *

At three fifteen p.m., when Pendragon was pacing the study, and not knowing whether to be furious or worried by the lateness of the boy, he received a letter, delivered by private messenger.

It was in a long narrow grey envelope, sealed with black wax. The seal was blurred and gave no hint as to the sender. Pendragon slit the envelope and shook out the letter. It was heavily perfumed with musk, and for a brief second Pendragon suspected it was an angry note from Lady Zara, complaining of his recent neglect. He unfolded the paper, and frowned. Clipped to the upper edge were two blond curls, one of which was bloodstained. The blood had been wet when the curls had been clipped to the paper, and had left a scarlet smear.

The writing was large and extravagant.

It read, 'Captain John Pendragon, I trust you will find yourself free to dine with me tonight. I shall expect you at 8 p.m.'

It was signed, 'Mikhailovich'.

12

So MIKHAILOVICH HAD Ted Blower; the blond curls clipped to the notepaper unmistakably belonged to the boy. The blood? Knowing Mikhailovich's reputation, it could well be genuine! The inferences of the letter and the hairpiece were clear. Mikhailovich obviously knew that Pendragon was Rambolt's replacement; and that he was close on his heels. The man could not be so naïve as to believe Pendragon would take no action on receipt of the note, and so the blond curls served a double purpose; firstly, to inform Pendragon that the Russian's knowledge was positive, and secondly, a hidden threat to the boy's life if Pendragon should be foolish enough to either refuse the invitation, or continue with his efforts to frustrate the Russian's plans.

'Damn and blast!' Pendragon bit on his thumbnail. What was behind the Russian's invitation? He must be coldly certain of himself to invite Pendragon simply for the satisfaction of meeting his enemy face to face. Was he so sure of his immunity he could afford to do so? Surely a knife thrust in Pendragon's back, dealt by one of his henchmen, would be a better way of settling matters? Unless, decided Pendragon, Mikhailovich was uncertain who else might already know of his involvement, and of the plot. That was information which poor young Ted would have been unable to supply, and Mikhailovich had to learn.

Suppose a message could be got to Cloverly or Herbert?

No chance of that, thought Pendragon. Mikhailovich must surely have men watching the house. He walked across to the window and stood behind the curtain looking down into the road. It was busy with afternoon traffic, but across in the park were two men sitting chatting. From their position, they must have been able to see both the front entrance to the house, and the gate to the coachyard, and though Pendragon could see their mouths moving they kept their heads facing the direction of Park Lane. Pendragon went up to his room and collected his telescope. When he returned, the men were still in their former position. He slid out the sections of the telescope and focused it on them. One of the men wore a thin drooping moustache and had pronounced cheekbones. It was a facial structure he'd seen before, common amongst some of the Russian Crimean regiments.

Pendragon rang for Cox. When the man arrived, he showed him the invitation.

'The bastards, Captain,' swore Cox. 'I'm sorry, Captain, I shouldn't speak like that, not in this house, but I surely mean it. The poor young beggar. I'd like to get my hands on that Russian swine. Let me collect the coachman and groom, and we'll get along there and finish them once and for all.'

'They'd finish Ted first, Cox,' warned Pendragon. 'I'm almost certain we're being watched, and if that is the case, then any move we make which they think is a threat will result in Ted's death, and probably ours as well. Look down there.' He handed Cox the telescope. 'Those two men on the grass under the lime tree.'

'I see them,' said Cox. 'A pair of sallow-skinned polecats.'

'I think we'll check my theory about them. You see that flower seller a hundred yards farther up the road? Well, go and ask the housemaid to go up there and buy a bunch of flowers. Tell her I want them to decorate my room or something. And tell her not to dawdle, but to return at once. On no account must she go farther up the road.'

Cox was back in only a couple of minutes. 'She'll be going directly, Captain.' He stood by the window, beside Pendragon. 'There,' he said. 'By the corner.'

Pendragon could see the housemaid hurrying across the junction of Green Street, straightening her hat as she did so. He looked back at the two men beneath the tree. They had also seen the girl for they both pushed themselves to their feet. One of them pointed; the other began moving up the park in the opposite side of Park Lane to the housemaid, but level with her. The other remained at his post.

'You were right, Captain,' said Cox.

'Wait,' said Pendragon. He took up his telescope again and

watched the man who was following the maid. He saw her across the road to the flower seller. The man held back and pretended to be adjusting the fastening of one of his boots. The maid examined the bunches of flowers, chose one, spoke to the flower seller for a few moments, then began to walk back. The man straightened himself and followed her again. When she crossed the road to the coachyard, he joined his companion under the lime. 'Yes, Cox, I was right. Mikhailovich has no intention of letting any of us out of his sight before this evening. You'd better go down to the kitchens and tell Wolfgang that on no account are any of the staff to leave the house again today; not for any reason whatsoever. Tell him those are my express orders and must be obeyed. The only exception will be the coachman later this evening when I need him.'

'Yes, Captain,' said Cox. 'But what will you do? Surely not accept that Russian devil's invitation? It strikes me as most dangerous, Captain. You'll be taking yourself into the enemy camp. Far be it for me to tell you how to win battles, but your father used to say battles were best fought on ground of your own choosing. The Russian's house is his ground, Captain.'

'I think we will employ cunning, Cox. Can I count on some physical help from you?'

'As physical as you care for, Captain,' replied Cox, grimly. 'As far as Russians are concerned, I have some extremely physical ideas.'

'Then I promise you we will discuss them later,' Pendragon assured him.

* * *

Georgina returned from a visit to one of her friends at a little after five. She breathed a sigh of relief at the cool of the house after the oppressive heat outside, and flopped down on to a chair, fanning herself with her hat.

'John dear,' she said. 'I met Zara an hour ago. You may be pleased that she is to dine with us tonight. I hear you have been a naughty boy and have neglected her of late. I explained that you had some strange business that occupied your time, and she sends a message that you are quite forgiven.'

Pendragon laughed. 'She'll have more to forgive me for yet then Georgina, yourself too. Unfortunately, I must dine out this evening. An invitation of only two hours ago.'

Georgina pouted. 'Oh, John. How aggravating.'

Pendragon was serious. 'Georgina, may I ask a favour, and also ask that you do not question me as to the reason for it?'

'I suppose so,' said Georgina peevishly.

'I want you to remain in the house for the rest of the day. Don't leave at all.'

Georgina frowned at him. 'Not leave my own house? I had no intention of doing so this evening, but I do not like the request. I come and go as I choose.'

'Promise me,' insisted Pendragon.

'I will do nothing of the sort. It is a stupid request.'

'Then I am forced to give you part of the reason,' said Pendragon. 'But only a few words. Georgina, indirectly, this concerns the safety of the country.'

'What nonsense! How can my being confined to my own house possibly affect the state of England?'

'No more information, Georgina, but I assure you that it is true.'

Georgina was silent for several minutes. Pendragon thought it wisest not to interrupt her thoughts. When she spoke again, it was in a cold tone of voice. 'I do not like the line of work you have chosen to follow. But because I have never known you either to lie or to exaggerate to me, I will agree to your request, but I feel that it is an imposition, and I am most cross. My house is for pleasure and not for business. In future the two must be kept separated.'

'Thank you, Georgina.' Pendragon knew she was right. It was unfair of him to involve either her or her staff in what he now realised was a dangerous game. Soon he would have to move away. There were too many sacrifices. He could picture Rambolt in the small dirty attic room near Smithfield. Perhaps Rambolt had once loved, been loved in return, planned for some future, and found it an impossibility. He must have died a very lonely old man. Pendragon felt sad at the thoughts.

* * *

A little after seven o'clock, Pendragon called Cox to his room. 'The plan I have is this,' he told him. 'I shall leave here

151

at a quarter to eight, by carriage. You will accompany me.'

'Good,' said Cox, grinning with satisfaction. 'I didn't like the idea of you going there alone, Captain.' He paused. 'But the men who are watching? Surely if there are two of us in the carriage they'll be warned and not let me in with you. It would be better if I dressed as the coachman, perhaps, Captain.'

'I think that's what they believe will happen. They must expect us to try something, and will endeavour to anticipate us, Cox. I noticed only a few minutes ago the two men have been joined by a third, on horseback. I suspect his job will be to watch the carriage and accompany it at a discreet distance to Mikhailovich's house. The other two will continue to watch here, at least for a while after I've left. They will want to be certain no one follows me, or goes elsewhere with a request for help. I doubt very much if I will be allowed to keep the carriage waiting for me at Mikhailovich's. They will probably insist I dismiss it, and the coachman. No, Cox, my idea comes from an exploit of young Ted's. There's a manhole cover in front of the house; it leads to the cellar where we store coal. I want you to direct the coachman to stop the carriage with the rear axle exactly over the cover. I want you to be waiting under the cover, and to slide it aside, quietly, when the carriage is in position. If we time things correctly, the man on the horse and the others will be watching me. Get yourself balanced on the axle until we reach Mikhailovich's drive, then get off and out of sight as best you can. If I can help by causing them a little trouble at that time, then I will do so.'

'It might work, Captain,' agreed Cox.

'I suggest you bind the axle spikes with sacking,' suggested Pendragon. 'There's no need to make the journey more uncomfortable than necessary. Have you a weapon besides your brass knuckle?'

'Oh yes, Captain,' said Cox enthusiastically. 'No need to worry on that score. What am I to do once there?'

'What I want you to do, Cox, is somehow to effect an entrance to the house, unnoticed. They won't be expecting anyone; the attentions of the household will be concentrated on myself and the Count. Doubtless there is a window at the back that will prove susceptible to your experienced hands.

Break in, Cox, and find the boy. I pray he's still alive. Once you have him, get him out of the house and back here. Here, in my room, there's a letter to Mr. Cloverly; take it to him at whatever the hour; fight your way past those men outside if needs be. It explains in fullest detail everything we already know about this case. Mr. Cloverly will know what shall be done.'

Cox looked horrified. 'And of yourself, Captain? I'm not for leaving any officer in trouble on a battlefield.'

'Don't worry too much. I shall make my moves with great caution.' He opened his bedside table drawer and brought out his pistol case. He flicked up the lid, and lifted out the ivory-handled weapon. 'I shall have this for company. The odds are less against me than at my last battle against Russians. Now go and arrange the carriage.'

Cox nodded unhappily. 'Yes, Captain.'

* * *

It was dark when Pendragon heard the carriage pull round the corner. He was already dressed in his topcoat and hat, and as the carriage drew to a halt with its two nearside wheels on the paving slabs, he opened the front door and walked down the steps. Half-way down he paused, turned and walked up again as though he had forgotten something, feeling in his coat pocket as he did so. He brought out his door keys, tossed them in his hand so they jingled, dropped them back in his pocket and then made his way to the carriage. With luck, all the watchers' eyes would have been on him. The coachman held the door for him.

Pendragon sat back in the seat. Cox must now be stationed below him on the axle. Pendragon took a deep breath. He had the same strange feeling he'd had before the Balaclava charge; seconds changing themselves into long minutes, and minutes to hours. He pressed his hand against his pocket, and felt the comforting hardness of the pistol. For a brief moment, he wished himself back on a battlefield, Dasher Charlie beneath him keen and muscular, and a sharp-bladed sabre in his gauntleted hand; ahead, an enemy who stood in the open and waited.

'Duke House, Cambridge Square,' called Pendragon. The

words somehow managed to sound like an order for his old troop to advance.

* * *

Duke House stood at the northern end of Cambridge Square, a mile from the Uxbridge Road and a twenty-minute drive from Park Lane. Cambridge Square itself was badly lit, and shadowed by the tall lime trees in the small private park it contained. The houses had been built some thirty years before, but the yellow stone was blackened by grime. Even the trunks of the limes were layered with sulphurous deposits, carried west from the chimneys of the City. There was a slight evening mist giving a warning of approaching autumn.

The coachman slowed the carriage and read the house name, then swung the heads of his two horses into a narrow drive. As he reined them to a halt, two men who might have been grooms stepped out of the shadows and grabbed at the horses' bit rings.

'You won't be needed more, man,' one of them shouted to the coachman. 'Our master's carriage is . . .'

'You there!' Pendragon seized the opportunity to divert the men. He called angrily. 'Any orders for my coachman will be given by me, damn you. I will not tolerate interference with my employees.'

'It's our master's . . .' began the second man.

Pendragon interrupted him. 'Let go those horses' heads, you louts.'

Pendragon was aware of the arrival of a third man beside him.

The man stepped partly in front of Pendragon, hard-eyed and dressed in the clothing of a butler. 'Forgive me, Sir. You will be Captain Pendragon?'

'Yes,' said Pendragon. By now, Cox must be away from underneath the coach and Pendragon realised if he continued to harangue the grooms his action must cause suspicion.

'It is my master's wish you dismiss your coachman,' said the butler. 'Should you require a carriage later, then my master's will be placed at your disposal, Sir.'

'I see.' Pendragon turned to the coachman. 'Very well, you may go back to Park Lane. I shall not need you more tonight.'

The coachman nodded and touched his hat.

'Thank you, Sir,' said the butler, softly. His voice was completely flat and toneless. He led Pendragon up the wide steps and showed him into the hall, took his hat and coat and bowed him towards another door. As Pendragon walked towards it, the butler reached past him and swung it open.

Page Cloverly had warned Pendragon of the strange decoration in Duke House, but even so he found it quite extraordinary. The room, once he was past the door, appeared to be some strange attempt to reproduce an Egyptian temple, complete with its bas-relief representations of ancient kings, hunting scenes, gods and goddesses. Tall pillars stretched to the ceiling, their lotus scrollwork gilded and enamelled. The floor and the walls, where they were unadorned by the carvings, were of black marble. The ceiling was deep blue, studded with hundreds of gleaming gilt stars. The furniture was sparse, black like the marble floor it rested upon, padded with loose cushions of some gold material.

The room was lit by suspended bronze candelabra, cast in the shapes of winged lions, and the flames of a hundred candles smoked and flickered, filling the air with the heavy scent of incense.

There was a faint metallic click; Pendragon turned and saw two sections of panelled wall slide apart to reveal a man standing motionless, watching him.

Mikhailovich! Pendragon's memory had been accurate. The man was indeed a giant, built more like a country peasant used to hard physical work than an aristocrat. With long hair and a jet-black beard, his face was pale by contrast. His shoulders were broad and heavy like those of a street wrestler.

Mikhailovich stood unmoving and silent for so long Pendragon began to think perhaps the man was blind, or unaware of his presence. He stared in Pendragon's direction, but with his eyes blank and cold, giving no hint of either welcome or recognition.

Pendragon moved slightly. It was as though he'd activated the switch that controlled a mechanical toy. Mikhailovich's face jerked to a smile. He bent his head slightly and stepped forward, both his hands held towards Pendragon. 'Ah,' he said. 'My guest, Captain Pendragon. Forgive me if I kept you waiting, but I was a little preoccupied by a matter of business.'

One of the hands clasped Pendragon's; the grip was a painful indication of the enormous strength of the man.

'I don't believe we've ever been formally introduced,' said Mikhailovich. 'We share acquaintances, though. Your face is familiar, no doubt we have seen each other at some time?'

'Once, I believe,' replied Pendragon, coldly. 'Some time ago, before the war.'

'Yes, the war. I'm led to understand you are a hero, Captain Pendragon, and single-handed you massacred thousands of my countrymen.' He paused, then laughed. 'Don't misunderstand me, I am little concerned by the deaths of common soldiers. It is their lot to be the pawns of those who make war their business. What regiment were you, Captain Pendragon? You have the weight of a lancer.'

'A hussar,' answered Pendragon. 'The 11th.'

'The 11th!' Mikhailovich half closed his eyes and looked closely at Pendragon. 'Do they exist any more, Captain? I heard they suffered badly at Balaclava. No, forgive me, I quite understand; a regiment may suffer terrible losses, and yet survive, if only in name. Men are soon replaced, eh, Captain?' He paused. 'So you are a horseman, and you favour a sabre, not a lance. I agree with you; a lance is a clumsy and unwieldy weapon, fit only for spearing pigs. Now a sabre, that is quite a different thing; a sabre is the weapon of gentlemen. I enjoy sabres myself. I had the pleasure to train as a pupil of Paul de Levaille, at the Paris academy. An amusing couple of years.'

There seemed little for Pendragon to say; he was content for the moment to let the Russian do the talking. He had to give Cox time to break in, if that was possible, and to find the boy.

'And how do you like my home?' asked Mikhailovich. 'A little eccentric, do you think? But then I am eccentric; an ex-patriot Russian whose lot has been cast in with the British; such lovely people, the British. Do you like the British, Captain Pendragon? Of course you do! You kill Russians. And so you should; if I had nothing better to do with my time, I might also kill Russians. I had a great-grandfather whose pleasure was to kill Russians, and he was a Russian himself. He used to tie them in bundles and toss them into the Volga, but only when he was feeling generous. At other times, he devised rather more intriguing and ingenious ways of disposing of them; all for his amusement. Are you at ease, Captain Pendragon? Are you a person who finds no distress in fresh company? I see that you are. Then, let us sit and talk while we dine.'

Mikhailovich led the way through the sliding wall into a long narrow room. Its décor was similar to that of the other, but its oblong shape made it even more like a temple. A table of black marble, matching the material of the floors and walls, stretched along its centre.

A servant, another man with Mongolian cheekbones and an almost oriental moustache, held Pendragon's chair, and stood back until Mikhailovich had settled himself before pouring a little wine from a decanter into a glass. Mikhailovich tasted it and nodded at the man. The servant filled Pendragon's glass, and then the Russian's.

'You will find no women in this house,' said Mikhailovich. 'I have an aversion to women servants. Amongst other things, they always seem to smell. My entire staff, including my cook, are males. They have my express instructions never to smell. You will also notice that they wear gloves. I do not enjoy being touched by the inferior classes, Captain Pendragon; another small eccentricity. And now, Captain, shall we find a mutually interesting subject to discuss throughout our meal? Do you hawk? Perhaps difficult around London! You ride, of course, yet I do not. My bulk, Captain Pendragon; a curse, for there are few horses capable of carrying me. Carthorses, yes,' he laughed. 'A carthorse to carry my two hundred and eighty pounds; what a sight it would make in the Ladies' Mile of the park! Now you know part of the reason for my marble furniture, Captain; the flimsy wooden pieces of today's society are hardly able to support me. Shall we talk about race horses? They interest me. Or, perhaps we can find some common scandal to discuss; the ladies? Surely we must share at least one feminine friend, Captain?'

Damn you for a cool swine, thought Pendragon.

* * *

Had it not been for the thought of young Ted Blower, tortured or perhaps even now dead somewhere inside the house, Pendragon would have found the meal, though not the company, pleasant enough. As it was, he had to force himself to accept each mouthful. Mikhailovich's evil presence made him feel physically ill.

Mikhailovich himself was in an obviously good mood; confident and assured. By his attitude he considered the game won, and could afford at this moment to be generous to his conquered enemy. He hurried his conversation from subject to subject, hardly giving Pendragon a few seconds to slip in comments. He was an attentive host, keeping a close eye on Pendragon's glass, and theatrically concerned he should make a good impression. But even through the mask of congeniality Pendragon could sense Mikhailovich's true feelings, and there were fleeting seconds when the mask slipped and Pendragon would find himself staring at eyes that shone with hatred.

Pendragon became aware of Mikhailovich's intentions; the man was behaving like the Commander-in-Chief of an enemy division contemplating a full attack on a well-defended position. He would bring the conversation swerving towards Pendragon on a subject that could only prove offensive, then at the last second divert it by some amusing, irrelevant or even self-effacing comment. His near insults were skirmishes, lightweight patrols sent to probe the defences. Each skirmish, each reconnoitre, became a little stronger and more determined. He knew Pendragon must be burning with anger inside, must be frustrated by his position, and perhaps even fearful for his life. Mikhailovich clearly wanted Pendragon's nerve to crack, but he had underestimated his quarry. Pendragon fought only to control the most intense hatred he had ever felt in his life.

'Let us take our port in my gallery,' suggested Mikhailovich at last. 'Once eaten, I find the smell of food, like unwashed bodies, unpleasant. It also has quite a repulsive affect on the taste of a good cigar, and I assure you mine are not to be surpassed. I have the leaf especially imported from the Americas, and rolled by Treyers of the Haymarket. If you would care to follow me, Captain Pendragon.'

He led the way out into the entrance hall, and along a passage towards the rear of the house. At the top of a flight of stairs that might have led down to a cellar he paused. 'Have a care, Captain. These are a little steep.' Pendragon followed him down. Mikhailovich opened a heavy door. 'My target gallery,' he said. 'Some men prefer billiards, but I prefer to shoot. I trust you also find it enjoyable? Port, a good cigar, and a few rounds at the target, are most relaxing after a meal.'

The gallery was some eight feet wide by thirty long, reminding Pendragon of a luxurious version of the range in Westley Richard's gun shop. However, unlike Richard's range, it was furnished with lounging chairs and a small table, on which was set a decanter and glasses and an opened box of cigars. Beyond the table were two gun-cupboards, with glass fronts, set against the wall.

'Shall we shoot first?' suggested Mikhailovich. 'I find even a solitary glass of port can play hell with one's concentration and accuracy.' He opened the fronts of one of the cupboards. A dozen pistols hung on racks inside; they appeared to match. Mikhailovich lifted them down carefully, and laid them in a line on the table. Six in front of Pendragon, six in front of himself. They were all single shot percussion pistols, finely built and long barrelled; undoubtedly French target pistols.

The Russian pointed down the range. 'Two targets,' he said. 'One to the left for yourself, and mine to the right.' The targets were black and white circles on cards clipped to the farthest wall. 'Would you care to fire first, Captain?'

Pendragon thought quickly. If he took the first shot, it would leave Mikhailovich with the last. Pendragon would have an empty pistol in his hand, and might not have time to reach for his own in his pocket. As politely and casually as he could manage, but with his heart pounding Pendragon said: 'As my host, perhaps you will take the first shot. It will give me the opportunity to get used to the weight of the pistol.'

'As you will,' agreed Mikhailovich. 'But shall we have a little bet? Shall we say five guineas for the shot nearest the centre of a target?'

'Of course,' said Pendragon, with a feeling of relief.

Mikhailovich picked up his first pistol. He raised it and fired down the range, the shot loud and deafening in the confined space. The blue smoke of the gunpowder swirled. Pendragon could, at first, see no signs of the bullet in the target, then spotted a dark hole within the centre black.

'A poor shot,' grumbled the Russian. 'At least two inches from dead centre. I hope to see you do better.'

Pendragon lifted the target pistol. It was beautifully balanced and seemed a perfect fit in his hand. He looked along the sight and squeezed the trigger. He caught a momentary glimpse of the ball as it flashed in the light, then the target was obscured by the smoke of the charge. He waited until it had cleared.

'Bravo, Captain,' congratulated Mikhailovich. 'An excellent shot. I swear it is half an inch nearer centre than my own.' The Russian raised his second pistol and fired again.

When both men had fired five shots, and the visibility along the range was poor because of the smoke, Mikhailovich picked up his sixth pistol. 'Captain Pendragon,' he said. 'Before we examine the boards and decide which of us is the richer by the other's gold, might I suggest a change of target for the last shot? Please take up your pistol.' Pendragon did so willingly, and kept a close watch on the Russian. 'One moment only,' said Mikhailovich. He reached sideways and pulled a length of cord. The wall at the far end of the range, where the targets were clipped, split down the centre and slid apart. 'Perhaps you would care to try a shot at that.'

Stripped naked and spreadeagled to metal rings in the wall, his back and shoulders striped with bloody weals, was the boy Ted Blower.

* * *

'Is that not an excellent target, Captain?' asked Mikhailovich. His voice was cold, brittle.

Pendragon turned quickly, his pistol aimed at the Russian's broad chest. 'Put up your gun,' he said.

Mikhailovich laughed, but without humour. 'You refuse to shoot some filthy urchin, Captain Pendragon, but you seem quite happy at the thought of sending my own aristocratic soul to its maker. Please pull your trigger if you will, for I can assure you it will do little good. The sixth pistol, which you hold so aggressively, contains no charge.' He raised his own pistol and pointed it at Pendragon's head. 'Mine, on the other hand, Captain, contains the same charge as the others.'

Pendragon squeezed the trigger of the target pistol. There was the sharp crack as the percussion cap exploded, but nothing more. He threw down the weapon angrily.

'I would imagine, Captain Pendragon, you would hardly choose to come here unarmed,' smiled Mikhailovich. 'I notice that the right-hand pocket of your coat seems a little heavy. I must ask you to turn and place your hands against the wall. If you make any sudden movement, I regret I will have to blow off your head.'

Pendragon turned, and put his hands, palms flat, on the wall. He felt the Russian take the pistol from his pocket.

'You may turn around, Captain. Please have a seat; will you have your port now? I think I shall do so.' He poured himself a glass and sat opposite Pendragon, keeping his pistol still aimed at Pendragon's face. 'And now we can talk sensibly to each other. So, you are Rambolt's successor. How sensible of Mr. Sidney Herbert to choose a gentleman. I found it so degrading to be chased around London by an ex-Bow Street Runner. A very uncouth gentleman; in fact, no gentleman at all. He caused me no end of embarrassment; the thought of that dirty unwashed body always a few yards from me. I was quite relieved when he met his end.'

Pendragon looked down the range at Ted Blower.

'Don't worry yourself about him, Captain Pendragon. He's simply sleeping. Unconscious, I believe. They have very little stamina, these gutter-snipes. Any discomfort he may have, should he ever awaken, will be quite brief. As a matter of fact it was my intention to set him directly behind your target, Captain; but then, I thought, he might well come in useful if I need to persuade you to tell me anything. After all, Captain, no doubt you are a gentleman in the truest British army manner. You might well kill someone else's urchins, but you will die to protect your own.'

'Mikhailovich, you're a bore,' snarled Pendragon. 'If you

want satisfaction, then give me a pistol and we can fight it out here and now.'

'Or a sabre, Captain?' Mikhailovich raised an eyebrow. 'Captain, really! Do you expect *me* to behave like a British gentleman? You forget, I'm a Russian Count. I'm not expected to behave like a British gentleman in these circumstances; nor shall I. You have been a dead man since two o'clock this afternoon; which was the exact time when that urchin down there decided he would like to inform on you.'

'Inform is hardly the word I would use,' said Pendragon, glancing at the deep whip marks on the boy's back.

'Does it really matter? You British seem to think every other nationality is foolish. The boy! Rambolt's boy! D'you think we hadn't seen him? I saw him in the early hours of this morning, hanging around the drive; skulking. Later today when I took a trip to my colleague's establishment, there was the same boy again. Dear me, Captain Pendragon, does the British secret agent department consist of one scruffy boy? No, of course it doesn't, it also employs crippled army veterans who are glad to do its dirty work to augment their inadequate pensions and small private incomes.'

Pendragon moved slightly and Mikhailovich swung his pistol quickly, focusing it on Pendragon's forehead.

'Your night of fire is already a failure,' said Pendragon, coolly. He prayed Cox, once he had failed to locate Ted Blower, had hurried to take his letter to Page Cloverly.

Mikhailovich's eyes narrowed fractionally. 'Ah! So you have proved in your somewhat brief career. Captain Pendragon, to be quite a passable agent, though your description of my plans waxes a little poetical. I would have referred to it myself as the wrecking of the British port system, and the destruction of the home-based British fleet. Quite a sensible ambition, would you not say, Captain Pendragon? Even Napoleon didn't manage that! He might have ruled more of Europe had he done so.'

'But why?' asked Pendragon. 'The war is almost over. Russia and Britain will soon be at peace.'

'At peace, the British gentleman says.' Mikhailovich chuckled. 'My dear boy! You don't mind if I refer to you as a boy, do you Captain? After all, your ideas are somewhat naïve;

boyish. You speak about one small military action and say it is over. The Crimea, Captain, wasn't a war, it was merely a battle. You think because there are connections between your Queen Victoria and our Czar, that we should be friends, Captain? This is the age of expansion, Captain Pendragon; the age of growing powers. There is no time left now for small countries. You think there is to be no war between Russia and the other European powers? There will always be war, Captain, until Russia controls every country. It is our ambition and we will succeed. Look at you ... the British, the French, the Italians, the Austrians, Prussians, all of you chasing round over half the world trying to establish ridiculous colonies you choose to call Empires. Subjugating black men, brown men, yellow men, red men. You fight your wars of expansion against inferiors; children, Captain Pendragon. You send your soldiers a thousand, no, even ten thousand miles away, and settle a small section of land you have no hope of ever holding. Fifty years from now, these colonies will have split away from you; you will have lost them. That, Captain Pendragon, is not the way of Russia. We are expanding outwards from our centre. We colonise the next field, absorb the next street, expand to the next town, take the nearest country and turn it into part of Russia. We will go on and on expanding until we cover the whole of Europe. And we have no intention of stopping until such time as the eastern and western outposts of Russian territory touch and intermingle, and the whole world becomes Russia. It may take us a hundred and fifty years, Captain Pendragon; it may take us a dozen Czars and three dozen changes of government or politics, but have no doubts our basic aims will remain constant and unswerving.'

'All this accomplished by the destruction of our ports?'

'Your ports? Not only yours, Captain Pendragon! You think the British are so important? Yours first, Captain, because it is convenient for us; because of Sebastopol, Captain Pendragon. Do you think it likely for us to forget that a hundred thousand Russian soldiers were recently killed in that town? Shall we forget that even more hundreds of thousands of our men died during the winter marches over our plains to the battlefields? The foolishness of the British escalated the Crimean War, Captain Pendragon. It was not of our asking. The British will pay first, and the French second, then the others. We will destroy your Empires, your so-called colonies will dismember your armies, we will starve your people, and we will over-run you, as we will over-run the whole of western Europe.'

'And your Chinese friends, are they to be your allies and share the world with you?'

'The Chinese, our allies? The Chinese, Captain Pendragon, like yourselves, and like your late colonials of the Americas, will cease as such to exist. They will be called Russians. Future generations of them will learn to loathe their past, and honour their present. The Chinese?'

'Wan Hei and the members of the Green Serpent society,' interrupted Pendragon.

Mikhaikovich laughed again. 'Wan Hei? Of course, you know about him, too! Wan Hei works for money, or at least, Captain, he works for payment. He has a certain hatred of the British, but he hates anyone with a white face and a large pose. Wan Hei is simply a bandit disguised as a merchant. He is useful, because of his connections. He provides me with manpower, Captain. Wan Hei is nothing more than a mercenary. If *you* offered him four cases of opium, plus one extra crown piece, he'd tear *me* apart and feed me to your ravens on Tower Hill.'

'And now?' asked Pendragon.

'And now, I regret I am unable to enjoy your company longer, Captain. You see, I don't suffer from the British scruples of honouring their guests.' Mikhailovich reached out and twisted a bell-pull on the wall. 'You will not be kept waiting long.'

The door of the target gallery was pushed open and two men entered. One was the servant who had waited at table; now that Pendragon was able to examine the man more closely, it seemed probable he was a Cossack. His long drooping moustache and almost oriental cheekbones gave him a sinister appearance. The second man was Chinese, sallow-faced, and with his scalp shaved; he was a heavy, stocky man, who moved with a shuffle that was simian. One of the men closed the door, then the two of them paused and waited for Mikhailovich's instructions.

'Take this British gentleman down the range,' ordered Mikhailovich, curtly. 'Strap him to the wall directly in front of the boy.' He turned to Pendragon. 'I have a few questions to ask, which you will, eventually, be pleased to answer. Do you recognise the nationality of my moustached servant? No? You will have obviously heard of the Cossacks, though I doubt if you know one thousandth of their reputation as experts with their razor-sharp knives, Captain. He will play very interesting games with the most sensitive parts of your body. I have seen Orientals, who are normally noted for their stoicism in the face of torture, cry like babies and plead for quick death in the hands of my Cossack. You will certainly answer my questions, and then both you and the boy will die. The quicker the answer, Captain, the cleaner and more comfortable your deaths. I have a loaded target pistol here, and as you have seen, I am an excellent shot. One well-placed ball will end your agonies. One ball for the two of you; I expect it to pass through your heart, and that of the boy as well. I assure you that you will be glad when I fire. I may even insist first you thank me for my mercy.' He spoke again to the two men. 'Take him and begin your work.'

The two men stepped forward to take hold of Pendragon. He had just time to notice the head of a serpent tattooed on the hand of the Chinese when the door of the gallery seemed to explode inwards, crashing back against the panelled wall. A hunched figure, trailing a black cloak like the wings of a demented bat, hurtled through the doorway with a deep-throated roar. It hit Mikhailovich in the small of his huge back, slamming him sideways; his pistol clattered along the black floor of the range and exploded as the hammer jarred free, the sound of the shot adding to the confusion.

Pendragon ducked and twisted himself, bringing his fist up sharply into the throat of the Cossack; the man's head jerked back. The Chinese grabbed Pendragon from behind, his arms circling him, his hands locked on Pendragon's chest. Pendragon rammed his elbow back hard and felt ribs crack. The grip around Pendragon slackened as the man yelped in agony. The Cossack manservant began pushing himself to his feet. As he did so, the light flashed on a steel blade which seemed to spear past Pendragon. A sabre, thrown skilfully, hit the man just below his rib-cage and lanced upwards. The man shrieked and grabbed at the blade. Blood spurted from his chest wound, and from deep cuts on his hands sliced open by the razor sharpness of the blade he struggled to remove. He screamed again, gasped and fell sideways.

Pendragon dropped his shoulder and grabbed at the clothing of the Chinese. He drove his arm upwards, at the same time wrenching the man across his hip. The man shouted and somersaulted forward. There was scuffling behind Pendragon but he had no time to look. He snatched the sabre from the dying man's chest; blood ran as he jerked out the blade. The Chinese was on his knees and had pulled out a long wedge-shaped dagger. He drove it upwards towards Pendragon's stomach. Pendragon sidestepped, and cut diagonally downwards with the sabre, his full weight behind the blow. The keen-edged weapon took the man's shaven head from his body.

Pendragon brought the blade up and turned to face Mikhailovich but the man was gone. The cloaked figure was pushing itself to its feet.

'Cox!' Pendragon stopped the swing of the sabre. 'God bless you, Cox.'

Cox stood and rubbed a bruised chest. 'Sorry I was late, Captain, but those grooms hung about outside, and I had to deal with them first. I'm afraid I didn't do them a lot of good. I laid them out with a brick I found, but I fear I hit one too hard.'

'Never mind,' said Pendragon, warmly. 'I'm glad you made it. Did you search the rest of the house?'

'I broke in through a window over a second floor balcony, Captain, so I began with the top of the house; mostly servants' quarters, I believe. I was working my way down when I heard a few faint shots. I followed the sound down to here, and then kept hidden for a while until I thought it was the best opportunity.'

'Where's Mikhailovich?' asked Pendragon.

'Like a bloody ox that man, begging your pardon, Captain. He just lifted me and tossed me aside, then ran out. I thought I heard a carriage leave just after.' He glanced down the range and saw the small figure fastened to the end wall. 'My God, Captain. Is that the boy?'

'Yes, come on,' said Pendragon. He hurried down the range.

Cox followed him.

'Christ!' gasped Cox, examining the boy's wounds. 'Look what they've done to the poor little blighter.'

Pendragon unfastened the straps holding the boy's wrists to iron rings set into the wall. Cox stooped and loosened the ankle straps. Ted Blower slid downwards but Pendragon caught him.

'He's still alive, Cox, but only just.'

'Damn and blast the cowards,' breathed Cox, staring at the deep whip marks. 'I wish we hadn't dealt with them so swift. I'd have liked to have given them a taste of their own medicine, Captain.'

'You didn't do too badly with the sabre,' said Pendragon. 'Where did you get it?'

'My own, Captain. Your father allowed me to keep it when I left the regiment. Seen a lot of service, that blade. Brought it with me under the coach.'

'Well, God knows what Cloverly and Herbert will have to say, but Mikhailovich didn't leave us much choice.' Pendragon stood, lifting the boy in his arms.

'Can I take him off you, Sir?'

'No. The child weighs nothing. We'd better get him back home where he can have some treatment, then we've got to find Mikhailovich and the Chinese.' The boy groaned, softly. 'It's all right, Ted, it's Cox and myself; friends.'

The body of one of the grooms lay in the coachyard at the side of the house, in a pale yellow circle of light cast by the coachyard gas lamp. There were the sounds of nervous horses in the stable. Pendragon lowered Ted Blower on to a bale of hay. 'Saddle up a couple of the horses,' he told Cox. 'I'm going back into the house.'

'Your pistol, Captain,' said Cox, passing over the weapon. 'Better not take a chance.'

Pendragon ran back into the house. Where, he wondered, would Mikhailovich keep his private papers? There might be no other opportunity to find them, if they existed. He remembered a black-stained desk in the first room, where he'd waited for Mikhailovich. He found it. The top of the desk was locked, but he broke it open with the base of a heavy unlit oil lamp. It contained only writing materials. He tried the drawers. The first contained a collection of Russian newspapers; the second was empty. Pendragon looked at the top section of the desk again, then ran his fingers along under the sill below the broken top. He picked up the heavy lamp base and smashed it down on to the front of the desk. More woodwork shattered. Pendragon tore at it. A long sliver of wood broke away to reveal a narrow drawer. Inside was an envelope. Pendragon pulled it out. There was an official-looking seal on the back, and Mikhailovich had carefully slit the paper rather than destroy the wax impression. It was an eagle above a crown. Pendragon frowned; the design was the same as on standards flown by the Royal regiments of the Russian army. He shook out the letter. The eagle coat of arms was repeated on the top of the notepaper. The letter was in Russian, seemed brief, but was quite unreadable. Pendragon put it back into the envelope, tucked it into his pocket, found his topcoat and hat in the butler's cloakroom, and hurried out to the stable yard. Cox had two horses saddled.

'Mount,' said Pendragon. 'I'll pass the boy up to you.'

Cox did so, settling himself into the leather. The boy was so light Pendragon passed him up to Cox with no effort. Cox turned the boy on his saddle so he rested against his chest and was cradled in his arm.

Pendragon swung himself on to his horse and dug his heels into its sides.

* * *

Realising it was possible that Mikhailovich's two men might still be watching the Park Lane house, Pendragon led the way down Park Street and entered Green Street from the east. The two men rode the horses so fast into the coachyard that Pendragon's horse skidded on the cobbles, nearly throwing its rider, but Pendragon leapt from its back and landed lightly. The yard was in darkness though the house itself was lit. He took Ted Blower from Cox until the man had dismounted, then went to the kitchen door. It was locked. Pendragon hammered on it. It was opened within seconds by the housekeeper. She looked startled at the unexpected sight of Captain Pendragon.

Pendragon pushed past her followed by Cox with the unconscious boy in his arms. Pendragon swept crockery from the kitchen table with one long movement of his arm. 'Put him down here, Cox. And gently.'

Wolfgang appeared in the doorway to the servants' living room. 'What is? Captain Pendragon? My God!' He saw Ted Blower and hurried across the room. 'The boy? Who should do such a cruel thing? My God!'

'Cox, go and see if those two villains are still waiting near the front.' He spoke to the housekeeper. 'Wake the groom. Tell him to go and get a doctor; fast. Wolfgang, clean up the boy's wounds a little, if you can. Is Miss Carr alone?'

'No,' said Wolfgang. 'She has guests. A Mr. Cloverly and Lady Cashell.'

Pendragon left the kitchen and climbed the stairs to the hallway. He knocked at the salon door and entered. Page Cloverly sat in a lounge chair facing both Georgina and Zara. They looked up at Pendragon as he entered.

'Good heavens, John,' gasped Zara, wide-eyed. 'John, what on earth has happened to you? You're covered in blood.'

'He is wounded yet again,' said Georgina, raising her eyes as though Pendragon made a daily habit of injuring himself.

'The blood's not mine, Zara. I'm unhurt. Page, forgive my intrusion, but I'm glad you're here. Zara, you claim to be half Russian, do you read the language?'

'Of course,' replied Zara.

'Then read me this,' said Pendragon, passing her the letter from Mikhailovich's desk.

Zara glanced at the undamaged seal, frowned questioningly, then opened the letter. She looked at Pendragon, her frown deepened.

'Well, can you read it to me, please?' Pendragon was impatient.

'It doesn't make sense,' she said, bewildered. 'It says simply: "If all succeeds as we have planned, then I will give you England as your province."'

'And it is addressed to whom?' asked Pendragon.

'"To my dearest cousin," it says.' Zara licked her lips with her tongue before she continued. 'It is signed by the Czar Nicholas, or purports to be so.'

'It makes sense,' breathed Pendragon. 'Does it not, Page?'

Page Cloverly nodded, silently.

'Please excuse me, Zara, Georgina, but I want Mr. Cloverly to come and have a look at some of Count Mikailovich's handiwork.' He turned from the room. Page Cloverly followed him, bewildered.

Pendragon led him down to the kitchen. 'Mikhailovich's methods of interrogating children,' he said, pointing at Ted Blower resting face downwards on the pine table.

'Dear Lord,' swore Cloverly. 'Is the poor lad dead?'

'Not quite,' said Pendragon.

There was the sound of a quick in-drawn breath from behind them. Pendragon turned. Georgina stood in the doorway. She looked at Pendragon. 'Did you say Mikhailovich? Count Mikhailovich?'

'The man has proved to be a Russian spy, my dear,' said Page Cloverly.

'He's a barbarian.' Georgina walked across to the boy and stared down at the lines of whip marks. 'Did he do this?'

'Yes.'

Georgina turned to face Pendragon, her face pale with fury, her eyes moist. 'Then I hope you have killed him, John.'

Pendragon frowned. 'Not yet, Georgina, but it is my intention to do so when we next meet.'

Wolfgang, who was cleaning the wounds on Ted's back, stopped suddenly and put his head close to the boy's. 'He whispers something.'

Pendragon listened. 'Captain?' asked the boy. His voice was little more than a soft hiss.

'You're quite safe now, Ted,' said Pendragon warmly. 'You're at home with us. You'll soon be all right.'

'I found the place, Captain,' whispered the boy. 'One Eye's. Tuffer's Alley, off Wallbrook.'

'Tuffer's Alley! Good lad, Ted.' Pendragon looked at Cloverly. 'That's where Mikhailovich has probably gone, and it's where I shall go, too.'

'And you intend to go there alone?'

'I have no intention of allowing the police to settle the matter,' said Pendragon. 'Those were your original instructions, and now they are my wishes.'

Cox, who had entered the room a few moments previously,

spoke. 'No sign of the men who were outside, Captain. Nor will you be going alone, Sir. After what they've done to the lad, I've more than a little reckoning to do.'

'Then you must let me help too,' insisted Cloverly. 'Let me accompany you.'

'It's a job for fighting men, Sir,' said Cox. 'Begging your pardon, Sir, and Captain Pendragon's.'

'And fighting men are what I intend to find, Page. Quite unofficially, I assure you.' Pendragon looked at Cox. 'Get a saddle on Dasher as quick as you can. I'm going to pay a visit to my club.'

'One thing, Captain Pendragon, Sir,' said Cox, hesitating and looking down at the boy on the table. 'You wouldn't go riding off and fighting without me?'

'That I promise you, Cox.'

* * *

It was a little over a mile from the Park Lane house to the Guards and Cavalry Club in Pall Mall. Pendragon rode it, bareheaded and in his bloodstained clothing, in less than five minutes. He rode furiously, shouting encouragement to Dasher Charlie as he thundered along the streets. There were still people about, and they turned to stare at Pendragon as though he were some lunatic escaped from the Battersea Asylum. As he thundered down Duke Street and turned towards Saint James's Square, two policemen leapt into the roadway to stop him, but instinctively Dasher Charlie swerved around them as easily as he would have done had they been enemy infantrymen. Their angry shouts were lost in the echo of his hooves on the cobbled streets.

Pendragon spun Dasher into the driveway of the club, and reined him to a sliding halt in a shower of gravel. He leapt from the saddle and tossed the reins to an amazed groom, then ran up the steps. The club doorman watched his approach, wide-eyed.

'Sir; excuse me, Sir, your dress, Sir . . .'

'Damn my dress, man. Is Captain FitzPatrick here?'

'But . . .' began the doorman.

'Don't but me,' roared Pendragon. 'Answer my question.'

The doorman was terrified. 'The . . . the billiard room, Sir,' he stammered.

Pendragon strode quickly through the lounge, watched by a dozen startled club members who had been drinking near the fireplace.

'I say . . .' began one. Pendragon ignored him. 'Well, I'll be damned,' said the man to his companions. 'Did you see the feller?'

Pendragon hurled open the billiard room door. A player bent over the table with his back to Pendragon mis-cued at the sudden sound, and swore. The figure turned. 'Good Heavens! Pendragon! What in the name of . . .'

'FitzPatrick,' Pendragon said sharply. 'Are you game for some sport?'

'Game? For what kind of sport, dear fellow?'

'A little of the kind we know best; fighting.'

'With my fists? Dear fellow you must be making a joke? Have you been drinking, perhaps? You certainly look as though you have.'

Pendragon was angry. 'I'm serious, and sober. I need help. This is Government work.' He tossed his platinum warrant on to the billiard table. It flashed brightly in the gas-lights.

FitzPatrick picked it up. 'God! You really are serious.' He passed it back.

'It's work for pistol and sabre,' warned Pendragon. 'I don't know the odds; but you'll be pleased to know that the ring-leader is Russian.'

'When?'

'Now,' said Pendragon. 'I want a few men with their horses. Men who can fight.'

'Then I'm with you,' said FitzPatrick. 'I'm not quite as fit as I used to be, but dammit, I'd like the chance to swing a sword again.' He looked across the billiard table to his opponent, a young fresh-faced man of about twenty. 'Do you fancy joining us, Beauchamp?'

'Why not? It saves my present defeat at your ruthless hands.' He looked across at Pendragon. 'Beauchamp, Lieutenant of the Dragoon Guards. Pleased to meet you.'

FitzPatrick stacked his cue in the rest. 'Crighton and Lumley are in the gaming room.'

'Get them,' ordered Pendragon. 'And see if Howard and

Carlton are in the club. Invite them too. Bring them if they're willing. Armed, and on horseback; at my house in an hour.'

'Done,' promised FitzPatrick, grinning broadly.

Pendragon turned to leave, then looked back. 'Ask them all to keep silent about this business. You'll get the reasons when we meet.'

'On condition you have stirrup cups ready for us,' smiled Beauchamp. 'Make them brandy!'

13

THERE WAS A full moon, high over the park; so bright the grass seemed winter-frosted and the leaves of the tall elms slivers of pure ice.

It was after midnight, and Georgina's salon at her Park Lane house looked more like the field headquarters of a military campaign than a private residence. She had wisely sent Zara home. Now she was hostess at a strange gathering: with the exception of young Beauchamp, all the other officer friends of Pendragon had arrived. There were five of them, standing around a table, glasses in their hands, waiting. None were in uniform, but they carried their sabres on belts worn over their waistcoats, and the weapons were hidden by their topcoat tails. At first sight it could have been any evening meeting of gentlemen friends. They spoke cheerfully, made jokes, laughed quietly and teased Georgina.

There was the sound of hooves outside in the road, and a few seconds later, Beauchamp, wearing his own sabre slung outside his clothing by a wide gold bullion and crimson sword belt, stamped into the room, red-faced and perspiring.

'Oh, my God, Beechy,' said Crighton, slim and elegantly dressed as always. 'You look like the hero of a comic opera. Put that damned blade out of sight or someone might just think you're contemplating mischief.'

Beauchamp blushed an even deeper colour, and fumbled with the gilt fastening of his belt.

FitzPatrick flicked the hammer down on a pistol he'd been examining, and pushed the weapon into his trouser pocket. 'The last of us,' he said to Pendragon.

'Good.' Pendragon tilted his brandy glass and drained it. He unfolded a copy of Cruchley's map of London, and spread it on the table. His friends gathered closer. 'Gentlemen, here's where we're heading for, just below Poultry; my valet, Cox, is familiar with the route, and will direct us. Don't be concerned about him, he's an ex-military man like myself, but with almost ten times as much service, I should add. You are probably all very curious at my invitation, and I'm grateful you have all come along with so little explanation.' He waved a hand towards Page Cloverly and introduced him. 'Cloverly is of Mr. Herbert's staff. I shall leave it to him to explain the purpose of tonight's action.'

Page Cloverly bowed his head and shoulders towards the men. He smiled slightly. 'I was unaware the British army could produce such a villainous-looking selection of young officers at such short notice.' The men laughed. 'Well, gentlemen, this is what it is all about . . .' He spoke quickly for several minutes. The men listened in silence although when he explained Mikhailovich's intentions, there were a few angry mutters. He finished his explanation without a warning. 'Gentlemen, by now you will all have realised what is to be done. I must, however, make quite clear the official thoughts on this matter; if any of you are killed or wounded, then you can expect no recompense for either your families or yourselves; from an official point of view, this will be nothing more than a serious brawl. If any innocent civilians are injured, then it will be most difficult for me to protect you from the normal course of the law.' He looked at Beauchamp who was still holding his sabre. 'You are all armed, and this I know is essential. Remember, though, the carrying of sabres is only lawful on official business, and at this moment, I can give no government approval. Be as cautious in displaying them as possible. I can promise you nothing in the way of protection, but I will do my best to clear matters at the highest level should there be repercussions. No guarantee, mind you.'

'Having heard Mr. Cloverly, if any of you feel it wiser to leave now . . .' Pendragon left the sentence unfinished.

'Leave, damn it! I've only just arrived,' grinned Beauchamp. 'I'd no more miss this outing than ride through Piccadilly without breeches. I've an unused sabre blade to christen.'

'Mind that it's not yourself who's christened.' FitzPatrick looked at the men. 'None leaving, then? Pendragon, you have your army.'

Page Cloverly raised his glass. 'A toast, gentlemen, before

you go. I give you Her Majesty Queen Victoria, Prince Albert, and the long continuance of the British Empire.'

* * *

To avoid the appearance that they were a night patrol, the men rode in groups thirty or forty yards apart, at a smart trot. The shadows were so sharply defined in the moonlight the riders seemed part of some strange life-size shadow theatre.

Henry Cox, riding Georgina's black gelding, took the men across the northern part of the city, avoiding the busier roads where the passage of so many horsemen might have aroused comment.

There was little talk amongst the men, although Lumley raised amused comments when he spun his high hat away in some shadowed square, complaining it kept slipping over his one good eye, and he could think of no way in which it would prove useful in the anticipated fight.

Pendragon rode alongside Cox. 'How do you feel?'

'Quite contented, Captain,' replied Cox, keeping his head to the front as he answered, as though Pendragon was his commanding officer. 'Always did prefer being out on patrol to staying in barracks, Sir. Though I admit I never before managed to fight in such high-ranked company as this. Feel it quite an honour, Captain, Sir.'

'If we fight, Cox. It could turn out to be a goose chase. Though, with luck and God's grace, we should see an end to the business tonight.'

'With God's grace, and British sabres, Captain,' said Cox.

* * *

East of the city, the roads narrowed as they approached the area just north of the Thames wharves. Once there had been fields and swamps here, but now, this whole section of the city was crowded with badly designed estates where greedy developers had pushed building against building, to take advantage of London's rapidly swelling population. Warehouses, meagre stores, blank-walled factories, six-storeyed slum dwellings, courts, alleys, thin terraces, were squeezed together into a squalid and dirty shambles.

Cox now kept to the main road, the side streets being unlit, and containing the usual heaped refuse, open sewers and gutters that might easily break a horse's leg in the darkness.

At last he raised an arm and halted his horse. 'Somewhere about here, Captain. But I've no idea where. London has changed a lot over the years, Sir.'

There was a man staggering along the pavement carrying a bottle from which he swigged at every few steps. Pendragon pointed at him. 'Better ask him, Cox.'

Cox rode his horse up on to the flagstones and reined it to a stop just in front of the startled man.

The man cowered backwards, protecting his bottle with a crooked arm. ' 'Ere!'

'Tuffer's Alley? Where is it, please?'

The man muttered something and turned to lurch away. Cox nudged his horse in front of the man again. 'Tuffer's Alley, I said, man.'

The man stopped and swore. 'Down there. One, two, three roads on your right. Down there.' He clutched his gin bottle as though expecting Cox to snatch it away.

Cox backed his horse, and jerked his head up the road. 'This way, gentlemen,' he said, digging his knees into the animal.

* * *

Tuffer's Alley was narrow and unlit except for one gas lamp at the farthest end. The flags of the alley sloped inwards to provide some crude drainage. There were small dilapidated shops on either side, their windows rough boarded. Three rusted cannon, set into concrete breech downwards, made posts to prevent the entrance of carriages or carts. Cox dismounted and dropped his reins over one of the posts. The other riders followed suit.

'Let me go ahead, Sir,' Cox suggested. 'To reconnoitre.' He didn't wait for Pendragon's approval, but slipped quietly along the alley, unsheathing his sabre as he did so. Pendragon could just see him silhouetted against the distant gas lamp. After a few moments, Cox returned. 'I found it, Sir. The fifth place along. Shuttered, like the rest, but I think we can manage the door.'

There was the soft ringing of steel as the men quietly drew

their swords. Pendragon pulled his pistol from his pocket, and checked the percussion cap on the first chamber of the cylinder. 'Let's go.'

They reached the door and Pendragon signalled for silence, then listened. There were no sounds from inside Wan Hei's. 'Are you all ready?' he asked the men. 'Cox, get that door down.'

Cox leapt at the door. It shuddered, but failed to open. 'Kick it down,' ordered Pendragon, but there was no need for silence; the sound of the door being broken would certainly arouse anyone within. Cox kicked at the woodwork. He was joined by Lumley, who added his weight to the assault. A panel of the door splintered.

'What's goin' on down there?' shouted a voice from a high window behind them. Other questioning voices joined the first.

The door shattered inwards. Pendragon pushed past Cox and Lumley. Inside there were no sounds of movement. 'Careful, Captain,' warned Cox. 'They'll be hidden in the darkness.'

Pendragon kept himself close to the damp-smelling wall, and moved slowly along the narrow corridor, his pistol held ready in front of him. A faint light showed under a door ahead; he reached it, paused for a moment, then thrust it open and jumped into the room. The room was empty; the light was from an unshaded gas jet burning high on one wall. Cox and the others followed Pendragon into the room.

'Seems like the birds have flown, Sir,' said Cox. 'They haven't left much. The room's been cleared.'

'Check the others,' ordered Pendragon. 'The cellars, too.'

Beauchamp's disappointment showed in his face. He slapped a hand angrily against his thigh.

'Easy, boy,' advised Lumley. 'The night's not over yet.'

Cox was back a minute later. 'Everything gone, Captain. Not a stick of furniture or stores in the place. Got this, though, Captain; take a smell of it.'

It was a thin sliver of cedar-wood, perhaps from the side of a small box which might have been made to hold cigars. Pendragon sniffed at it. He looked at FitzPatrick, then passed him the scrap of wood. 'Opium,' he said.

There were shouts from the alley. Pendragon led the men

outside. A small crowd had gathered. One of them pushed himself close to Pendragon. ' 'Ere, what the 'ell you think...' He noticed Pendragon's pistol, then saw the sabres in the other men's hands. 'Strike me,' he said, stepping back suddenly against those behind him; they moved aside. 'H'it's the law,' he shouted. 'Bob Peeler's men 'ave come down here.' He peered closely at Pendragon and the other man. 'No, it ain't the law, it's the bleedin' army come here.'

'Where did they go?' Pendragon asked the man. 'The owners of this property.'

'The owners? You mean them Chinese?' asked the man, cockily. 'Search me, Mister. I don't know nothing about anything, least of all Chinese people.'

There was a sudden bustle of movement beside Pendragon. Cox pushed himself forward and jerked the sharp tip of his sabre up under the man's chin.

'Christ!' squeaked the man at the top of his voice. 'Jesus Christ, they're killing me!'

'Talk,' snarled Cox, bristling like a furious terrier cornering a rat.

'They've gorn.' The man squealed his reply. 'The 'ole lot of 'em. A full hour past. It's God's truth, I swear it.'

Cox dropped the sabre point slightly allowing the man to lower his chin. 'Where have they gone?' He let the sabre rest on the man's chest, and prodded it hard enough to bring beads of sweat to the man's forehead.

The man swallowed. 'I don't know, Mister. I swear I don't know. They went in the direction of the river. Dowgate Wharf, I'd say.' Cox pressed the sabre point a little harder. The man's eyes opened wider in terror; white in the dim light of the alley. 'God, Mister! I don't know no more; honest I don't. Dowgate Wharf. Straight down the high road, then right. I swears I don't know more.'

'Let him go,' ordered Pendragon, afraid Cox might become too enthusiastic in his questioning.

Cox lowered the sabre to his side. The man stepped back against the wall and rubbed at his chest.

'Let's away,' shouted Beauchamp.

*　*　*

Ia was a mad gallop, now. Pendragon, crouched low over Dasher's neck, led them in a wild charge, shattering the silence of the dark streets and alleys. Behind him rode Beauchamp, determined to be first at any kill, if he could manage it; his sabre was still in his hands, pointed forward as though he were going into full battle against enemy thousands.

As they neared Dowgate Wharf, Cox drew level with Pendragon and together the two men charged into the small area of dock immediately above the river. The others followed. Several waggons and carts stood around the edge of the narrow dock, unattended. Pendragon rode Dasher to the edge of the wharf, and looked down. The Thames below, oily and swilling with rotting debris licked against wide stone steps. There were no boats.

Beauchamp swore loudly and swung himself down off his horse. 'Where do you think . . .' he began a shouted question. There was a movement behind him.

Three Chinese leapt from one of the waggons. One of them, wielding a narrow-bladed axe that glistened in the moonlight, hurled himself at Beauchamp.

'Look out!' Lumley yelled a desperate warning.

Pendragon dug his heels into Dasher's side and charged him at the attacking Chinaman. Beauchamp turned to face the leading man just as his axe began swinging in a silver arc. Before it reached Beauchamp, Dasher hit the attacker, at full gallop, with his muscular flank. The man hurtled sideways, the axe clattering across the paving flags. Howard and Carlton took the staggering man together, scissoring in from left and right; Howard leaning far out of his saddle to strike downwards from the left side of his horse. Their blades bit into the man simultaneously. He dropped without a sound.

The second of the Chinese thrust a curved broad-bladed sword upwards at Cox's horse. Cox jerked the animal sideways then kicked the man in the face. As the Chinese stumbled backwards, Lumley ran him through the neck. The man shrieked and fell.

Beauchamp leapt away as the third man stabbed at him with a short knife. He managed to parry the blow with the hilt of his sabre then, because the man was too close to permit him a swing with the sabre blade, punched at him with the guard. The man dropped to one knee and brought up the knife again, slashing through Beauchamp's shirt.

FitzPatrick shouted and spurred his horse, leaning down from his saddle as he passed, and grabbing at the man's clothing, to drag him away from Beauchamp. The man's weight broke his grip. The Chinaman twisted in his grasp and stabbed his knife deep into the stomach of FitzPatrick's horse. The horse stumbled and collapsed and FitzPatrick rocketed over his shoulder to crash down on the dockside.

Beauchamp ran in from behind the Chinese and struck at his head, but the man rolled sideways and Beauchamp's sabre rang on the stones. The Chinaman kicked wildly at Beauchamp, and the young officer fell. The Chinese raised his knife, but before he could drive it downwards Pendragon shot him in the chest. The man stiffened, then slumped over Beauchamp.

'Search the other waggons,' shouted Pendragon. He wheeled Dasher towards the nearest.

'They're empty over here,' called Lumley.

'And here,' reported Cox. 'I think that's all of them.'

'What about FitzPatrick?' asked Pendragon.

'I'm all right,' groaned FitzPatrick, staggering to his feet. He rubbed a bruised arm. 'My damned horse is dead, though. Where's that idiot Beauchamp?' He saw the dark figures on the ground a few yards away and ran across. He dragged the dead Chinese off the young officer. 'You hurt?'

Beauchamp, covered in blood from the dead Chinese, shook his head. 'I don't think so.'

'Well, you damned well ought to be, you young idiot,' raged FitzPatrick. 'If you were one of my officers, I'd have you up before the Colonel for that. You might have been killed—or had one of us killed. You owe me a horse for your foolishness.'

'What the gentleman is trying to tell you,' said Crighton politely, and leaning down from his saddle, 'is that you don't get off your horse in open action unless the thing is blown away from under you, dear chap. You're too damned vulnerable on your feet. By rights we should be mourning you now.'

'Did I kill one?' asked Beauchamp, shamefacedly.

'Sorry old boy,' said Lumley. 'You missed out. Howard and

Carlton share a kill between them. Pendragon has one bird in the bag, and I skewered the other. Your score is Fitz's horse. Cost you a guinea or two, I'd say.'

Cox's voice was urgent. 'The rest of them are in that barge.' He pointed out into the river. Three hundred yards off shore the brown sails of a Thames sprits'l barge were just catching the soft night breeze. An oil lamp swung on her masthead and moved a little downstream against the dark skyline.

'Gone away,' groaned Crighton.

'Perhaps not yet,' said Pendragon, looking down-river. He offered a hand down to FitzPatrick. 'Ride behind me.' Fitz-Patrick took Pendragon's arm and swung himself up on to Dasher's rump, grabbing at Pendragon's waist as he knee'd Dasher to a canter from the dock.

'Hey, wait!' shouted Beauchamp, running for his loose horse.

London Bridge was deserted. Pendragon and FitzPatrick dismounted at the downstream side of the centre arch. The others joined them. Pendragon hitched Dasher to the balustrade.

'The barge is still upstream of us,' he said. The masthead light of the barge glowed some half a mile up the river as she made her way down slowly with the breeze and the outgoing tide. 'She can't clear the bridge with her mast up, she'll lower it a fraction, and drift through.'

'God almighty, Pendragon,' growled FitzPatrick staring at the water below the bridge. 'It's thirty feet down to the river. I've no intention of jumping it, if that's what you have in mind.'

'Nor I,' said Lumley. 'I leave the heights to birds and balloonists.'

'We've got a chance,' Pendragon encouraged. 'They'll only drop the mast enough to give her clearance. Perhaps only a foot or two below the span of the bridge. We don't have to jump thirty feet, if we drop on to her rigging. It's a chance I've got to take, anyway. The barge has to be stopped.'

'I'm in for a try, Captain,' said Cox.

FitzPatrick shook his head. 'You're absolutely mad, Pendragon. No wonder your crowd had such a tough time at Balaclava; you all have suicidal tendencies. All right, I'll give it a chance, too; though if I break my leg as well as losing a good horse, don't expect me to be too happy.'

'The rest of you?'

'In for a damn penny, in for a crown,' said Carlton, peering down from the bridge at the oily river.

* * *

There was a narrow parapet outside the balustrade of the bridge. Pendragon, Cox and the others crouched in the darkness on the downstream side. The barge would pass under the tunnel of the arch and appear below them. The only sounds were the lapping of the river against the stone buttresses. It seemed to be an age before the barge reached the bridge. Pendragon heard a shouted order, in some foreign tongue, echo from beneath the arch.

'Wait,' he hissed. The sound of water splashing seemed to increase. A man's voice, hollow and strange, spoke below them. Something blacker than the surface of the river slid into view. Pendragon tensed himself and prayed the mast wouldn't have been lowered to deck level, to his relief, the thick trunk of the mast, and a net of ropework appeared, tilted backwards under the bridge, seeming to raise itself towards them. It got closer, until it was within six feet. Pendragon waited as long as he dared, then he said: 'Now . . .' He jumped, his arms spread wide, his fingers clawing. A rope sawed across his wrist, burning skin; another caught at the crook of his right elbow. He hooked his arm, and thudded against the narrow yards. The mast swayed and sagged. There was a shout beside him. The mast moved more, jerking and pitching, then from below someone yelled. The mast dropped as the unexpected weight of the men proved too much for the crew on the deck tackle, and then swung downwards, crashing against the boom, which splintered on the hatch cover as the heavy pine standard hit the deck. The mainsail billowed outwards; the heavy tarred canvas ripped away the light mizzen mast before flapping over the side, to drag the barge beam on to the current.

For a few moments Pendragon was dazed.

'Captain Pendragon?' Cox's voice was beside him.

He grunted an answer.

The barge crew were shouting in confusion, only one or two of them at first realising they had been boarded. Pendragon struggled to his feet and pulled himself free from the loose ropes. A man holding a needle-pointed cargo-loading hook leapt at him. He ducked and pulled out his pistol. It was difficult moving on the loose mountains of canvas and rope beneath his feet. The man's sharp steel hook whistled past his face and dug into the woodwork of the mast. Pendragon shot him at close range, the bullet folding the man forward and the burning gunpowder setting fire to his short tunic. He pushed him out of the way.

There was a shriek from his right. He half turned his head to see Beauchamp on one knee, with his sabre clean through the belly of a man in front of him. The sabre was wedged into the back ribs and Beauchamp was having to use both his hands and a foot to pull the weapon free. The man, still struggling, was trying to stab Beauchamp with a sharpened iron marlin-spike.

Flame burst from the stern of the barge as the masthead light spilled its fuel oil on to the tumbled canvas and rigging. The flames spread forward with a dull explosive thud.

Cox was fighting near the barge's tiller. Pendragon caught a glimpse of him just as he sabred the first of two huge Chinese who were trying to trap him between them. The man screamed as Cox's blade bit deep into his shoulder. Cox spun to slash the second man low across the thigh, before driving the sabre point through the man's chest. Pendragon just had time to see Cox turn to finish off his first assailant, when a slimly built Chinese, better dressed than the others of the crew, and with a wispy beard, swung himself over the fallen mast. The man moved like a trained fighter and faced Pendragon with his shoulders squared towards him, his knees slightly bent. His hands were held forward almost like a fist-fighter's. He carried no obvious weapons.

Pendragon realised he was facing Wan Hei, the Green Serpent leader; Wan Hei moved sideways too quickly for Pendragon to react. The Chinese kicked and the heel of his foot jarred high into Pendragon's chest, just below his throat, ramming him backwards to crash down on to the deck. He struggled to his knees. Wan Hei struck at him with the edge of his hand, the blow catching Pendragon with surprising force on his left shoulder and numbing his arm. The man kicked again, his foot glancing from Pendragon's chin; he fell, his pistol arm trapped beneath him. The Chinese dived forward, to kneel above him, forcing his fingers into Pendragon's mouth and wrenching his head sideways. Pendragon felt his neck muscles straining; he twisted his head using all his strength to do so. He found Wan Hei's fingers between his teeth and bit hard on them. The man's hold relaxed a little enabling Pendragon to free his trapped arm. He brought his knee up into the man's groin. Wan Hei gasped, but rammed his head against Pendragon's face. For brief seconds, Pendragon was stunned. He felt the triad leader's fingers close around his throat; the grip tightened like steel cord. Blood pounded in the veins at Pendragon's temples. Pendragon brought his pistol upwards, praying it would fire; in another half second he would be totally unconscious. He squeezed the trigger. Wan Hei was blown upwards. His fingers relaxed their terrible hold on Pendragon's chest. He stiffened, kneeling above Pendragon, then slid sideways. Pendragon pushed himself shakily to his feet.

The flames had spread now, enveloping the whole broad stern of the barge, and licking their way fast along the tar-filled deck seams.

Lumley, FitzPatrick and the others were fighting on the for'ard section where there was less debris from the tangled rigging and sails. Crighton was leaning against the deckhouse, holding his hands to his stomach. As Pendragon climbed forward, he saw Lumley slice the last of the Chinese across the throat; the fighting ceased as the man slumped. FitzPatrick was resting against the bulwarks, his face gleaming with sweat in the light of the flames. He waved weakly at Pendragon as he arrived.

'John,' he said, breathing heavily. 'If you ever choose to invite me out again, I may well refuse your invitation. Your idea of entertainment is a little over-strenuous.'

Lumley laughed. 'It's a little more entertaining than cock fighting, Fitz.' The man he had just killed was lying across the barge's rail. He pushed him over into the river.

Pendragon clambered across to Crighton. 'Are you all right?'

'If someone will find me a bit of rope, yes,' said Crighton, wryly. 'I burst all my damned trouser buttons when I slid down the rigging. Makes it difficult fighting when your trousers are around your ankles.' He looked at a body lying face downwards on the deck. 'That feller damn near castrated me.'

'Any wounded?' called Pendragon.

'A few cuts and bruises, that's all,' said Carlton.

'I think I've broken a wrist, Captain,' said Cox, his voice giving no indication of discomfort.

Pendragon looked around the deck. The centre and after part of the barge was blazing fiercely, making it uncomfortably hot even on the foredeck. The painted and oiled woodwork was spluttering and crackling; sparks showered upwards in breeze-drifted spirals. 'Did anyone see the Russian?'

Beauchamp said: 'A big man? Someone went over the side a couple of minutes ago. I couldn't get to him fast enough across the mast.'

'Damn!' Pendragon peered across the river. After a few seconds he could make out the white splashing of someone's arms, a hundred yards from the barge and heading for the northern shore. 'Cox, lend me your sabre.' He took the weapon and passed Cox his pistol. 'Can all of you swim?'

Beauchamp made a sour face. 'In this filthy water? It'll be like swimming in a sewer.'

'Unless you can walk on the water,' said FitzPatrick, 'I would think it's the only way we're going to get ashore.'

'Then don't waste time,' warned Pendragon, urgently. 'Remember this barge's cargo. If the twenty-four tons of powder are in her holds, she'll blow herself to matchwood.'

'My God!' exclaimed Beauchamp. 'I'd forgotten.'

'Can you manage, Cox?' asked Pendragon.

'Yes, Captain.'

'Then all of you make your way back to the horses. Wait for me there.' Pendragon turned and dived over the side.

* * *

It was hard work swimming after the exercise of the fight. After a few yards, Pendragon paused, shrugged off his waistcoat and kicked away his shoes. The sabre wasn't helping him.

He tried swimming with it across his teeth, but it was too heavy. He trod water and jammed it through the top of his trouser waistband. He could see no signs now of Mikhailovich, if indeed he was the swimming man. He struck out for the north bank as fast as he could, the current carrying him downstream. The water tasted of rotting vegetables. Pendragon kept his mouth closed as much as possible.

After some ten minutes he thought he saw splashing ahead of him and struck out harder. His arms were aching, and the old wounds on his leg sent burning pains up his thigh. He was only eighty yards from the northern shore, and facing a high white-stone wall that ran alongside the river, when he saw movement against the wall. Someone struggled to find a handhold, failed and floundered farther downstream. Pendragon altered his course to bring him to a gate in the wall some fifty yards down-river. The swimmer ahead must have heard him because he turned, and Pendragon could see the white of his face in the moonlight. The man splashed at the water, wildly, and Pendragon saw the glint of steel in one of the man's hands. The man reached the gate in the wall, and pulled himself up on to the steps. He stumbled out of sight.

Pendragon felt mud beneath his feet and waded forward. The water shallowed. He reached the steps. It was black above him. He pulled out Cox's sabre and climbed cautiously.

He moved into the shadow. The steps were black slime. He trod them silently, his back against the slippery walls of the arched gateway. He dived the last two steps to the top, rolling as he hit the hard ground, and spinning to his feet. There was no sign of the man. Now, from the top of the wall, Pendragon could see the barge, alight from stern to bow, burning furiously in midstream. He thought he could see the heads of the other men in the water, but could not be certain. The narrow road where he stood was strangely familiar; the Tower! Its walls and battlements stretched above him.

There was movement in the shadowed foot of the white stone building thirty yards ahead.

'Mikhailovich!' shouted Pendragon, standing with his legs straddled, water dripping from him. His hair was streaked down his face; he wiped it aside with his arm.

The shadow moved again. 'Ah, Captain Pendragon.' Mikhailovich stepped into the moonlight. Like Pendragon, he had shed some of his clothing. He was naked to the waist, and his huge barrel chest was dark with hair; his shoulders gleamed, wet with the river water. He carried a wide-bladed oriental sword, and walked towards Pendragon, swinging it slowly across the front of his body. 'I knew you were on the boat, and when I heard someone following me in the water, I rather hoped it might be yourself. What is your intention now? No doubt you expect to capture me, and take me in chains to your fat Queen.'

'When you surrender your sword,' said Pendragon.

Mikhailovich blew water from his beard, then laughed. 'Surrender my sword?' He glanced at it. 'I might well, as it's a clumsy weapon; a Chinese sword, in fact. But I'm afraid I won't surrender it, Captain Pendragon, inelegant as it might be. No member of the Mikhailovich family has ever surrendered the sword he carried. No; instead, I believe I shall kill you.'

Before Pendragon could answer, Mikhailovich leap forward swinging the blade of the sword so fast Pendragon heard it hiss past his chest. He jumped backwards. Mikhailovich laughed again. 'One must agree, Captain, this blade is made more for slicing ham than one of Her Majesty's officers.' He pivoted suddenly, fast for a man of his huge bulk and weight, and the sword blade whistled downwards, Pendragon caught it against his sabre, the shock of the blow almost carrying his weapon from his hand. 'Very neat, Captain Pendragon.'

Pendragon attacked, but Mikhailovich parried the blows easily, and Pendragon nearly took the point of his sword in his face. He realised that although the Chinese sword was heavy and perhaps clumsy Mikhailovich's great strength allowed him to handle it as though it were a light fencing blade. He stepped back a pace, hoping to draw Mikhailovich into a move that might give him an advantage. Mikhailovich was in no hurry.

'An interesting situation, Captain Pendragon. However, I fear you are quite outclassed. I trust you are leaving no dependents; it distresses me to learn of officers' wives and children forced to live in unfortunate circumstances.' He swung the sword again, changing the direction of the cut in mid-swing, so the blade drove Pendragon's aside and cut a furrow down his bicep. 'First blood, I believe, Captain Pendragon.'

Pendragon couldn't feel the wound, nor risk glancing at it. He could feel blood, warm, running down his arm. He dived forward, forcing Mikhailovich to step sideways and parry a high attack, then thrust in at him from below the Russian's blade. Mikhailovich grunted as the point of Pendragon's sabre scored into his side. Pendragon carried his movement past the Russian with a long stride so his sabre point turned and cut a larger exit wound as he used its length as a lever.

Mikhailovich was silent now; his only indication that Pendragon's sword had done him injury. He brought the curved sword swinging across him, then turned it to bring the keen edge up towards the pit of Pendragon's stomach. Pendragon leapt out of the way, the blade glancing from the back of his sabre only half an inch from his body. He attacked again and forced Mikhailovich backwards along the narrow roadway. He was finding his arm tiring rapidly after the swim, and with its fresh wound; he wondered how long he could maintain the effort. A moment's hesitation and Mikhailovich would kill him.

By the gateway with its steps to the river, Mikhailovich turned the attack, and struck out strongly at Pendragon, his blade hissing fractionally above Pendragon's head. Mikhailovich sensed Pendragon's fatigue; his experience told him the wound in Pendragon's bicep must be weakening the arm. He swung a backhanded blow at Pendragon's shoulder, forcing him to take the weight of the blow high on his sabre, near the guard, and at an angle which focused maximum strain on his injured muscle. It was Mikhailovich's opportunity. He brought the blade round in a full circle, and struck diagonally at Pendragon's neck, with the full weight of his body behind the blow. Pendragon wrenched himself sideways, off balance; Mikhailovich's blade sliced through the lobe of his ear, and hit the stonework of the arch. The blade snapped just below the hilt, singing across the road, like a piece of spent shrapnel.

Mikhailovich smiled almost apologetically, and stepped back as though expecting Pendragon to lower his own sabre. Pendragon drove the blade forward, his full weight behind the weapon, hitting Mikhailovich just below his breastbone.

Mikhailovich's eyes widened fearfully. He stood, facing Pendragon, the blade of the sabre buried eight inches into his chest. His lips twitched, then tautened into a grimace of agony; blood ran from the corners of his mouth and dripped down from his chin. Pendragon stepped away and jerked out the blade. Mikhailovich stood motionless, his eyes fixed on Pendragon with the same unseeing stare Pendragon had seen when he first visited the man. The Russian suddenly screamed; a long and unearthly cry as though his soul was tearing itself loose from his body. His body quivered and swayed forward, like the tall trunk of a felled oak, to crash stiffly at Pendragon's feet.

* * *

It was a bright morning a week later, with just the hint of sharpness in the air, and a touch of autumn in the fading colouring of the leaves on the trees lining Constitution Hill. Pendragon and Cloverly sat together in the berlin, its coach-work freshly beeswaxed, and its two horses so well groomed their gleaming coats seemed to have been painted with fresh pitch. The coachman, in his best uniform of green velvet, kept the animals to a fashionable high-stepping trot that gave a slight bounce to the soft springing of the carriage.

'I have a little of Rambolt's money,' said Pendragon, 'gold coin found amongst his belongings. About a hundred and fifty guineas. Does the department want it?'

Page Cloverly shook his head. 'He's no one to pass it on to, and what's a little gold to us? Give it to the boy, Ted Blower. Better still, invest it for him.'

'That's what I was hoping to do.'

'Now, don't say too much,' warned Cloverly. 'There's plenty that Mr. Herbert didn't dare to tell their Majesties. God, man, they'd have your neck if they thought you'd gone charging across half of London swinging your sabres as though you were going into battle. The general purpose of our department is to protect British interests, and British citizens. If you knew the amount of talking I've done on your behalf in the last week, you'd be amazed. Eleven corpses floating in the river, most of them with sword wounds, are hardly the things to endear the department to the constabulary. And Mikhailovich; how on earth did you think I'd manage to talk his death away? You could at least have lost his body instead of just leaving it there. Fortunately, I've managed to have it recorded as an unidentified person, and no doubt it's in a pauper's grave by now. As far as the Russian government are concerned, they've been informed he has disappeared leaving a small fortune in unsettled gambling debts. We're hoping that will satisfy them. We had his house cleaned up, and that was a messy business, too. Can't you cavalry chaps ever kill some-body cleanly! Chopping off heads in England went out with the Tudors.' Page Cloverly sighed deeply. 'Thank God at least the barge sank and didn't explode.'

'Don't thank God, thank FitzPatrick. He stayed on board and opened the sea cocks. It was a good piece of thinking, and brave, too. Anyway, Page, at least we settled the matter.'

'Settled it?' Page Cloverly groaned. 'You very nearly settled the careers of both Mr. Herbert and myself. Herbert's had the best idea for you so far. Send you to France.'

'France? Exiled?' Pendragon sounded startled.

Cloverly laughed. 'Exiled! God damn you, that's an even better idea! We hadn't thought of that one. No, John. Herbert thinks a few weeks with the French Corps d'Intelligence might help you a little. He's arranged it with Colonel de Bagneau. They're expecting you in two weeks' time. Think of it as a training course, although, I admit, it will be sensible for you to be out of the way for a little while. You've caused more ruffling of the waters in a fortnight than Rambolt managed in his whole lifetime.' He looked sideways at the walls and gateway of Buckingham Palace. 'Don't forget, John, discretion at this Royal meeting.' He clicked his fingers. 'I'd forgotten, John, discretion isn't one of the words in your vocabulary. I had better describe its meaning to you. Discretion, Captain Pendragon, means . . .'

GENERAL FICTION FROM CORONET

NIGEL TRANTER

☐	18768 9	The Clansman	40p
☐	18767 0	Gold For Prince Charlie	40p
☐	20299 8	The Wisest Fool	£1.25

R. F. DELDERFIELD

☐	15623 6	God Is An Englishman	£1.25
☐	16225 2	Theirs Was The Kingdom	95p
☐	02787 8	Farewell The Tranquil Mind	35p
		Give Us This Day :	
☐	18818 9	Book 1 – Three Score Years And Ten	50p
☐	18819 7	Book 2 – Reconnaissance	50p

MARK RASCOVICH

☐	19985 7	Falkenhorst	£1.25

All these books are available at your local bookshop or newsagent, or can be ordered direct from the publisher. Just tick the titles you want and fill in the form below.

Prices and availability subject to change without notice.

CORONET BOOKS, P.O. Box 11, Falmouth, Cornwall.
Please send cheque or postal order, and allow the following for postage and packing :

U.K. – One book 19p plus 9p per copy for each additional book ordered, up to a maximum of 73p.

B.F.P.O. and EIRE – 19p for the first book plus 9p per copy for the next 6 books, thereafter 3p per book.

OTHER OVERSEAS CUSTOMERS – 20p for the first book and 10p per copy for each additional book.

Name...

Address..

....